*What the*

ↂ

DANCE OF THE CRYSTAL was the first erotic romance novel that PLAYGIRL chose to excerpt in their magazine (January 2007 issue).

5 stars "…a great contemporary erotic romantic suspense. The characters are three-dimensional. The dialogue is superb." ~ *Just Erotic Romance Reviews*

5 hearts "Wonderful tale!" ~ *The Romance Studio*

5 angels "Awesome job, Ms. Anson." ~ *Fallen Angel Reviews*

"Filled to the brim with humor, steamy erotic scenes, passionate emotions, and thrilling action…with a depth that I don't see very often!" ~ *EcataRomance*

"Cris Anson has successfully written another beautiful and tumultuous love story." ~ *Romance Junkies*

"This story is hot and riveting." ~ *Coffee Time Romance*

"…an all around, highly erotic, wonderful read." ~ *Joyfully Reviewed*

"…a good and hot story that will keep you captivated till the last page." ~ *Love Romances*

DANCE OF THE BUTTERFLY

5 stars "Sexy, passionate, emotional, intelligent and fun…this one is a keeper!" ~ *EuroReviews*

5 pleasure cupids "Kat and Magnus are two very likeable characters, the chemistry between them is explosive and the sex scenes are scorching hot and erotic." ~ *Cupids Library*

"Full of life and character studies, this book is filled with intense emotion and wonderful scenes. Great job, Ms. Anson." ~ *Enchanted in Romance*

"…endearingly well written and emotionally charged…definitely a keeper." ~ *Romance Junkies*

DANCE OF THE SEVEN VEILS

5 unicorns "The storyline was well written and the characters captivating. Not to mention the sex was hot!" ~ *Enchanted in Romance*

5 hearts "(It) is not only incredibly, sinfully erotic, but it features two characters that all readers will feel a strong connection to." ~ *The Romance Studio*

5 angels "Lyssa's struggle to overcome the low self-image she has from her loveless marriage was handled wonderfully. Savidge was…so sexy that I wanted to keep him for myself." ~ *Fallen Angel Reviews*

"…an intriguing exploration of a woman rediscovering her sensuality and her power as a female." ~ *Romance Junkies*

Dance of the Crystal

Cris Anson

ELLORA'S CAVE
ROMANTICA PUBLISHING

An Ellora's Cave Romantica Publication

www.ellorascave.com

Dance of the Crystal

ISBN 9781419956171
ALL RIGHTS RESERVED.
Dance of the Crystal Copyright © 2006 Cris Anson
Edited by Sue-Ellen Gower
Cover art by Syneca.

Electronic book Publication March 2006
Trade paperback Publication January 2007

Excerpt from *Dance of the Seven Veils* Copyright © Cris Anson
2005

Content Advisory:

S – ENSUOUS
E – ROTIC
X - TREME

Ellora's Cave Publishing offers three levels of Romantica™ reading entertainment: S (S-ensuous), E (E-rotic), and X (X-treme).

The following material contains graphic sexual content meant for mature readers. This story has been rated E–rotic.

S-*ensuous* love scenes are explicit and leave nothing to the imagination.

E-*rotic* love scenes are explicit, leave nothing to the imagination, and are high in volume per the overall word count. E-rated titles might contain material that some readers find objectionable — in other words, almost anything goes, sexually. E-rated titles are the most graphic titles we carry in terms of both sexual language and descriptiveness in these works of literature.

X-*treme* titles differ from E-rated titles only in plot premise and storyline execution. Stories designated with the letter X tend to contain difficult or controversial subject matter not for the faint of heart.

Also by Cris Anson

∞

Dance of the Butterfly
Dance of the Seven Veils

About the Author

∞

Cris Anson firmly believes that love is the greatest gift…to give or to receive. In her writing, she lives for the moment when her characters realize they love each other, usually after much antagonism and conflict. And when they express that love physically, Cris keeps a fire extinguisher near the keyboard in case of spontaneous combustion. Multi-published and twice EPPIE-nominated in romantic suspense under another name, she was usually asked to tone down her love scenes. For Ellora's Cave, she's happy to turn the flame as high as it will go—and then some.

After suffering the loss of her real-life hero/husband of twenty-two years, Cris has picked up the pieces of her life and tries to remember only the good times—slow-dancing with him to the Big-Band sound of Glenn Miller's music, vacations to scenic national parks in a snug recreational vehicle, his tender and fierce love, his unflagging belief in her ability to write stories that touch the heart as well as the libido. Bits and pieces of his tenacity, optimism, code of honor and lust for life will live on in her imaginary heroes.

Cris welcomes comments from readers. You can find her website and email address on her author bio page at www.ellorascave.com.

Acknowledgments

ℬↄ

I'd like to acknowledge the assistance of my terrific editor, Sue-Ellen Gower, in the writing of this book. It was a time of great personal upheaval, which engendered crippling self-doubt, but she steadfastly insisted that I had the ability to bring Soren out from under Magnus' shadow into the hero he became.

Thanks also to Kristin, the model for my heroine, from her unruly hair and dazzling smile to…well, you know.

And last, my everlasting love and gratitude to my two Adolphs — so different, yet so much alike. I miss you both.

Cris Anson

January 2006

Dear Reader:

To learn how newlyweds Kat Donaldson and Magnus Thorvald met, pick up a copy of DANCE OF THE BUTTERFLY. And for an introduction into The Platinum Society, along with Lyssa Markham and Robert Savidge's story, don't miss the first book in this series, DANCE OF THE SEVEN VEILS.

Trademarks Acknowledgement

The author acknowledges the trademarked status and trademark owners of the following wordmarks mentioned in this work of fiction:

Beetle (VW): Volkswagon Aktiengessellschaft

BMW: Bayerische Motoren Werke Aktiengessellschaft

Bucks County Coffee: Bucks County Nut and Coffee Company

Caroline Herrera: Carolina Herrera, Ltd.

Dos Equis: Cerveceria Moctezuma, S.A. DE C.V.

Escalade: General Motors Corporation

Guinness: Arthur Guiness, Son & Co., LTD.

Jacuzzi: Jacuzzi Inc. Corporation

Jaws of Life: Hurst Performance, Inc.

Kahlua: The Kahlua Company

Kevlar: E. I. du Pont de Nemours and Company

Lalique: Lalique Corporation, France

Maglite: Mag Instrument, Inc.

Philadelphia Inquirer: Philadelphia Inquirer Co., The

Popsicle: Lipton Investments, Inc.

Ritz Carlton Hotel: Ritz-Carlton Hotel Company, L.L.C.

Sevres: Compagnie Francaise du Cristal - Daum

Speedo: Speedo Knitting Mills Pty. Limited

Styrofoam: Dow Chemical Company

Victoria's Secret: V Secret Catalogue, Inc.

DANCE OF THE CRYSTAL

૭૭

Chapter One

༺༻

"But I don't *want* to buy a bachelor!" Crystal D'Angelo stamped her dainty, stockinged foot to underscore her point. And promptly regretted it. She had stubbed her little toe on the carved post at the foot of her canopy bed. Again.

"Don't take me literally, young lady. You're not buying a bachelor. You're just buying the opportunity to buy a bachelor a dinner."

Crystal tried to give her grandmother the evil eye. She'd never gotten the hang of it so wasn't surprised it didn't work. Looking like a queen in a white sequined gown covering her from neck to wrists to ankles, Rowena D'Angelo sat on the antique wedding ring quilt and calmly waved two tickets in the air. "You know I support the Battered Women's fund-raiser every year. It just so happens that this year they came up with the bachelor auction idea. Call it kismet that it occurs on the eve of your thirtieth birthday. I'm giving you a birthday present you won't soon forget. Now put your shoes on and let's go. We don't want to be late."

With a sigh, Crystal slipped into the three-inch heels she wore to lengthen her five-foot-three height. She gave herself a quick once-over in the cheval mirror. Another inch or two had been added by virtue of having her curly black hair piled atop her head and held in place by dozens of pins. A red satin sheath with delicate spaghetti straps covered her well-rounded curves in an unbroken line to the floor, another trick to make her look taller. What she called chandelier earrings dangled from her pierced ears, throwing off many-colored sparks as light bounced off their crystal facets.

She caressed the large, asymmetrical crystal dangling on a delicate golden chain around her neck. As far as she could tell, none of the magic ascribed to it had ever touched her since her thirteenth birthday when Grandma had passed it on to her.

As if reading her thoughts, the older woman said, "Like fine wine, the best things happen in their own good time. Tonight may just be the night for magic. And you'll know when it happens."

Crystal shook her head as if to say, *I doubt it.* She heard a *ping* as a hairpin bounced onto the dresser, and felt an ebony curl fall down to her ear. "Darn it, can't I even once fix my hair and have it stay there?" Retrieving the errant pin, she jabbed the curl back into place.

Picking up her tiny, red silk evening bag, she checked its contents—lipstick, compact, car and house keys, ten dollars for emergencies, grabbed her matching red wrap and followed her only living relative downstairs and to the front door of her cozy Cape Cod home.

They walked outside to a mild April evening in suburban Philadelphia. Crystal flicked the remote opener to her sun-yellow Beetle and helped Rowena into the passenger seat, smiling at the fact that Rowena had taken her unique, hand-carved cane with her. Crystal knew for a fact that her grandmother didn't need it, but used it as a prop.

What she didn't know was what was inside that prop.

* * * * *

"I haven't worn a tie in years," Soren Thorvald grumbled as he tried for the third time to master the knot on the red silk tie he'd borrowed from his younger brother. The only place he felt at home was behind the bar at his pub. All a bartender had to do was fill orders and act as though he was listening. What the hell was he doing, getting ready to go on stage in front of a live audience and pretend to be a social animal? Good Christ, he'd have to actually smile at the woman who won his ticket. And, worse yet, *talk* to her, sit across a dinner table from her. He hoped he and not the winner chose the restaurant. He'd pick a pizza parlor. Or a fast-food joint. The faster, the better.

"It's like riding a bike," said Rolf with a wicked grin. "Or fucking. You never forget how."

Soren turned an ice-blue glare at him. "Just because you hump everything in skirts."

"Uh-uh. Get with today's fashion, bro. Women don't just wear skirts. They wear slacks, capris, shorts, minis, midis, maxis, bikinis…" he paused for emphasis "…thongs…"

"Stifle it, okay? I'm done fussing with this noose. If they kick me off because my tie isn't knotted right, I'll be one happy camper." Soren ran a finger inside the collar of his brand-new white dress shirt. Damn size seventeen neck was too tight. "I still can't believe I let you talk me into this."

"How many times have you told me that a successful businessman should give something back to the community? Don't go turning into a grinch just because you have to wear a tie."

In lieu of a comb, Soren ran his hands through the blond waves on his head, grabbed the navy blazer he'd just taken the price tag off of, and shoved his arms into the sleeves. That was all the concession he'd make. Shirt, tie, blazer. And jeans. If they didn't like it, they could just bar him from the hotel. Damn blazer was too tight too. Well, when you're six-three and a forty-four long and need it the same day, you take what's on the rack. "Let's get it over with."

* * * * *

"Our next bachelor is an ex-Marine who owns Thor's Hammer, a bar-restaurant in nearby Allendale."

Seated at a small round table near the front of the stage, Rowena perked up as the announcer hawked his wares at the podium. "This one sounds like a winner."

"Oh, puh-leeze." Crystal fingered her amulet, as she often did when nervous. "Ex-Marine? Bar owner? He's probably a tobacco-chewing redneck who drives a big truck. I think you're going to have to be satisfied with just the price of our tickets for your donation. There's only a couple of slabs of beef left."

Rowena chuckled. "It's more than a meat market, child. I'm getting vibes from my cane."

"What?" Crystal swung her head toward her grandmother, dislodging another couple of pins from her upswept hair. She sighed and relegated them to the "lost" pile on the floor, tucking the fallen tresses behind her ear.

"Here." Rowena handed the cane to Crystal. "Feel it. The knob."

Like a dutiful granddaughter, Crystal accepted the cane. And felt the blood drain from her face. The head of it felt like...like...

She thrust it back to Rowena and made a big show of turning her attention to the stage. It felt just like she imagined a cock to feel, smooth, hard, a ridge running around the head, the opening like an omniscient eye—

And then it hit her. It was warm. The cane was warmer than wood should be in this air-conditioned ballroom.

Well, of course it was. Grandma had warmed it with her hands and tried to suggest something otherworldly was happening. Crystal took a long sip of her white wine to slow her accelerated heartbeat. She shouldn't be so suggestible.

"Soren Thorvald," said the announcer.

Grudgingly Crystal raised her gaze to the latest bachelor. And gasped.

It felt like her amulet had sent out an electric shock to the skin between her breasts.

She leaned forward, the crystal swinging away from her body, and rubbed her skin where the stone had lain.

"Is something the matter, dear?" Rowena asked her.

Take a deep breath. "No, Grandma, I'm fine." She fought the impulse to look at Bachelor Soren Thorvald. And lost.

The moment she raised her lashes and looked to the stage, a pair of glacier-blue eyes laser-locked onto her gaze. Oh God, he was so…big.

She noted how he towered over the announcer. Noted how his broad shoulders and square jaw reminded her of Dudley Do-Right, the cartoon mounted policeman. How his tie, the same bright red color as her gown, lay loose and askew under his unbuttoned collar. How the worn jeans molded to muscular thighs.

A sharp nudge to her shoulder broke her concentration on this giant, and she realized she was holding aloft the numbered paddle the ticket-taker had given Rowena when they entered the ballroom. Her heart stuttered then pounded back double time.

Her grandmother had won the bid for Soren Thorvald.

And she'd put the paddle in Crystal's hand while she'd been in never-never land.

Ohmigod, what was she going to *do* with him?

"Will the winning bidder please come on stage and claim her prize?"

Crystal jerked her hand down and thrust the paddle into Rowena's lap. The slight dip of her shoulder caused her spaghetti strap to slide down and drape across her upper arm, dragging some of her bodice with it to expose more of her breast than was proper. Feeling her face flame, she tugged and jiggled until everything was back in place.

"Your prize awaits you, Crystal." Rowena looked almost…smug. "Go on now."

"You bid on him," she whispered rawly. "*You* collect the prize."

Rowena's face took on that intimidating glare that had always cowed Crystal as a teenager. She squirmed in her seat. Clenched her fists in her lap. Uncrossed her legs. And felt one high-heeled, backless sandal fall to the floor under the royal blue-draped table.

"Don't you start going into a tantrum, young lady, or I'll go up on stage and show the emcee the sexy cane you bought me for my seventieth birthday."

Crystal's eyes widened to shimmering O's. "I did not—"

"Get your tushie up there! Your bachelor looks like he's ready to come get you."

Crystal snapped her gaze to the bachelor in question. He was doing a credible impersonation of a bull who'd just seen a swirling red cape and was building up steam to charge. "Oh God, he looks so *angry*. Grandma, what have you done?"

"Move!"

"I can't! My shoe…" Swallowing a building panic, she gingerly explored the area under the table with her foot, searching for the elusive shoe. And kicked it further away. In desperation, she shoved back her chair, ducked down to her knees and all but disappeared under the tablecloth. *There!* She grabbed the errant sandal and carefully began to edge backwards on hands and knees.

Suddenly she let out a piercing yell.

Huge hands had gripped her waist. She felt herself being dragged back until her head reappeared from under the tablecloth. Then she was unceremoniously yanked to her feet and twirled around. Unbalanced by the three-inch differential between a shod and a bare foot, she fell forward onto an unyielding wall of powerful male flesh.

"That's enough grandstanding, dammit!"

The intimidating wall of flesh had a voice to match, she had time to think, right before she was hoisted up like a sack of potatoes and flung over a linebacker shoulder.

"Put me down!" With her torso hanging upside down, Crystal felt the swinging amulet hit her nose with every step her captor took, the heat of the crystal startling her. Curl after curl released its hairpin and she could feel swaths of hair tickling her face and neck as she bounced.

With mounting indignation, she pummeled whichever parts of his back she could reach—and was evilly delighted when she realized she still held her stiletto in one hand—but the juggernaut plowed through the noisy crowd without slowing down. Dimly she realized the noise was applause.

Darn it, did they think she orchestrated this?

With an effort, she lifted her bobbing head to seek out her grandmother. Rowena could be as imperious as a tsarina. Surely she'd be a match for this Neanderthal.

But when their gazes met, Rowena D'Angelo sat regally on her chair, hands tucked one atop the other on the head of the cane, looking very like the Cheshire cat in Alice's Wonderland.

Crystal felt as though she'd fallen through the rabbit hole.

* * * * *

"Did you enjoy your little game of humiliation?"

"Let me go, you big bully!"

Soren released the woman's wrist and took a deep breath. Oxygen. He needed lots of it. He should have had it earlier—to regulate his brain, before he'd done something so uncharacteristic that he still didn't believe it. Rolf had always accused him of being too buttoned-down, too rigid. And Rolf was right. He'd kept his emotions on a tight leash ever since he was nine years old.

But when this pixie made a fool of him by hiding under the table rather than claiming her prize, something inside him snapped. Yeah, sure, when their eyes had met across that proverbial crowded room, he felt his cock snap to attention. Any red-blooded man would have done the same. She'd looked at him as though she was starving and he was a sizzling steak.

More fool he.

A slender thread of sense penetrated his wrath as he dared a glance at the woman he'd flung so cavalierly into a wing chair outside the ballroom. The four-star Ritz Carlton Hotel was not a fitting backdrop for his caveman behavior. Hell, no backdrop would be fitting for what he'd just done. It was so unlike him to lose his cool over a—

He swallowed hard. His "owner". Her heart-shaped face was sheened with a rosy glow, like she'd just been made love to by an expert. Her curly black hair, half piled on her head and half dangling in sinuous curves around and across half her face, whispered of wild and wicked sex. Eyes the color of dark melted chocolate stared at him from under gracefully arching brows.

But what made his cock swell inside his jeans was a mouth made for sucking him, wide and soft with a cupid's bow outlining the upper lip, stained a red as deep as her dress. He plopped down in an adjoining chair and dragged the fingers of one hand through his hair. He *never* thought of things like that. He didn't *like* women. At least that's what he'd told himself over the past score of years.

"Look, I'm sorry. I don't usually—" Hell, he didn't have a clue how to apologize to a woman.

She just stared at him, eyes wide and lower lip trembling, her hand grasping whatever it was that dangled on the end of a gold chain around her delicate neck.

"I didn't mean to frighten you. Really." He reached out a hand to her, tentative as an uncoordinated infant. There was something so fragile about her. Something that awakened in him a deep desire to protect her.

Crap. She probably needed to be protected from *him*.

"Would you like something to drink?" Yeah, right. As if she needed any liquor to dull her wits around the likes of him. "A glass of water maybe?"

"You…you're the one?"

She'd said it so quietly that he almost didn't hear her over the background hum of a busy hotel lobby. He cleared his throat, remembering the bang of the auctioneer's gavel that had sounded like a death knell. "Yeah, I guess I am."

Her death grip on the object around her neck loosened. Now he could see that her long, slender fingers were caressing what looked like an asymmetrical chunk of crystal. As she breathed—deep, shivery gasps like she was a mile above sea level in rarified air—the crystal shimmered and sparkled, mesmerizing him. He barely noticed the ample cleavage below it.

Until she let go of the crystal. His eyes followed as it nestled between plump rounds of flesh so inviting he actually licked his lips before he caught himself and tore his gaze away.

Thankfully she seemed not to notice his gauche behavior. Her long, thick lashes lowered. She let out a resigned sigh then looked back up at him. "Guess we'd better get acquainted then."

She placed her hands on the armrests as if to rise to her feet. "Oh." She looked at the high-heeled sandal in her left hand as if wondering how it had gotten there.

"Please. Allow me." Soren slid out of his chair and sank to his knees before her. He held out his hand, palm up.

Crystal's gaze flicked from her shoe to the Bachelor's face then noted his posture, like Prince Charming come to see if the glass slipper fit Cinderella's foot, then back to her stiletto. A frisson of alarm skittered down her spine. He was actually going to…he wanted to…

No. It struck her that there was something much too intimate about a man holding a woman's foot to slip a shoe on it, and this stranger, this man that the crystal had declared was The One, well, geez, she needed some time to absorb the enormity of the revelation.

She tried for a haughty look as she shook her head, but only dislodged the last remaining pins holding her hair up. Blowing an exasperated breath at the wayward tresses, she bent forward to place the shoe where it belonged. And heard a strangled gasp come from him.

Her peripheral vision told her a strap had slipped down her shoulder again. This time, in her forward-leaning position, the edge of her bodice had gapped enough that she could see what he'd reacted to—the tip of her dusky-rose nipple thrusting against the all-but-transparent lace of her strapless bra.

She jerked upright in the chair so forcefully that the spaghetti strap ripped from its anchor in back of the silk gown and dangled in the small space between them, gravity pulling the fabric down so that anyone nearby could see her exposed breast.

Heat spread over her cheeks, her shoulders. Mortified, she jockeyed the fabric back up to cover what it was supposed to cover, yanked the strap behind her neck and wound it around the other strap a few times, and sat back with her spine rigid against the chair. She couldn't bear to look at him. What must he think of her? Lordy, here they were, strangers in a public place and he'd seen her *breast*! Why, he didn't even know her name!

Her name. Yes. He would have to know who she was, so they could make the dinner arrangements. So...she'd use an alias.

Settle down. Use Grandma's imperious stare. Intimidate the intimidator.

Thrusting out her chin, she looked at him, still on his knees before her. "My name is Anne Dubois. I'm happy to meet you."

He threw back his head and laughed, showing strong white teeth. Little crinkles appeared at his eyes and gave him a totally different appearance. Instead of ferocious, he actually looked...approachable.

But why was he laughing?

The Bachelor—no, wait, she had to start thinking of him as Soren if he was The One—Soren sprang to his feet. Looming over her, he reached out for both her hands and gently pulled her upright. At least he hadn't lifted her by the waist and flung her over his shoulder again.

"Come on, Ms. *Dubois*," he said, emphasizing the name with a chuckle, "I'm ready for some coffee. How about you?"

"Tea, please," she said primly. "Chamomile, if you can find it."

"No problem, *Annie*. If they don't have it in a place like this, the concierge will run right out and dig some up for you."

She didn't like the way he was saying her name—uh, alias. But she valiantly walked alongside of him, taking three steps in her slender sheath of a gown to his one. Then he slowed down. A lightbulb must have popped in his head, she thought gratefully.

They wound up in a softly lit room with a row of leather banquettes and fat lighted candles glowing on the tables. The waiter assured her chamomile tea was no problem, and would she like wild honey with it? Soren ordered dark-roasted coffee and cognac.

"So tell me, Anne Dubois, who is Crystal D'Angelo?"

Crystal flinched, and hoped in the dim light he hadn't seen her reaction. She flicked her unmanageable hair behind one ear and looked yearningly in the direction where the waiter had disappeared.

"Are you a writer?" he persisted.

She glanced at him from out of the corner of her eye. "What makes you ask that?"

"I thought Anne Dubois was, you know, a pseudonym. To keep your professional life separate from your day-to-day life." He shifted closer to her on the soft leather.

She tensed. She couldn't move away from him without being obvious.

"Here you are, ma'am, sir." The waiter rested the tray on a corner of the table and placed a delicate china cup and saucer before her, then a matching teapot and honey jar. The cognac came in a bulbous glass set atilt in a holder over a low flame.

Grateful for the interruption, Crystal poured her tea and dribbled honey into it, then stirred. "So you were in the Marines?"

"Annie."

She worried her lower lip with her teeth. "I'm sorry. I shouldn't have done that."

"Done what?"

Lifting her cup to her mouth, Crystal paused then set it back down. "I was embarrassed, so I made up the name."

"A woman like you, what do you have to be embarrassed about?"

That innuendo got her back up like a cat about to unsheathe claws. "Like me?" Did he think she was accustomed to baring her breast before strangers? "What does that mean?"

"Man magnet. As beautiful as a sunset. Sexy as all get-out."

Crystal felt her mouth drop open. "I'm afraid you need a lot more light."

"I saw just fine from up on stage. You zapped me with those eyes. You looked like you wanted to eat me up."

"I didn't…I mean, Grandma told me to look at you, so of course I did. You were so big, I couldn't wrap my mind around it. But you were The One, so…"

She trailed off at the tender smile on his face. "Funny," he said. "I thought the same thing when you looked at me. I thought, if any dame there at the auction was going to win an evening of my time, it might as well be you."

"Really?" Her eyes grew huge and she groped for the crystal around her neck.

He leaned closer, casually slid his arm around the top of the banquette. "May I?"

"What?" He was too close. She wasn't ready for this! She needed some time to accept the fact that this was the man she would marry, whose bed she would share. Fighting panic, she dropped the crystal to press a protesting hand to his chest. Then couldn't bring herself to touch him.

He reached up to her shoulder, trailed a finger to her collarbone and the gold chain. He traced its path down her chest to the hollow between her breasts. She couldn't contain the little breathy sound that escaped her.

His knuckles brushed the warm swell of skin pushed up by her bra as he wrapped his fingers around her crystal. "This is lovely."

Crystal swallowed. She dared not look at him. He was too close. "It-It's been in the family for generations."

"I noticed that you played with it while you were bidding. Made me want to see what it was."

"Um." She could feel the soft puffs of his breath as he spoke, smelled the hint of coffee and cognac and some elusive scent she couldn't place. Her brain went foggy. "Now you know."

"Crystal."

The whisper of her real name from his tongue made her shiver. Grandma was right. She would know when she met The One. She turned her head just the slightest bit.

Just enough for his lips to graze her cheek.

"Soft. So soft," he murmured, nuzzling near her ear.

Heat sizzled through her, heat as strong as what she'd felt from the crystal when she'd first seen him. She couldn't help it. She leaned into him.

Soren's cock roared to life at her capitulation. She looked so innocent and sexy at the same time. He dropped the crystal and traced his fingers over the swells of her breasts, then up her throat to her jaw. He turned her face toward him and brushed his lips against hers. Once, twice. So soft, so pliant.

He shifted his angle and deepened the kiss. Her eager yet unschooled response sent flames to his groin. His tongue licked the seam of her lips.

"Oh." Her breathless sigh opened her mouth just enough for him to delve into that delectable cavern.

He wanted to drown in her, wallow in the scent of her hair, the femininity of her. He let his tongue taste the inner softness of her mouth, felt the rasp of her tongue, the sharpness of her teeth as he explored. Wrapping an arm around her shoulders, he nudged her closer to him and felt her tilt off balance. Instinctively she planted a small hand on his thigh, much too close to his zipper. Heat exploded into fire in the vicinity of his cock.

Danger signals blared across his mind even as he drove more deeply with his tongue. What the hell was he doing? These were the actions of a seducer, not a businessman supporting his community. Not a man who didn't even want a woman. He was just supposed to have dinner with her, for God's sake.

The heat of her small hand on his thigh intensified his lust as she kneaded his flesh in uncoordinated, jerky movements. Without breaking the kiss, he skimmed his hand down her shoulder, her arm and wrist, until his fingers covered hers. Without a thought of where he was, Soren nudged and prodded until she covered the unbearably hard bulge under his jeans. Vaguely he wondered how long it would be before the tablecloth burst into flames from his raging erection.

He felt a jolt run through her as she realized what her hand was caressing. He opened his eyes in time to see her eyelids flutter upward. She looked at him, eyes unfocused, mouth all ripe and wet and soft, breath coming in short gasps. Damn, he had to reach hard to find the gentleman lurking behind the seducer, but he managed to release her hand.

"Oh." She blinked as if coming out of a trance, still rubbing his cock like the magic lamp that would produce a genie to do her bidding. "It's so…hot."

Through gritted teeth, he hissed out, "Baby, I'm barely two seconds away from spontaneous combustion."

Oblivious to his pain, she continued rubbing his cock in soft, squeezing motions. Her eyes took on a dreamy quality. "It feels like…"

"Ah, there you are, young lady. You left your wrap on your chair. I was hoping I could catch you before—"

Crystal jumped to her feet at her grandmother's voice. And bumped the table with her hip. Her teacup clattered in its saucer, then toppled over, spilling its contents over the edge of the table. Soren didn't move quickly enough to avoid having the lukewarm liquid drip smack-dab on his jeans-imprisoned cock.

"Oh dear," the young woman said. "I'm so clumsy. Here," she grabbed a linen napkin, "let me wipe it off."

Soren grimaced. *Not bloody likely. At least not with your chaperone watching.* "It's fine," he said hastily. "No harm done." Yeah, right. If he was lucky, he'd be able to walk in about an hour.

"I must say, young man, you made quite an exit. In fact, you brought down the house. A couple of the bidders asked me if my granddaughter and I planned this." She shifted Crystal's red silk wrap to her other arm and offered a hand to Soren. "My name is Rowena D'Angelo. I'm happy to make your acquaintance."

Soren swallowed. What the hell was he supposed to say now? He cleared his throat, reached across the table reluctantly and accepted her handshake. "I'm sorry if I messed up the auction. I wasn't—"

Rowena waved away his objection. "You did the audience a favor. All those old fogies were ready for a shake-up, if you ask me." Without missing a beat she turned to Crystal. "Did you get what you needed?"

"I haven't—"

She ran right over Crystal's words. "No, you probably didn't. My granddaughter's kind of an ethereal thing, you know," she switched her attention to Soren, "like a wood nymph—or a sylph. I can never remember which is which. She doesn't get the nitty-gritty out of the way first. Do you have a business card? She'll need to be able to contact you to set up the dinner. You haven't set a date yet, correct? It's a good thing I found you in time to help, dear. We'll just exchange particulars and then you can give me the keys to the Beetle so I'll be able to get myself home and you two young ones can get acquainted without worrying that I'm losing my beauty sleep."

Crystal blinked. "Grandma, it's a stick shift."

"Yes, dear, I know. It's a perfectly sturdy car that will get me where I'm going."

"I can take her—" Soren said at the same time that Crystal said,

"But you can't drive a stick—"

"Bosh! Your grandmother can do anything she sets her mind to." She turned to Soren with what he thought was a gleam in her eye. "Besides, this young man has just offered to take you home, so we're all set."

"No."

"Now, Crystal, don't get uppity with me. You know how I get headaches if you're cross with me."

"Grandma, I respectfully request that we continue this discussion *in private*." She tossed a meaningful look Soren's way. He bit back a smile at the subtle way her spine straightened, the way her mouth firmed. Apparently she didn't often best her Grandma, but it wasn't for lack of gumption.

"Here's your wrap, dear. Now give me—"

Soren saw the flash of rebellion in Crystal's eyes as she ignored her grandmother's outstretched hand. "I *will* drive you home. Just give me a minute." She turned to him with determination written on her face. "*Do* you have a business card? It will make things simpler than having to write your phone number on a cocktail napkin."

The smile crept up one side of his mouth at her prim tone of voice. He dug into his back jeans pocket and fished out a wallet that had seen so many years of wear, it conformed to the shape of his butt. He pulled several cards out and shuffled through them. "Ah. Here. This one has my private office number on the back."

"Thank you." She accepted the card, careful, he noted, to keep her fingers from touching his. "Do we do the 'my assistant will contact your assistant' thing? Or can I call you direct?"

"By all means, Ms. *Dubois*, please feel free to call me yourself. I'm usually at Thor's Hammer by noon, and more often than not, I'm the one closing up at two a.m. My days off, when I take them, are Monday and Tuesday. So you can reach me most anytime."

"Thank you," she said again, then turned to Rowena. "May I have my wrap?"

The sly old woman pushed the swath of red silk into Soren's hands. It took him a moment to realize her meaning. Hell, he wasn't a gentleman, what did he know from wraps? He fumbled with the fabric, wondering if there was a right and a wrong side, an up and a down, then thought, *the hell with it*. Holding it up helter-skelter, he draped it over those delectable shoulders, wondering if shoulders could blush or if it was just a reflection of the silk.

* * * * *

Sitting at the vanity table of her art deco bedroom set, Crystal paused in the act of brushing her hair and stared at herself in the mirror. What did her Bachelor see when he looked at her? Unruly corkscrew curls that would touch her shoulder blades if she ever decided to iron her hair. A rather large mouth. Porcelain skin that blushed too easily. A little too ample in breast and hip.

What had Grandma called her—a sylph? Wood nymph? Where did she get such ideas? They conjured up a vision of Audrey Hepburn flitting through a wooded glade in a diaphanous negligee. Not a thirty-year-old slung over a lumberjack's shoulders like a log he'd just felled with an axe.

Not a woman wearing a granny nightgown printed with tiny, boring daisies.

She laid the brush down on the vanity and pushed to her feet. She was really too wired to sleep, but tomorrow would be a busy day. Maybe a cup of warm milk…

The ringing phone startled her. She glanced at the bedside clock. It had to be a wrong number, someone calling at two in the morning. She hovered near the answering machine, just in case she needed to pick up after the beep.

Her blood ran cold when she heard the message.

"Slut! Have you no shame?"

Chapter Two

§

"Whoooo-eee! Here comes the man himself!"

Soren stopped in his tracks and groaned at the uproar that greeted his entrance. Ordinarily the pub was a refuge, a place where he could keep the bar between himself and humanity and blend into the background.

Not today. It was barely eleven on Saturday morning. The bar had just opened its doors to the public, although the kitchen staff had been working for an hour. And the place was packed. He scanned the smiling faces. It seemed all the regulars had come by to add to the cacophony. "What the hell—"

Rolf stepped to his side and thumped him on the back. "Boy, does your still water run deep! We never knew you had it in you."

"What in blazes are you talking about? And what are you doing up before the crack of noon? I never see your homely face around here before dinnertime."

Instead of answering, Rolf lifted his sudsy mug of beer. "Hip hip!"

"Hooray!" the crowd answered as one. Soren dazedly noted that each person hoisted a drink as well. And all the grinning bunch of them were staring at him as though he were a celebrity.

"Dammit, have you all gone mad? What's going on here?"

"You, my dear, silent, back-of-the-room brother, made the front page of the *Philadelphia Inquirer* this morning." Rolf slapped said newspaper on the bar in front of him.

Soren grabbed it and stared at the full-color photo in disbelief. Feeling the blood drain from his face, he groped for the nearest barstool and slid his sorry ass onto the leather seat. The first thing to catch the eye was the red-covered derrière facing the camera. Then came the shapely calf kicking up from the side slit of her gown. He groaned. The photographer caught not only her bare foot but the questionable location of his huge hand keeping her from sliding off his shoulder.

He tossed the paper aside, plunked his elbows on the bar and pressed the heels of his hands into his eye sockets. God, how could he have been so stupid? How could a pair of innocent brown eyes make him such a laughingstock?

A glass of seltzer over ice appeared at his elbow. "Here," said Rolf, chuckling, "you might as well get it over with. We'll drink to your celebrity, ask you all sorts of embarrassing questions then let you get on with your work."

But Soren wasn't listening. He was reading the caption and groaning again.

At the highly successful Dinner With a Bachelor Auction, Soren Thorvald, owner of the Allendale bar-restaurant Thor's Hammer, carries his date off to their rendezvous. Socialite Crystal D'Angelo, highest bidder of the night, paid $2,200 for the privilege. The auction raised over $75,000 for the Battered Women's Shelter of Philadelphia. Story on page 3.

Twenty-two hundred…

Soren shook his head like a dog shedding water after a bath. "The world's gone mad. How can some broad pay more than two grand for a freakin' *date*!"

"Hey, if Magnus can hook up with a rich one, why shouldn't you?"

Soren glared at Rolf. Magnus, oldest of the three siblings, had just gotten engaged to the Main Line art dealer who handled his wood sculptures. "Magnus didn't get embarrassed on the front page of the *Inquirer*."

Unrepentant as usual, Rolf shot back, "What Magnus did to Kat at the Platinum Society couldn't be reported in a family newspaper."

"Mind your audience." Soren glanced meaningfully around him.

"So tell us," Rolf segued neatly, "what did she do to merit this Tarzan reaction?"

Soren closed his eyes for a moment. "Guess I just got hot under the collar. I was the next-to-last one on the auction block. Spent over an hour listening to the auctioneer jabber away. Looking at all the rich women in the audience, with their fancy gowns and fancier jewelry, hearing their sexist comments, I wondered what the hell I was doing up on the stage."

"So you chucked your purchaser over your shoulder as a kind of revenge?"

Soren clenched his fist around the glass. It wasn't until he'd actually seen the shoe in her hand that he realized she'd just been searching for her shoe under the table, and not hiding from him. He raised the glass and downed half the seltzer, more to postpone further talk than to quench a thirst.

"Phone call for you, Soren," Trang, the day bartender, yelled in a singsong voice that hinted of a certain woman on the other end.

An anticipatory hush fell over the revelers. Soren tamped down a hint of panic. Why had he given her the pub's number? Why hadn't he just told her to leave a message on his private office number? Why hadn't he just made the damn dinner arrangements last night?

Hell, why hadn't he opened a bar in Oregon instead of in Pennsylvania?

"I'll take it out back," he bit out, and headed for the kitchen, which had no more than three pairs of ears eavesdropping on every word.

He picked up the cordless extension and said, "I've got it, Trang," and waited to hear the click that ensured she had hung up. After a deep breath, he said into the phone, "Soren Thorvald here."

"Oh, Mr. Thorvald," gushed a breathy feminine voice, "I'm so glad I caught you. I'm Sarah Lane from Channel Five. What a great human-interest story in today's *Inquirer*. I'm on my way to Thor's Hammer with a cameraman and wonder if you'd kindly grant us an interview for tonight's news. We'll be there in fifteen minutes."

"No! I mean, no," he said with slightly less panic. "I'm afraid I have an appointment that will take up most of my day."

"Oh, please, just a few minutes. We'll be in and out before you know it."

"No, really, I'm leaving soon."

"But you're still here, right?" said the perky voice. Suddenly he heard a lot of commotion through the phone. He snuck a peek through the window in the kitchen's swinging door in time to see a guy with a videocam on his shoulder, doing a slow pan of the bar area.

Shit! She had sneakily kept him on the phone to be sure she'd catch him there. Well, she guessed wrong. With a couple of panicked hand motions to the chef, he slunk out through the employees' entrance while talking to the reporter. "Look, Ms. Lane, why don't you talk to the bartender. Trang, her name is. She'll set something up on my calendar for next week. I really, really can't take the time now to talk with you."

He disconnected the phone, flicked the remote button to open his truck, and hauled his ass out of the parking lot like the hounds of hell were chasing him.

Because they were.

* * * * *

Jack Healy carefully combed his wavy brown hair as he scrutinized himself in the small bathroom mirror. Not bad for fifty-one, he thought. Most people guessed him to be no more than forty, with his Charles Atlas physique and thick head of hair with touches of gray at the temples. And if he was only five-foot-six, he carried himself with the panache of a much taller man.

Life was good.

Today was especially good. Crystal D'Angelo was bringing him another "find". Over the five years they'd been associates, she'd consigned many antiques to sell in his shop on trendy Lancaster Avenue in Devon, Pennsylvania. He wasn't one of the Philadelphia Four Hundred, but he counted many of them as his friends and clients. They knew a Healy was quality.

He frowned at his image then opened a small cupboard over the towel rack and withdrew his manicure scissors. It wouldn't do to have Crystal distracted by a nose hair. A few judicious snips and he was perfectly groomed again.

The bell over his front door tinkled like wind chimes. Jack straightened his rep tie over his snowy white shirt and went to greet his customer.

One look and he knew the woman was a browser. She gazed around like a camera panning a scene, touched a Sevres bowl here, an arrowback side chair there, and in two minutes walked out without having said a word.

"I'm here," Crystal sang out a half-hour later as she all but danced through the entrance, her raven black hair flowing out behind her. "Augie's driving the truck to the alley. Can you give him a hand?"

"So nice to see you, my dear," Jack said as he took her hand and brought it briefly to his lips. "Your eyes sparkle as much as your crystal today."

"Thank you." She air-kissed his cheek and headed toward the back storeroom. "The fund-raiser was great last night. Raised over seventy-five thousand dollars."

Crystal continued talking about the event as he followed her, but Jack heard only the husky music of her voice. Above calf-high boots, she wore a swirling blue paisley skirt and matching fringed shawl that covered the white turtleneck sweater beneath.

She had the back door unlocked by the time Jack got there, and was walking toward a scruffy white truck of uncertain vintage, with a dent in its rear bumper and patches of rust along one fender. He shook his head. Crystal D'Angelo could well afford to purchase an appropriate van for her business, but seemed unaware that the current battered vehicle was tarnishing her image. The fact that the young man she used for occasional hauling lived in this affluent area added to Jack's pique. The kid must not still live at home, or his parents would have seen to it that he drove a current model. On the Main Line, he knew, image was everything.

A tall, muscular redhead in gray T-shirt and worn jeans, Augie bounded onto the truck bed, which held two large objects wrapped in mover's quilts. Dismissing the twinge of jealousy at the younger man's agility, Jack turned his attention to his new consignment and rubbed his hands in anticipation. Because of her trust fund, Crystal only worked, he knew, for the thrill of the hunt. He himself had the same sense of excitement over a new piece.

"This one's a beauty," Augie said when he spied the proprietor.

Jack nodded an acknowledgement, although he wondered how much the kid knew about antiquing. He couldn't be more than twenty-two or -three. Probably got all his buzzwords from Crystal. The kid was unfailingly cheerful every time he brought in another piece of hers. Such a saccharine disposition had to be faked, he mused.

They carefully lifted first one, then the other object off the truck and carried them into the storeroom. When both sections were unwrapped and fitted one over the other, Jack walked around the cherry corner cupboard in silence, evaluating, assessing.

Finally he said, "All nine panes are original glass. Excellent patina. No nicks or dings. This will fetch a good price." Close to five figures, he added to himself. He looked at Crystal, whose eyes were aglow at her triumph and whose self-satisfied smile dazzled. God, she was more beautiful than the antique.

"Come." He extended his hand to her. "Let us toast this newest acquisition." He'd inaugurated a ritual with her to celebrate the delivery of each new consignment, imbibing in a salubrious glass of extra-dry sherry, using a pair of treasured Lalique glasses he'd vowed never to sell.

"Oh, Jack, I'm sorry. I know we've established this lovely tradition, but today I don't have the time. Grandma's waiting for me. The poor thing has no sense of direction, and she needs to go down to Wilmington. You know how imperious Rowena D'Angelo can be when things don't go her way."

"She runs your life," Jack grumbled. "You should be able to come and go as you please without being her lackey. She can afford a cab. Or even a chauffeur."

Crystal gave him a hug, as if it was an acceptable substitute for more of her time. "She's my grandmother and I love her."

He held onto her as long as he dared, until he felt her pull away.

"You ready, doll?" Augie stood at the passenger's door of the truck, frowning at their embrace. "Your chariot awaits."

"I'll talk to you soon," she told Jack, touching his cheek even as she turned to go.

As Crystal lifted her foot onto the running board, Augie put his huge hands around her waist. Jack was sure the cocky youngster tried to make it look like he was simply getting a good grip on her, but to Jack's eyes, he was caressing her, damn him. "Up you go."

Jack gritted his teeth as he watched her smile at the kid, tucking her skirt inside the cab. Then he trudged back into the shop and sat at his cluttered desk, staring at the photograph on the front page of the *Philadelphia Inquirer* and shaking his head.

* * * * *

"He's a little old for you, don't you think?"

Crystal looked at Augie with a mixture of exasperation and affection as they flowed with the stop-and-go traffic of a Saturday afternoon in suburbia. The sprinkling of freckles across his nose made him look like a college freshman, but his green eyes held a man's knowledge of the world. "He's a colleague, Augie. There's nothing personal between us."

"He sure thinks there is."

"Oh, come on, now."

Suddenly Augie turned into a fast-food restaurant and drove to the back. "I need some coffee. But first." He pulled crosswise into a couple of hash-marked slots, braked hard, and shoved the truck into Park. "C'mere, doll." He snapped off his seat belt, leaned across the console and pulled her roughly to him. "You want some excitement, you come to Augie."

Before Crystal had time to do little more than blink, his mouth latched onto hers, alternately thrusting his tongue inside and sucking on her lower lip. His right arm tightened around her shoulders. With his left, he groped for her hand and rubbed it against a raging erection. "You turn me on like nobody's business," he whispered hoarsely. "Look how much I want you."

"Augie, please don't—"

"Come on, doll. You know you like it rough. Hell, that caveman stunt in the picture, it made me hard just looking at it."

"What are you talking about?"

But Augie just clamped down on her again, opening his mouth like a leech, teeth clicking against hers as he sought even more access to the inside of her mouth.

Struggling against his sudden, misplaced passion, Crystal managed to yank her hand away from his zipper and shove her palm against his chest. It was as ineffectual as trying to move a mountain with a stick. Eyes wide open in shock, she twisted her head from side to side trying to escape, but Augie gripped her skull tightly as he thrust his tongue further inside.

In desperation, she bit down on it.

"Hey! What the fuck—"

Crystal took in a deep, gulping breath. "Augie, I'm sorry. I didn't mean to hurt you. You just…" She raised her hand to her heart, felt it thumping wildly. "You frightened me."

"You bit my tongue!"

"I'm sorry," she said again, wondering why she was the one apologizing. She inched away from him until her back hit the door, and crossed both arms over her chest as some kind of flimsy protection against any further assault.

He glared at her for a moment, making her feel like a deer in headlights, unable to move yet sensing danger. Then he shifted in his seat, pulled a folded handkerchief out of his jeans pocket and pressed it to his mouth. "Look." He held it out to her. "Blood."

"I'm—" *No.* She would not apologize again. She tried to take a deep breath without expanding her chest—she would *not* do anything to further provoke him.

Although what brought on his attack, she had no clue.

Oh. Maybe she did. "What picture? What caveman stunt?"

His mouth turned up in a smirk. "You mean you haven't seen today's paper?"

"No. I got—" She was going to say she'd gotten up late today because of the events following last night's auction, but prudence dictated that she not refer, even obliquely, to her sleeping habits or her bed. Who knew what would set him off again?

"I had to run some errands before you picked me up. And, by the way, I do thank you for helping me with the corner cupboard. With you and Jack moving my antiques, I know they'll be handled with kid gloves."

"I still say he's too old for you."

She made a little impatient sound. "I repeat, we're just colleagues in art. And what picture are you talking about?"

With a smirk, Augie reached under the driver's seat and pulled out the daily newspaper, folded so the page-one photo held center stage.

Crystal gasped. Her eyes widened to big O's as she read the caption. Then she smacked the paper on her knee with a force that would have killed a dozen flies. "Take me to Grandma's. I am so going to give that woman a piece of my mind. She hoodwinked me every step of the way last night."

Her eyes snapped to him. "And wipe that grin off your face."

Easing the truck into gear, he saluted her. "Yes, ma'am."

God, his balls hurt like a son of a bitch. The little tease made him harder than an iron girder in a skyscraper. She kept flirting with those sexy brown eyes and killer smile then pulling back when a guy tried to take her up on it.

He'd been walking around with a boner ever since he'd seen the picture in this morning's paper—her heart-shaped ass with that red material clinging to it like saran wrap, outlining every lush inch of it, slung over an Arnold-type shoulder with the guy's hand very near where he wanted his own to be. Augie imagined the feel of her crack as his hand ran up and down the valley between her ass cheeks, driving her wild with each stroke. Especially if she was damn near helpless, like she was in the picture.

One of these days, he was sure, she'd give in to him. No one resisted a Quillan for long. He'd just have to bide his time and keep on her good side. Which reminded him. He'd better apologize.

"Hey, Crys, I'm sorry. I let my imagination run away from me." He tossed her one of his naughty-little-boy half-smiles that had gotten more debutantes to spread their legs for him than he could count. "You gotta admit, though. That picture's gonna sell a lot of newspapers."

There it was again, her cheeks going all red. Why would something like that make a woman blush? Hell, surely she knew she had everything a man would want. Not just an ass made in heaven, but the headlights too. He'd bumped up against her, accidentally on purpose, enough times to know she hadn't had a boob job.

"I promise. It won't happen again, Crys. I like helping out, 'cause I'm learning so much about the business side of antiquing. We got shit like that all around the house, but to me it's just, you know, things to sit on or to store stuff in. You're showing me all kinds of little tricks to pick out what's worth bidding on."

She turned to him, a small smile chasing away her scowl. *Good. Distract her by talking about things she likes.*

"I do get a kick out of finding a treasure in someone's attic," she said.

"But I'll never know as much about it as you do. You seem to have a knack."

"You forget, Augie. I grew up with that 'stuff' too. We were just interested in different things."

He let his eyes rove shamelessly over her body, her arms now relaxed in her lap rather than tightly crossed over her chest. Then he looked up at her and grinned. "Yeah. You don't look much like a football player."

Damn, there it was again. It was way too easy to make her blush. She punched him ineffectually on his biceps. "Stop that."

Augie didn't respond. They had arrived at her grandmother's house. He swore as he eyed the black Escalade in the sweeping driveway near the front steps. "Your gramma don't watch out, she's gonna be the next Mrs. Courtland A. Quillan the Third."

Crystal laughed. "Don't be silly. She's a dozen years older than your dad."

"Yeah, but don't forget, she's rich. So were his three other wives."

"You're so cynical for such a young man. They're probably discussing last night's Bachelor Auction."

Then her smile dimmed. Thinking, no doubt, about how she'd exited said auction.

He pulled the truck behind the SUV until he nudged it with his rusty front bumper. It was the most disrespect he could get away with at the moment without jeopardizing his allowance. He shifted gears, turned off the ignition and jumped out to give Crystal a hand with the dismount. He loved this old truck. It was so high off the ground, women almost always waited for an assist from his two big, willing hands. And usually got a kick out of sliding down his hard young body on the way to the ground.

Crystal was a good deal shorter than he, but she was ready to jump down when he reached her. "Hey, you don't want to twist your ankle. Here. Let me." Planting his hands on her waist, he whisked her off her feet and set her down gently on the paving bricks arcing across the driveway. Not a hint of hanky-panky. He hoped she appreciated how good he was being.

She rummaged in the little change purse she had on a belt around her waist and turned to him. "Here." She handed him an envelope, which usually contained fifty dollars. "Thanks again for your help. I'll be in touch."

Augie watched her sweet ass sway as she marched up the stairs, tossing his keys in the air as he debated whether to leave now or to follow her inside and cause more trouble for his father.

Chapter Three

ℬ

"Did you orchestrate this, Grandma?"

Crystal stormed into the elegant study off the front hall and tossed the newspaper onto the Louis Quatorze desk behind which Rowena sat. "Did you pay the photographer to take this kind of tabloid-trash picture?" She speared a glance at Courtland—or Trey, as everyone called him, since he was the Third—sitting on the brocade wing chair alongside the desk, one ankle crossed over his opposite knee. "And you, Trey. Were you part of this circus too?"

Her grandmother just smiled mysteriously, like a cat who swallowed a canary and had another in its sights.

Crystal leaned forward, slapped her palms down on the desk. Her hair fell forward into her eyes. Impatiently she flicked it back with a toss of her head. Her shawl slipped off her shoulders and slithered to the floor.

"And that muscleman you hired. Where did you find him, central casting? Did you figure that since I didn't like any of the trust-funders you keep setting me up with as blind dates, that I'd go for an uncouth brute with more muscle than brain?"

"And did you think I relished the idea of being bought like a slab of meat by a spoiled brat of a socialite?"

Crystal whirled around to see Soren rising from the sofa against the far wall. She'd been so focused on her grandmother's face when she'd stalked in a moment ago, she hadn't even glanced around the room. "What are you doing here?"

The smile he showed was more like a snarl. "Your grandmother seems to have tentacles all over eastern Pennsylvania." He pointed with his chin at Trey. "They staked out Thor's Hammer and caught me running out the back door from a Channel Five reporter."

She threw him a disparaging look. "And what, they overpowered you and forced you to come here?"

He took a few menacing steps toward her. "'Forced' me? In a way, yes, they did. Ms. D'Angelo suggested, very forcefully, that we get the 'transaction' completed as soon as possible."

At the threat implicit in his approach, she instinctively took a step back. And caught her boot heel in the shawl lying in a tangle on the floor. Off balance, she flailed her arms, trying to get her feet back under her.

In an eye blink, Soren was at her side. He scooped her up, one arm under her knees, the other around her shoulders.

Without conscious thought, Crystal wrapped her arms around his neck.

Time stopped. She looked into his fathomless blue eyes and felt the amulet pulsing warm against her chest through the soft wool of her sweater. The heat of his torso spread to her hip, her waist. She wanted nothing so much as to snuggle against the strength of him until the end of time.

"What the hell is this, a Grade-B movie?"

Crystal felt her feet slap to the floor as Soren let go of her. Augie stood in the archway, fists on his hips, glaring at the tableau before him.

"Augie, dear, how nice to see you again." Rowena stood and walked around her desk, regal in a dark blue long-sleeved sheath with three strands of exquisitely matched pearls at her neck, her arms outstretched to him.

He suffered her handclasp while he glowered at Crystal.

"I tripped," Crystal explained, nonplussed at the resentful look in Augie's eye, as though he thought she'd willingly go into any man's arms except his. "He saved me from another bruise." To punctuate her statement, she bent forward to retrieve the shawl from where it had dropped when Soren rescued her.

"Well, at least it wasn't Trey trying to play hero," Augie sneered. "Father isn't in any shape to physically pick up a woman. He can only do it with money."

"Money always seems to loom large to those who have none." Trey stood and shot his French cuffs from under his linen blazer as he glared at his son. "Perhaps that's Fourth's problem. I can see," he said, turning to Rowena, "that it's impossible to continue our discussion with so many interruptions." He took the older woman's hand and lifted it to his mouth. "Come walk me to the front door."

"It will be my pleasure," Rowena said. "And you, my strong, handsome Augie," she turned her smile on the young man, "I would be much obliged if you would help me bring down a cumbersome package from the attic."

Augie reluctantly pulled his glare away from Crystal and Soren and allowed himself to be nudged toward the pocket doors, carefully avoiding any contact with his father.

"And as for you, my dear, remember, a D'Angelo always honors a commitment." She gave Crystal one of her imperious stares. "I suggest you and Mr. Thorvald stay in the study and work out the details of your agreement. In fact," she pushed down a lever as she slid the doors closed, "I'm locking you in until you do."

When the doors met, the lock mechanism clicked loudly. Retreating footsteps, muffled by the oriental runner on the parquet floor, faded into silence.

Crystal barely held back the smile that threatened to twitch the corners of her mouth. She knew, although Soren probably didn't, that the door couldn't be unlocked from the hallway, but only from inside the study. Grandma had truly given them privacy.

The thought sent her pulse racing. She reached for the talisman at her throat. The crystal now lay silent and inert in her hand, as if in tacit approval.

They stood no more than two feet apart. Crystal had the strongest urge to reach out to him, to run her fingers through his wavy blond hair. Hers. This man was hers. Did he know it too?

"I didn't mean—"

"I'm sorry I—"

They had spoken simultaneously. Crystal thought he looked as hesitant as she herself felt.

"Ladies first."

She cleared her throat. "You're really not a brute. And...and you're not uncouth, or any of the other horrible things I said. I was just...I mean, when I saw that front-page photo, it made me pretty upset. The paper could have been merciful and said 'unknown woman'. But to see my name in the caption and have it linked to that huge derrière, well, I never realized my butt was so big, and the—"

Soren raised his hand in a stop-sign gesture. "Your butt isn't big. It's—" he cut himself off before he could say *It's perfect the way it is*— "It's not big," he repeated. God, how lame was that?

"Oh, heck." Crystal waved a hand in the air. "I don't really care how big my butt is. It all has to do with camera angle, anyway. What I do care about is the image created by that photo. Poor Grandma. She's always tried to remind me of the decorum expected of, well, the upper class, and I came across looking like an exhibitionist on one of those tell-all, bare-all television shows."

Soren tried to keep his thoughts pure. He really did. But having seen Springer when his patrons clamored for it on the bar's big-screen TV, his long-dormant imagination had Crystal ripping her sweater over her head and baring her lush breasts to an audience before launching herself at the "other woman" with claws unsheathed, and him being one of the bouncers keeping the combatants apart, having to put his hands on her soft skin to hold her back and maybe, just maybe, copping a surreptitious feel...

Jesus. He spun on his heel and flopped down on the wing chair that Trey had so recently occupied, shut his eyes tight and gripped the brocade arms until his knuckles showed white.

"Are you all right?" Crystal's soft, concerned voice sounded right at his ear.

Cautiously he opened his eyes. Mistake.

She was bent toward him, breasts at his eye level. He could see the slight difference in color where the white bra pushed against the white sweater. He could also see—God, the lump in his throat felt like a fist—her nipples poking twin tents in the fabric.

"Soren?" Her warm palm grazed his cheek. "Can I get you something? Brandy? Water?"

His groan came out like a growl. As if of their own volition, his hands reached out to cup her firm ass cheeks and draw her in between his outspread thighs. He pillowed his head between her breasts and inhaled the aroma of her, a flower-and-orange scent along with a subtle musk that was definitely female. He felt her lean down and put her cheek on the crown of his head, hands resting lightly on his shoulders.

Oh man, he was a goner.

With great delicacy he ran his palms up and down her ass, explored the contour of her hips melding into the curve of her waist. His thumbs caressed her rib cage, circling higher and higher until he reached the heavy weight of her breasts. He moved his head until his mouth grazed one nipple. The feel of that hard nubbin through the sweater made hot blood surge to his cock. He closed his lips around the tip of her breast.

She drew in a halting breath and whispered his name.

Taking that as encouragement, Soren increased the pressure, alternately suckling and lightly raking it with his teeth. She snuggled him closer into her embrace, her hands cupping the back of his head, her breath coming in shorter gasps.

He tilted his head back, slid his hands beneath her sweater and shoved the material up over her breasts. "Tell me I'm not

45

dreaming," he murmured as he flicked his thumbs back and forth over the silky bra enclosing what surely had to be the most glorious tits he'd ever seen in or out of a magazine.

The sudden revving of an engine broke into his befogged brain and he realized where he was. Where they were. He dropped his hands to her hips. "Crystal, we have to stop."

"Mmmm, why's that?"

"Your grandmother's likely to come barging in any minute to see what's going on."

Crystal laughed, a slow sultry sound. "She can't."

"No, really, we have to—"

"Soren, read my lips. Grandma didn't lock us in. She locked herself and everyone else out."

Soren blinked. "Huh?"

"The door unlocks only from the inside. We can stay here until tomorrow if we want and nobody will interrupt us."

Soren's focus sharpened. "So she actually expected us to do…what we're doing."

"I think she was hoping."

Abruptly he stood. "I can't compromise you like that. She'll know. It's not right."

Crystal stood toe to toe with him, fists on her hips. Having to look up at him, however, took some of the sternness out of her reply. "I'm old enough to make that decision for myself."

"I can't do it. It shows a lack of respect to do…anything under her roof, knowing that she knows what we're doing."

She rose on tiptoe, snaked her arms around his waist and gave him a kiss that nearly blew his ears off. "You're so sweet, Soren, but I want more."

"No. You only think you do. You're reacting to your grandmother's subliminal suggestion, that's all. You're a…a…what did the newspaper call you? A socialite. You've got money, class, a pedigree. I'm a bartender, for God's sake."

She gave him a meltingly soft look. "I want you, Soren."

His teeth clenched. He could feel the panic building. Oh boy, was he out of his element. Why hadn't he had more practice with women in general? What the hell was he supposed to do now?

"But I'll wait." With that simple declaration she turned and walked to the pocket doors. A flick of a lever and she pulled the doors ajar an inch. "Happy?"

Soren swallowed. Or tried to. His mouth felt dryer than the Sahara at noon. "That's not quite the word I would use, but yes, that's better."

"So," she said primly, strolling to the Louis Quatorze desk and sitting in the plush leather chair, "let's do the other thing Grandma is expecting us to do."

He gave her a blank look.

"Where would you like to have dinner? I'm buying."

Chapter Four

ഇ

"Okay, Soren, out with it."

Magnus guzzled half the bottle of iced tea he'd pulled out of the cooler then looked at his younger brother. Soren's T-shirt was plastered to his back and chest from sweat, just like his own. They were taking a break from cutting a slab off a valuable black walnut log with a two-man saw.

"Huh? Out with what?"

"I can't remember the last time you took an afternoon off from Thor's Hammer to help me. Yet you've been slaving away for three hours without saying a word. What's bugging you?"

Soren leaned against the tree stump and rolled a frosty bottle against his forehead. It did little to cool the hot blood pumping in his veins. Hell, Magnus was in much better shape than he, hauling slabs of wood around his atelier while Soren himself only wrestled with a keg now and then.

He set down the bottle and pulled out a red handkerchief from his jeans pocket. Swiping it over his face and neck, he squinted into the woods surrounding Magnus' barn. "You ever think about Mom?"

He'd caught Magnus unaware, Soren saw, if the breath whooshing out of his brother was any indication. Magnus settled himself on the forest duff away from the pile of sawdust and stared into the distance, much as Soren was doing.

"Yeah. She's living in Alaska. Did you know that?"

It was Soren's turn to take a sharp breath. "No, I didn't. How did you find out?"

"Kat. She's an Internet whiz."

Kat. Soren still couldn't get over the fact that his big brother was marrying Kat Donaldson in a few weeks. They'd started out as such antagonists—Kat a sexually active, aggressive art gallery owner, Magnus a reclusive sculptor with a big stick up his ass—that he wondered if it would last. But then, what did he, Soren, know about relationships with women? His view had been tainted by the woman who'd up and walked out on three young boys and a heartbroken husband.

"Kat kept asking me questions about her," Magnus continued. "I told her what little I knew about her after she disappeared. At least, we think it's her. I haven't gotten up the nerve to contact her yet."

After twenty-some years, Soren wasn't sure he'd have the nerve to, either. What would he say? *Why did you leave? Who was the guy that made you carry on so?*

Maybe he was better off not knowing.

Magnus looked at him with a sober expression. "What brought this on?"

Soren picked up a piece of bark and began shredding it with his fingernails. "I don't know. Maybe I'm just wondering if she's the reason I've never had, you know, a relationship."

"You mean with a woman?"

Soren sighed. "Yeah."

A beat went by before Magnus asked, "You found someone?"

"Yes. No. Maybe. I don't know."

Magnus snorted. "Well, that covers all the bases."

"Seriously, Mags. I've been thinking about Mom. What she did to Pop. Remember how all the spark went out of him when she left?"

"Yeah, and then a couple of years later he has a fatal accident."

"Think it was an accident?"

Their somber gazes met. Erik Thorvald's truck had smashed into a railroad abutment at a high rate of speed. It had taken the Jaws of Life to pry his mangled body out of the cab. "I always wondered," Magnus admitted.

Soren had been nine, Magnus a year older, when Alana Hall Thorvald dropped her bomb on their family. In his mind Soren could still hear the harsh words between his parents in the dining room, could hear his mother's raw sobs as he cowered behind the kitchen counter where he'd gone in search of a snack, not wanting to listen but afraid to move for fear of adding to the maelstrom. He'd been old enough to understand love, and the withholding of it.

He'd withheld it ever since.

He thought Magnus had withheld love, too, especially after his brief, tragic marriage.

Then Magnus had truly found love with Kat. He was a changed man. Not possessive and jealous like with the first one, but being himself only better, easygoing and confident in her love.

It made Soren wonder if the same could happen to him.

The image of Crystal D'Angelo coalesced in his mind's eye. Her *joie de vivre*, the sparkle and snap in her eyes. Her sweet nature, her combination of innocence and unconscious sensuality. And that body...a man's wet dream.

"So, you want me to?"

Soren roused himself. "To what?"

"Contact her. Mom."

"Jesus, Mags. We've lived twenty years with the knowledge that she didn't want anything to do with us. Give me some time to absorb this new information. To steel myself to having her reject us yet again."

For a while neither man spoke. Birds twittered, flying in and out of the branches overhead as the brothers sipped their tea, each thinking his own thoughts. Finally Magnus stood. "Well. Break's over. Let's get this bugger on the truck." He stashed the empty iced tea bottle in the cooler and turned to the slab of walnut.

"Right." With a sigh, Soren heaved himself up as well.

"And, Soren?" Mags put a hand on Soren's shoulder. "You're as tight-assed as I used to be as far as women are concerned. Wouldn't hurt you to take a leap of faith and let one get close enough to spend the night. There's something to be said for waking up to a warm, cuddly body wrapped around you, even if there's no happy ever after in the offing."

Soren turned away. "Spare me the mushy details."

But he was thinking about it. Oh yeah, he was thinking about it.

* * * * *

"I can't, Deirdra, it's too revealing."

Crystal stood at the cheval mirror in her bedroom and frowned at her image. The underwired bra covered no more than a half-inch of skin above her dusky-rose nipples. And those might as well have been exposed, the ecru lace was so sheer.

"The point of a Victoria's Secret bra, dear heart, is to enhance your natural charms." Deirdra adjusted a strap to add a smidgen more of plumpness where Crystal thought none was needed. "And you said so yourself, you want to do the nasty with him. When he peels off your clothes, believe me, seeing you like this will bring him to his knees."

"Well, I don't want to hit him over the head with it."

"From what you've told me about this bachelor, he needs a good swift kick right between the eyes. But more to the point, this little getup will make *you* feel sexy. So you'll be giving out all the right signals while still acting demure. Just don't chicken out."

"I won't." She rubbed the crystal nestled between the plump cleavage. It was just barely warm, perhaps from her erotic thoughts and not from any magical message that it approved what she contemplated doing tonight. "Grandma told me it would let me know when I found The One. When I first laid eyes on Soren at the auction, it got so hot it almost left a burn mark on my chest."

Deirdra had been with her the day Grandma had given her the amulet. The two friends had met in fourth grade when a bully cornered Crystal and demanded her lunch money. Several inches taller and twenty pounds heavier than Crystal, Deirdra had come along and clunked the kid on the head with an unabridged dictionary she was returning to the library. They'd been inseparable ever since.

Today Deirdra was still several inches taller and twenty pounds heavier, but those pounds were well distributed on her five-foot-eight frame. They'd gone to different colleges, but managed to be as close as twins during the separation. Deirdra had come back to the area and ran a successful New Age shop, Good Vibrations, in Bryn Mawr. One didn't need to explain the power of crystals to Deirdra Zinman.

"Now. Lose those white cotton briefs. Here." She held up a bikini bottom whose minuscule front and back patches of lace seemed held together with almost invisible elastic.

"What, no thong?" Crystal asked, only half jokingly.

"Ick. Thongs go all the way up to your waist. Yeah, they make your legs look longer, but the newest look is a pair of panties that are so low down on your hips that you can see your butt crack."

She tossed the garment to Crystal. "It's a visual thing. Makes him think how much easier it is to pull them down."

Crystal groaned. "If you're trying to convince me to wear it…"

"Just do as I say. Time's getting short." Deirdra reached for the outfit she had browbeaten Crystal into wearing—a cream-colored sweater cropped at the waist, a row of tiny buttons down the front, a sweetheart neckline displaying a modest amount of cleavage, and a low-rise pair of snug stovepipe jeans with high-heeled slides.

"I can't," Crystal gasped when she got everything zipped and buttoned. "There's too much of my midriff showing."

"Not." Deirdra folded her arms across her chest like a stern librarian. "It's just right. Don't you browse through the fashion magazines at the supermarket checkout counter? I could have gotten you one with a two-inch rise. This one's mild compared to some of the styles."

The frown deepened between Crystal's brows. "I don't think…"

"Good. Don't think. Just do."

Crystal huffed out a breath that tickled a curly tress dangling down her forehead. "But isn't this…overkill?"

"My great-granddaddy used to tell me that before you can make a mule obey, you have to get his attention. That's why he always carried a two-by-four when he went into the mountains. Sounds like our Soren is like that mule. We're just getting his attention."

She put her hands on Crystal's shoulders and twirled her toward the bedroom door. "Now go, before you're late!"

"Okay, okay." She descended the stairs with Deirdra at her heels. Reaching the closet at the front door, she pulled out her raincoat. "It's supposed to get cold tonight."

"Ew, not that ratty old thing. Here. Take this." Deirdra scooped up her trendy vest, a rabbit-fur front and knitted back that skimmed the hips. "Just make sure to take it *off* in the restaurant. Don't forget, you do want to make an impression on the man."

Crystal rolled her eyes. "Yes, Mommy."

As they descended the porch steps to their respective cars, Deirdra called out, "And don't come back until noon tomorrow!"

* * * * *

"Boy, are you antsy tonight!"

Soren checked his watch again, then wiped down a spotless section of the bar, giving Trang a gimlet eye. "No, I'm not."

The assistant bartender shook her head. "You've barked at the chef twice for burning the burgers, you damn near bit off the head of that new waitress for getting the beer orders wrong, and you've gone out back to pee several times. Now what gives?"

"Just being the boss."

"You'd better adjust your attitude, or you'll be the boss over nothing."

When he merely raised an eyebrow, she added, "Everyone'll quit."

Talk about being on the horns of a dilemma. On the one hand, Soren wanted to do this right here, on his home turf, where he felt most comfortable. He knew the abundant selection of beers on tap was top-drawer and the food hearty and tasty. On the other hand, Trang and everyone else would be all over them if he brought Crystal here. He could just imagine them hovering around the booth, pretending to offer good service while eavesdropping on whatever conversation he might manage to have with her. No way, uh-uh.

So he'd chosen a Tex-Mex joint where he didn't have to wear a tie. One night a year dressed up was more than enough for him, thank you very much, and he'd already used it up. She'd better not be late. He'd gone out back three times to check the parking lot. After all, how many lemon-yellow VW bugs would be parking in his lot tonight? He'd specifically told her where to pull up so he could just dash out and jump in. Damn it, he should have insisted that he'd meet her at the restaurant. But she was as obstinate as a boulder about picking him up for their "date".

Date. The very word made him shudder.

He stashed the cleaning cloth on its rack and ducked under the counter. Skirting the tiny dance floor, he pushed open the swinging door to the kitchen. The chef pointedly ignored him, but the assistant eyed him warily as Soren made his way around the chopping table to the employee entrance.

There! His heart gave a hard thump. He looked over his shoulder and yelled, "Tell Trang to take over. I've got some errands to run."

And he was out of there as if the proverbial bats out of hell were chasing him. Just as he hit the asphalt, the VW stopped with its passenger door facing the entrance, as though it had been choreographed and rehearsed. He ducked his head, verified through the open window that it was indeed Crystal, and jumped in.

"Go." He grabbed the seat belt and hooked it around himself.

"Which way?" To her credit, she kept the car in motion, heading toward the parking entrance, oblivious to the fact that he was pulling a disappearing act.

"Turn right. About a mile and turn right at the first light."

When the lights from the Thor's Hammer sign had faded from his side-view mirror, with no little amount of relief that they'd escaped with no one the wiser, he turned to Crystal. "Hi."

She glanced over, gave him a tentative smile, and turned back to the road.

"I see you didn't have any trouble finding the place."

Way to go, Thorvald. Could his conversation be any more scintillating?

"No, your directions were very good. Is this the turn?"

"Yes."

She hung a right then followed his instructions until they were parked in front of Chica's. "It's a down-home place. I hope you like Tex-Mex."

"I like it fine."

He got out of the car and headed to the entrance. Then looked back when she didn't follow suit.

"Oh." He guessed she'd been waiting for him to open the car door. By the time his brain had shifted gears to go back to the VW, she was walking toward him.

He scratched his head, then opened the restaurant door and made himself stand there. "Sorry. I, uh, I'm rusty at this kind of stuff."

"That's okay." The smile she gave him made his eyes cross. She preceded him inside into an area with a counter and booths, then walked to the rear, where a quieter dining room awaited.

The hostess ushered them to a corner table. "Someone will be right with you to take your drink orders." She set menus down on the checkered tablecloth and left.

"Uh, do you want me to take your...fur thing? Or is that part of your outfit?"

"Yes, please. It's warm in here." She turned her back to him, unsnapping the front and slipping it off into his waiting hands.

The fur slipped all the way to the floor as synapses misfired inside Soren's head. His eyes took in what the fur had previously covered—six inches of creamy pale skin from her tiny waist down to...he gulped. Cleavage. The delicate bones of her spine ended at the point where the swell of her ass cheeks began.

Dammit, he thought as he snatched the fur off the floor, he'd seen women in his pub dressed in low-slung pants and hadn't blinked an eye. What was it about this one that made him all thumbs?

By the time his head cleared, she was seated, her chair pulled close enough to the table that the cloth hid whatever was bared in front, her belly button probably, and more smooth skin. He fumbled the vest onto the back of the chair to her left and went around the table to sit on her right, arguing mentally that if he sat across from her, his back would be to the door, and he didn't want to be in a vulnerable position.

Yeah, right.

She nudged his arm with a menu. He turned.

And zeroed in on the amulet nestled at the bottom of her neckline, sparkling with every breath she took.

Gulp. Talk about smooth, creamy skin. Talk about cleavage. He'd be less vulnerable with his back facing the door if he was a bail jumper hiding from a bounty hunter. But he couldn't move. He knew he was staring. Knew he had to drag his eyes away and look up to her face.

"Do you have any recommendations?" She leaned forward, her cleavage shifting with the movement.

"Scrambled brains. Uh, eggs! Scrambled eggs. With salsa."

She wrinkled her nose. "Maybe I'll check the menu anyway."

Doofus! Listen to yourself! He tried to backpedal. "That was a joke. I put salsa on my eggs for breakfast."

Her eyes widened. "Will we have breakfast too?"

He could feel the tips of his ears turning red. How could she tie him up in knots with a simple question? "Their chimichangas are very good," he said, trying to change the subject.

"We have a special on frozen margaritas."

They looked up. A waitress had materialized, placing a small basket of nachos and a bowl of salsa on their table. "Two for one if you order two entrees."

Crystal smiled. "I love margaritas." She looked expectantly at him.

He had been all set to order Dos Equis. But hell, he could get them anytime. Thor's Hammer was known for its selection of beers on tap, not for mixed drinks. He nodded. "Make that two."

"Coming right up." The waitress disappeared.

"So, tell me, Soren Thorvald," Crystal said, dipping a nacho into the salsa, "what kind of a bar do you run?"

Okay, *now* he was on solid ground. He thought he actually came out sounding coherent as he explained, "It's a pub, actually. Twelve stools at the bar, four booths, couple of tables. Small dance floor, sometimes we have live jazz. Pool table. Hamburgers, chili, fries. Easy-to-make, easy-to-eat food. Nine different beers on tap—"

She had been bringing the nacho to her mouth. A chunk of salsa slipped off and landed on the exposed curve of her right breast. Without thinking, Soren leaned over and swept it off with his index finger. Then jerked back, his face as hot as the beer mugs that came out of his industrial-strength dishwasher.

He glanced around. No one seemed to have noticed. Thank God. He grabbed his water glass and drank down half of its contents.

Then he snuck a look at Crystal. She sat there, mouth open, nacho poised in midair, probably pissed and unsure how to react. Until he looked into her eyes. They were meltingly soft, like warm chocolate sauce ready to drizzle on ice cream.

"Not fair," she murmured. "You'll have to let me return the favor. Later."

Soren knew his face must have paled, because he felt all the blood rush to his cock. This was so not him. He had to think before he acted. Then remind himself not to act. At least, not around Crystal.

"Here we go," chirped the waitress, setting down two humongous stemmed bowls with salted rims. "Are you ready to order?"

"Not quite," Crystal said as Soren sat there with his tongue too numb to speak.

Later, Soren would realize that he couldn't recall a single thing he'd eaten, a single thing he'd said. But he remembered the movement of Crystal's mouth as she forked a piece of enchilada into it, as she bit into a jalapeno, as she sipped her gigantic margarita through a straw. As she licked her lips after licking the salt off the rim of her glass with a glistening red tongue. As she smiled at him.

He awoke from his entrancement when she asked, "Do you have anything special planned for dessert?"

All he could think of was, he wanted Crystal for dessert. To touch her, to taste her. But that would be like entering a spider's web and getting all tangled up and ready to be spit-roasted.

"Since this dinner is my treat," Crystal was saying, "I have a suggestion."

Soren dragged his attention away from his thoughts and focused on the sound of her voice.

"Soren?" She placed her hand on his arm. Her fingers, he noticed, were long and slender, with short oval nails done up in a pale pink. As far as he could tell, she wore no jewelry except the crystal between her breasts.

The thought of her breasts drove his gaze to them, to the spot he had touched. A tiny streak of red remained where he'd missed. His cock, as stiff as the table leg, twitched remembering the velvety texture of her skin. Had he been that hard during the entire dinner? Damn, the woman was messing with his mind.

"Would you like some homemade apple pie for dessert?"

"Uh, homemade?" Soren asked cautiously.

She laughed, a delicate, feminine sound. "I even make my piecrust from scratch. With real butter, and to heck with what the so-called gurus say about trans fats or carbs or whatever diet is fashionable this month."

Oh boy. He rarely bothered with dessert, much less anything homemade. He took his meals at the pub, and while the food was hearty, dessert wasn't on the menu. Didn't go with beer, which was his big moneymaker. His mouth began to salivate at the thought of tart apples and cinnamon in a flaky crust, warm and fragrant from the oven. He'd have to dig way down deep in his memory to remember when he'd last had fresh apple pie.

"Sure. I could go for a piece of pie." He tossed his napkin onto his empty plate and pushed back his chair. Reaching for his wallet, he looked around for the waitress.

"Uh-uh. It's my treat, remember?" Crystal stood as well, digging into her handbag. "The auction. I paid for the privilege of buying you dinner, remember?" She pulled out a credit card, in the process dropping a folded bill to the floor.

He knelt down to retrieve it for her. And came face to face with her navel. He could visualize himself licking that navel, thrusting his tongue inside it, nipping at the edges of it.

A string of four-letter words dammed up behind his clenched teeth. What had they put into that margarita to make him think like that? He didn't even *like* women.

He felt her hand on his shoulder. He looked up. She looked down at him with a tender expression. Maybe he was so screwed up that he'd dreamed it, but he could have sworn she mouthed a soundless "Later".

* * * * *

Her heart was pounding so hard she wondered if Soren could hear it. *Tonight*, she thought. It would happen tonight.

Touching the remote mounted on her visor, Crystal waited for the garage door to lift then drove the Beetle inside. The overhead lights came on and the door descended behind them. With a hitch in her breath, she turned to Soren. "Ready?"

She unlatched her door, triggering the car's interior light, which illuminated half of his face. He looked slightly stunned. She wondered how often he drank margaritas. Admittedly, those portions at the restaurant were at least a double, even with all the ice. She'd left half of hers in the glass.

Well, he'd follow or he wouldn't. If he didn't, he'd be locked in the garage overnight. She made sure of that by stowing the remote in her purse. Fishing for her keys, she unlocked the inner door, flicked on some lights and waited in the hallway. With relief she saw him get out and close the door.

Still, she thought he dragged his feet like a man going to the gallows as he climbed the two steps to the house level.

"Just flick that dead bolt and engage the chain, would you?" she tossed off casually as she headed—at a slow pace, to be sure he wouldn't run back out—into the living-dining room. "I'll get a pot of coffee started."

Her seduction skills were practically nonexistent, Crystal fretted. She'd always expected that The One would make all the overtures and she'd just melt into his arms, the way they did in romance novels. Reality was different. Reality made her wonder if the crystal was wrong after all. It had been quiescent all evening.

On the other hand, maybe the way to a man's bed *was* through his stomach. She'd put up her apple pie against any other dessert east of the Mississippi. So maybe the crystal only pointed the way and she had to do all the work.

So be it. She wasn't afraid of work.

"I have regular Colombian, decaf, vanilla and—"

"Regular is fine." Soren had followed her through the dining area and into the kitchen, whose white oak counters made an ell around two sides of the room. He pulled out one of her French country chairs from under the round oak table near the windows and sat in it, watching her work. "Nice place."

"Thanks." She gave him a quick smile as she measured the grounds and flicked the switch to start the coffee perking. Then she turned to get cups. And smacked her hip into the opened cutlery drawer. She snuck a glance at Soren, hoping he hadn't noticed her clumsiness. It seemed to her that she went through life a half-inch off. Paper cuts, bruises, hairpins falling. More than once she'd gotten her fingers caught in a closing screen door or an elbow banged on a piece of furniture.

Resisting the urge to rub the bruised area—dang it, wouldn't you know it was on the exposed part of her hip—she arranged china, silverware, sugar, creamer, and linen napkins on a black lacquered tray. She lifted the tray and carried it to the table.

And almost dropped it when she saw the intent look on his face.

He popped up off his chair like a jack-in-the-box. "Uh, you want me to take that?"

"I've got it." She bent down to set the tray on the table. When she straightened, she saw he continued to stare at her. Specifically, at her boobs. "Something wrong?"

"No. I was just thinking."

She cocked her head to one side. "About what?"

His Adam's apple bobbed up and down as he swallowed, and his gaze finally swept upward to her face. "We aren't at your grandmother's house."

A smile blossomed on her face. "Why, no, we aren't. Is that significant?"

"Crystal." He looked as though he was waging an inner war. "Dammit, come here."

Instead of waiting for her to comply, he stepped forward and grabbed her shoulders, pulling her flush against him. He buried his face in her hair and mumbled, "Christ, you're more seductive than that apple pie on the counter."

He took her head in both hands and kissed her like a man who'd been away from civilization for years. His tongue thrust into her mouth, and she opened for him like a blossom unfolding its petals.

Her arms wrapped around his waist. She tugged at his blue polo shirt, pulling it from his jeans. Skin. She needed to feel his skin. There it was, hot and smooth under her palms. She thrilled to the intimacy of her hands roaming up and down the bumps of his spine. Shivers ran across her skin as he did the same to her waist, the exposed expanse of her hips.

His fingers dipped into the crevice of her buttocks. *Yes*, she wanted to shout. She moved artlessly against him, rubbing against his man's bulge, wanting to feel it with her hands, bare on bare, but didn't know how to ask, how to show him by deed what she wanted.

With a growl, he shoved her away. "Damn." He plowed the fingers of both hands into his blond hair, mussing it enough to make him look less formidable. "Look, I'm sorry. I'll just go and—"

He stopped. Just as if he had fallen off a cliff in the middle of a sentence.

"Hell. I don't even know where I am. If you could call a cab, I'll—"

"Oh no, you don't." She took a step forward. He backed up. Just enough for him to fall back into the chair when she gave him a nudge. "I spent a good deal of time making this pie, and you're not leaving until you have your fill."

The spitting and soughing of the coffeepot signaled the end of the brewing. "See? The coffee's ready." She shrugged. "Kismet."

Soren just sat there, feeling like he'd been hit on the head with a two-by-four. This little firecracker had apparently set her sights on him and he wasn't going to get out of here anytime soon.

So why was he fighting? Rolf would have had her pants off already. He'd have asked why Soren overanalyzed everything and then wound up taking no action. Hell, Crystal wanted him, he wanted her. No questions, no commitments. So what was the problem?

Should he lie to himself and say he'd stay only because he wanted some homemade apple pie?

The clanking of silverware on china roused him from his self-flagellation. He zeroed in on the dessert plate she'd placed in front of him. The rich scent of cloves and cinnamon teased his nostrils. In spite of himself, his mouth watered. Damn, but he did want some homemade apple pie.

Picking up the fork, Soren cut off a chunk and stuffed it into his mouth. He closed his eyes and savored the taste of tangy apples, sweet brown sugar, and something heavy, a splash of brandy maybe. Mmm, heaven.

His piece of pie was almost gone before he realized Crystal stood in front of him. Holding a round carton. Smiling a bemused smile.

"I guess it's too late to ask if you want some vanilla ice cream on it?"

He looked over at her place setting. She hadn't even had a single bite while he'd scarfed down his pie like a shredder sucks up paper. The tips of his ears burned again. Of social graces, he had none. A gentleman would have waited for his hostess to sit down before digging in.

Soren knew he was no gentleman.

She pivoted on a bare foot—when had she shucked off her shoes?—and walked away from him. Soren almost groaned aloud at the expanse of skin she exposed when she stretched upward to set the ice cream back in the freezer.

Then she returned to stand in front of him. "Do you want some more?"

Soren fought to keep from caressing her belly, her breasts, with his eyes. He forced his gaze upward to her dark, dark eyes, eyes that seemed to be all pupil, with barely a rim of brown iris. He swallowed.

"Yeah. I want more." But more of what, was the question he didn't want to answer.

"Soren, can I ask you something?"

"Sure." But he wasn't sure. Not at all.

"Are you afraid of me?"

He tried to manufacture a laugh. It came out like a scratch. "There isn't much I'm afraid of, babe." There. That sounded good. Fearless.

"Excellent." With no warning, she sat sideways on his lap and snuggled her luscious ass onto his crotch.

He was a goner.

She wrapped her arms around his neck and started placing artless kisses on his temple, his nose, his cheek, little nibbles on his ear, all the while wiggling, wiggling, as if trying to get the tip of his cock right…*there.*

On a groan, Soren took hold of her waist with his big hands to lift her off his boner, but succeeded only in moving her a slight inch for a better fit. Oh God, she felt wonderful, all soft and warm, her hands touching his shoulders, his arms, then around to roam over his back.

"Bloody hell." He half-stood and, holding Crystal by her hips, finagled their bodies so that her legs were splayed then sat down again, with her legs wide apart on his thighs and her pussy planted firmly on his rock-solid cock. Somewhere in the back of his mind was the thought that he'd make a mint if he could manufacture women's crotchless jeans for situations like this. He couldn't get close enough to her to suit him.

She took to lap-dancing as though she'd earned her way through college with it. She squirmed and wiggled and rubbed her pussy against his cock with seeming delight. What little finesse he'd ever learned deserted him. Instead of tackling that row of tiny buttons, he yanked up her sweater to expose her breasts.

The sight of those dusky-rose nipples made his cock even harder, if that was possible. He ducked his head down and captured one through the shimmery lace, tonguing it, sucking it deep into his mouth.

Crystal jerked and arched her back, as if giving tacit approval to his hungry movements. He fumbled his fingers around to the back of her bra, seeking the hook that would release the lacy cage holding her breasts. He moaned in frustration at the unbroken swath of fabric across her back.

As if understanding his goal, she leaned back a smidge. "The front," she gasped between kisses, "it's a clasp, not a hook."

Soren's lust-filled brain couldn't quite comprehend the concept of front clasp. His scrabbling got more frantic until he finally pulled one breast from its cup and let the pointed tip of it poke straight out from its hammock. He zeroed in on it, the finally bare skin of her breast, her naked nipple inside his mouth, and he licked and sucked and pinched like a starving man.

"Soren, wait." Crystal edged herself back a few inches on his thighs and grabbed the hem of her sweater with crossed arms. One yank and it was over her head and on the floor. "Here," she said, breathing raggedly, her hands going between her breasts. "See? A clasp." She flicked her wrists. The bra fell open. She wiggled the straps down her shoulders and let the bra fall to the floor.

Soren's throat closed up as he saw those soft, plump breasts jiggling mere inches away from him. "Beautiful," he whispered. He trailed his fingers around the areolas, inordinately pleased to see the little bumps on them swell. "So smooth. So creamy." He would have liked to stroke them, admire them, for hours, but he was thinking with his little head now, not his big one. He took a breast in each hand, kneaded them, squeezed them together. "I'd like to put my cock right in between them," he growled. Then dipped his head again, trying to get both nipples in his mouth at once, greedy bastard that he was.

"Wait," she said breathlessly, yanking at his polo shirt. "Your turn."

It took a moment for her comment to sink in. Reluctantly he released his hold on her breasts and shucked off his shirt. He glanced at her, ready to return to suckling the most delicious pair of breasts he'd ever touched. The fascinated look on her face stilled him.

"Oh. My. God." She trailed her splayed fingers down his hairy chest. "I've never seen a man with…" She lay her palms against his chest and swept outward, matting the hair, then inward to muss it again. Out, then in. Out, in. As if fascinated.

Soren couldn't stand being still a minute longer. About to explode with lust, he pulled her to him roughly, rubbed her breasts against the hair that fascinated her. His skin felt on fire. The scrape of her taut nipples against him only added fuel to his impending meltdown.

He wanted everything at once—his face buried in her hair, inhaling its subtle fragrance. The feel of her teeth scraping his neck, nipping his ear. Their mouths, fumbling blindly until they found each other's and fused them together with heat and suction and hunger. He needed skin to skin, all of it, from nose to toes.

With an urgency he couldn't contain, Soren stood, lifted Crystal by the waist and set her on her bare feet. He dropped to his knees, ripped open the snap and zipper on her jeans and jerked the denim down to her ankles. In some small, sane corner of his mind he knew she was the kind of woman who'd want hearts and flowers, sweet words whispered in her ear, a Rhett Butler gesture of carrying her up the stairs to the bedroom. But damn, he was out of practice, and she was so hot, she was all over him like honey on pancakes, even now fumbling at the snap of his own jeans as he stood—

"Whoa, babe!" His brain cleared enough to realize that she couldn't pull down the zipper around his swollen cock without his careful help. And if she so much as *touched* it, he'd come like a teenager with his first piece of ass.

With great care, he eased jeans and briefs around what felt like a torpedo about to launch. When the clothing got tangled at his ankles, he briefly wondered if Crystal had shucked her shoes in anticipation of avoiding the kind of circus he was now experiencing as he clumsily toed off his own shoes and lurched out of his clothes.

Then he looked at her. She stood with her hands half up and reaching toward him, as if wanting to touch him but afraid to, wearing nothing but her sparkling amulet and a tiny scrap of lace at her crotch. Somewhere along the line she'd stepped out of the tangle of her jeans. Her eyes were glued to his hard-on, but whether she was impressed or afraid, he couldn't tell.

Suddenly he felt awkward. He was hot as Hades, hard as a granite boulder, breathing like a blacksmith's bellows, and he knew she wanted it as much as he did. Jesus, he wished he was as experienced as Rolf. Rolf would say something glib and sexy and the woman would melt right into him. But he, Soren, didn't know—

Holy shit. Crystal knelt down before him, her mouth right at the level of his cock that pointed straight at her, her face a study in awe and wonder.

"It's so…big," she whispered.

He groaned. *No shit, Sherlock.* Then ground his back teeth. She had reached out one finger and stroked the hard length of it, from the ridge down to the base and back again. Involuntarily his hips pivoted forward.

"Tickles," she said, running her knuckles lightly over the darker blond pubic hair surrounding his cock then following the rough trail of hair down one thigh.

Soren didn't know which tease was worse, her touching his cock or touching everything *but* his cock.

"Crystal." He reached down and jerked her up, slammed her into the furnace of his body so her feet dangled a foot from the floor. Skin against skin, chest to breasts, hips to hips. He kissed her, hard, his tongue thrusting deep into the hot cavern of her mouth, showing her what he wanted to do to her pussy. She met each thrust with a sucking motion of her mouth, driving him nearly mad. Her arms and legs came around him, her lace-clad pussy wide open to the pressure of his naked cock.

Without breaking the kiss, he strode to the nearest kitchen counter and slid her sweet ass onto it, her legs still tightly wrapped around his hips. Mindless with need, he wrenched aside the sliver of lace covering her crotch and with the other hand guided his cock between her hot, swollen pussy lips.

She whimpered, a soft needy sound in the back of her throat. She tilted her hips, wiggling them so as to encourage his entrance.

On a prayerful curse, he plunged into her with all the pent-up force of years of reserve and denial and need and want. In a far corner of his mind he noted her slight resistance, her passionate cry at his first thrust, and accepted it as a sign of their mutual desire to finish what they started, this thunderous dance as old as time and as new as their touch. Over and over again he drove into her, her little gasps urging him on, until he felt on the edge of the precipice, ready to plunge into oblivion, and he remembered. With a last wisp of sanity, of knowing he couldn't take the chance of impregnating her no matter how much he wanted to shoot deep inside her, he pulled out his cock and felt himself gush his cum all over her belly.

And only after his pounding heart had slowed, after his breathing normalized, after he felt her rigidity, did he realize what his subconscious had processed in the heat of the moment.

He had taken a virgin.

Chapter Five

ಐ

"Jesus, Crystal, I feel like a heel."

Relaxing his death grip on her hips, he took a small step back, to examine her turned-aside face, her downcast eyes. "Are you all right? I didn't know you were…" His throat closed. How could he have not known she was a virgin? All those artless kisses, the fumbling touches, the awe in her face at the sight of his rampant cock—the signs were there. He simply chose to misinterpret them.

He didn't know exactly when she'd removed her arms from around his shoulders, but her hands were now planted on the kitchen counter, holding her upright, it seemed, by sheer force of her will. Her legs dangled down the sides of the counter in limp parentheses to his thighs.

"Jesus," he said again. "How can I make it up to you?"

She wouldn't meet his gaze. He couldn't tell if she was hiding tears of disgust at him or shame at herself. Or physical pain. He glanced down and winced. Not only at the globs of his cum slithering down her belly but, more to the point, traces of red—fresh blood, virgin's blood—on his wilting cock.

"Dammit," he said in a raw voice, "you should have been coddled, pampered, fussed over. Not taken like a tavern slut. I'm nothing but a piece of shit you should have scraped off your shoe." He took a deep, stabilizing breath and slid one arm under her knees. "I wouldn't blame you if you never spoke to me again, but I *am* going to do this one thing for you." He placed his other arm around her unresisting shoulders and lifted her into his arms. "Where's your bathtub?"

She felt like a limp child, her head now slumped onto his chest, the weight of her surprisingly light for how voluptuous she was to the eye. When she didn't answer, he walked down the hallway where they'd entered from the garage, and saw a stairway leading up at the far end. Flicking a light switch with his elbow, he climbed up with his precious burden, careful to keep her bare feet from hitting the walls.

The stairway ended at a small hallway with three opened doors. The one on the right showed the edge of a filing cabinet. An office, he surmised. The one in front of him was carpeted, probably her bedroom. Assuming that the third door would be the bath, he turned to the left and stepped into a spacious, up-to-date bathroom done up in soothing shades of green and blue.

Still holding Crystal in his arms, he bent down to run hot water into an oversized Jacuzzi, then sat on the closed toilet seat and settled her on his lap while the tub filled. He dropped light, remorseful kisses on her temple, murmuring soft apologies into her hair. With a pang of self-loathing he noticed she still wore the scrap of panties that he'd ruthlessly yanked out of the way of his deaf, dumb and blind cock.

God. How could he make it right for her?

When the tub was more than half full, he got up and walked to it, sat on the ledge and, balancing her on his lap, dipped one hand to test the water temperature. Perfect.

Turning off the tap, he stood and began to lower her into the water. Her arms came around his neck and gripped him in a vicious hold, her face buried in the crook of his shoulder. "No."

"Let me do this for you, honey. Let me wash away your pain and the evidence of my perversity. Then you can tell me to go to hell. Or worse."

"No." She clung to him in an unexpectedly strong embrace.

She lifted her face to him. He was not surprised to see tears shimmering in those soft brown eyes, tears of pain and humiliation that were certainly all his doing.

"What, then? What can I do to take away your tears?"

With a little shudder, she clung to him, tucked her face against his throat. "Us. You first. Together."

A long moment passed before he processed her meaning. "You mean, in the tub?"

Still hiding her face, she nodded.

He swallowed hard, felt the soft skin of her cheek pressing into his Adam's apple. "Sure. You got it." And stepped into the warmed porcelain, the water hot enough to relax but not to burn. Carefully balancing her, he knelt down then sat back on his haunches, lowering her into the water until her weight rested sideways on his thighs, her feet dangling over the side of the tub. Only then was he able to juggle her enough to stretch out his legs and settle her as well, her butt on his thighs, legs between his. He did not attempt to pull her back to lean against his chest for fear of her reaction.

He didn't know what to do with his hands. He didn't know what to do or say next. He didn't know what the hell he was doing here in the first place, sitting with his victim as if they were in a Pocono Mountains honeymoon suite drinking champagne. So he opted for something neutral. "How does one turn on the bubbles?"

With what might have been a tiny giggle, she reached over and turned the knob.

The water frothed around them. As she sat there quiescent on top of his legs, Soren became uncomfortably aware that his randy cock had begun to swell again from the nearness of her, both of them damn-near naked and sandwiched together, the jets of water caressing his skin like a woman's touch. God, did they make chastity belts for men? What did it say about him that he still thought with his dick even after he'd deflowered a virgin?

Her head was bent forward. The riot of dark curls had separated to flow down the front of her shoulders, leaving a swath of vulnerable nape that invited him to kiss it. An invitation he resisted by the skin of his toenails.

She leaned down into the water. He imagined her lovely breasts dangling, bobbing in the froth then mentally slapped himself. She was probably hoping the bubbling water would scrape off his pecker tracks from her belly.

"Soren?" Her voice came out muffled, absorbed by the water.

He couldn't help it. He rested his hands on her upper arms, testing. "I'm here."

It might have been wishful thinking, but he imagined she leaned into his touch just the slightest bit. "I'm sorry."

"What?"

She pulled herself into a smaller silhouette. "I'm sorry I wasn't very good."

Soren blinked. "What are you talking about?"

Crystal looked over her shoulder at him. "I-I didn't know what to do. I felt so awkward and stupid. I wanted you to kiss me, to touch me, the way you did. I liked it. More than liked it, even. But then, when you...did *it*, I didn't know how to respond, because it hurt and I was surprised and I didn't want you to think I didn't want you—"

"Oh, baby, I was the stupid one." He rotated her shoulders, forcing her to shift her body crossways so they could look at each other. "I should have known you were innocent. The first time I met you, I thought you were a flowers and candlelight type of woman and you deserved someone better than me. But tonight when I felt your skin on mine, I just went ape-shit. Uh, I mean—"

She gave him one of those thousand-watt smiles that made his knees weak. He was glad he was sitting down. "I know. And I loved it that I could make you lose control like that."

"Still, it was my responsibility to be in control. Whether it was your first time or your twenty-first. And I wasn't."

"But you pulled out so we wouldn't make a baby."

His gaze darkened, flicked down to her belly, where bits of translucent cum still clung to her smooth skin. "Yeah," he said almost to himself. "Hardest thing I ever did in my life."

Eyes sparkling like the ever-present crystal around her neck, she turned to face him, snuggling her feet astride his hips and leaning her elbows on her bent knees. Another little giggle. "It was the hardest thing I ever had in my life, too."

On a groan, he leaned forward and took her face between his palms. "Let me make it up to you, Crystal. Let me show you how it can really be between a man and a woman. I can't see how you got anything out of this little episode except pain."

She crossed the minuscule gap between them and touched his lips with hers. "Okay. Show me."

"Count on it."

* * * * *

Crystal's nerves hummed with expectation. After finally slipping off her panties, Soren had settled her back in the Jacuzzi with her butt on the porcelain, her back to him, his legs stretched out on either side of her like an embrace. She had twisted her hair into a topknot and held it in place with one of the spring clips she kept in a pink seashell on the tub's ledge.

He reached over to turn off the jets. In the sudden, intimate silence she could hear the rasp of his breathing behind her, felt the slight breeze of his exhale soft across her shoulder, an errant strand of hair scraping along her sensitized skin.

In her peripheral vision she saw him take her green-apple-scented soap in one of his big hands. Her eyelids fluttered shut. She hoped he would…

He did. Slick with soap bubbles, his hands roved lightly over her shoulders, her upper arms, her back. She felt him wiggle a bit closer. His head brushed against the tendrils of hair falling down her neck as he leaned forward.

His hands slid around to her front, caressing her skin through the thin, slick film of soap, slowly, oh-so-slowly gliding across her waist, her ribcage, up to her breasts. When he touched her nipples, firecrackers blasted through her, rocketed from the fullness of her breasts down to the spot between her legs that still throbbed. The pain when he'd entered her had been sharp, unexpected, but fleeting. She'd been glad to get it out of the way so they could concentrate on this, the thrill of Soren's hands on her, his man-heat at her back, the anticipation of fully becoming a woman at the hands and body of the man her crystal had chosen.

"Oh!" His fingers touched a spot that made her whole body vibrate with pleasure. She'd never felt anything remotely like it before. Unconsciously she let her legs fall open to give him better access, leaned back until her head rested against his shoulder. She lifted her arms and draped them over his knees, telling him without words that she surrendered her body to his will.

A deep growl in response made her feel powerful. This rough-edged man with a tender core was *hers*. She could hear the tempo of his breathing increase, as indeed her own did. He nuzzled her nape, taking tiny nips here and there with his teeth, sending delicious shivers down her spine. With his left hand he kneaded her breast, brushed his thumb over her nipple. His right hand massaged—dare she think the word?—her pussy, sliding his fingers between her lips now slick with soap, warm water, and her own juices.

She pressed herself into the solid wall of his chest, the back of her head nestling in the notch between his neck and shoulder, as he played with her, now teasing the nub that he'd rubbed into a hard acorn, now pinching her nipple until she began thrashing her legs helplessly. Her hips lifted into his hand, and he slipped one finger into her vagina.

"Soren!"

Immediately his hand withdrew. "Did I hurt you? Oh hell, I'm sorry I—"

Crystal grabbed at his hand, frantically guided it back between her legs. "No, no, it felt so good I couldn't stand it." She pressed his hand against her pubic bone. "Please. Don't stop."

"As if I could," he murmured, slipping one finger, then two, inside her pussy.

"Oh, my." She began to move her hips in counterpoint to his fingers, wanting more, wanting…something just out of reach. At her unschooled urging he increased his rhythmic thrusts, all the while squeezing and tugging at her nipple with his other hand, scraping his teeth on her shoulder, her neck, pressing the scalding hammer of his penis between her butt cheeks. Sensations washed over her like flames in a forest fire. Her heels dug futilely at the hard floor of the tub, trying to push herself closer to him, to his magic fingers, to that ladder she was climbing, climbing, soaring to some elusive goal high in the heavens.

Her eyes went unfocused as her world narrowed to him, to Soren, to the feeling that she would die if he stopped touching her. Nothing in this world mattered except to reach that peak, and she sobbed and tried to catch her breath as he rubbed her clitoris with his thumb, and then her mind went blank and she felt herself shattering into hundreds of fireworks lighting the sky, shimmering and dazzling and shifting to an ever-changing kaleidoscope of color until each individual piece burned out and floated down to the earth.

* * * * *

Finally, finally, she held him in her arms.

After her first wondrous orgasm, Soren had lifted her out of the tub, dried her off with such tenderness that her heart melted. Then kneeling before her, he had kissed and licked and nipped at her skin until she came again, her knees buckling as she pressed his head to her pussy to contain the uncontainable, the irresistible spiral up to the top of the mountain until she jumped from the pinnacle to soar over mere mortals, with his mouth and tongue sucking and lapping up the juices he'd coaxed from her. And he held her tight until she was able to groan a few indecipherable words of repletion, and he lifted her into his arms again and carried her to bed.

Her bed. Her man.

Soren lay atop her, resting the bulk of his weight on his elbows, his legs nestled between her thighs, his penis huge and hot and hard against her belly. He bent his head and dropped small kisses over her face until he reached her lips. His kisses became hotter, more demanding, and she opened her mouth to him. He thrust his tongue inside, mimicking the act of love. Her arms wrapped around him, pulling him closer and closer still. She ran her palms up and down his muscled back, over the indentations of his spine, the hollow at his waist, then lower to his firm buttocks.

Heat spiraled inside her. She wanted him. Wanted to feel him inside her, now that she knew what to expect, now that he'd prepared her so thoroughly. She lifted her hips in silent supplication while pressing her hands down on his butt.

His answer was a growl deep in his throat and a noticeable increase in muscle tension.

On the right track, she thought giddily. She arched her back, pressing her body into his. Ran her hands between their bodies, trying to reach the part she wanted him to move.

He groaned against her mouth. "Woman, you're killing me."

"I am?" Her hands stilled.

"But don't stop. God, I love how your hands feel on me."

"Soren, can we…?" She turned her head, embarrassed to be asking.

He levered himself up onto his elbows. She looked into eyes of such a deep blue in the dimly lit bedroom, she felt herself drowning in them. His gaze was intense. A muscle worked in his jaw. "It's too soon. I'll hurt you again."

It took Crystal a moment to understand. "Oh, that. It had to happen sooner or later. I'm glad it's over with. It doesn't hurt the second time, does it?"

Soren made a sound somewhere between a laugh and a groan. "I wasn't a Boy Scout, babe. I never expected to need protection tonight. If I stuck my cock inside you now, knowing how hot you are, how good it feels to be there, I wouldn't stop until I shot my wad. I'm not big on Russian roulette."

"Oh. I, um, I think I can help." She made an effort to sit up, no mean feat when one hundred ninety pounds of pure male muscle and bone pinned her to the mattress, but succeeded only in rubbing her lower body against the part of him that, as he put it, would shoot his wad into her. The very thought of it made her shiver in anticipation.

He made another sound deep in his throat, a low rumble embodying both hunger and frustration, rolled off her and onto his back, and flung an arm across his eyes. On his face was etched a look of pain.

Her gaze snapped to his cock. It rose straight up from a nest of dark blond hair. The shaft was long and thick, with purple veins standing out in sharp relief against the smooth skin. There was a pearl of creamy white fluid at the very tip. She had the sudden urge to lick it, to take the whole thing in her mouth and suck him the way he sucked on her, to see if she could make him come that way.

But she wanted something else even more. She scooted to the side of the bed and reached into the nightstand drawer.

"Here," she said triumphantly.

Cautiously he moved his arm to uncover one eye. And felt more blood rush to his groin as he processed what she held up. A condom packet. He jerked up like he'd been released from a slingshot. She'd been a virgin and she stashed condoms at her bedside? Hell's bells, had she *ambushed* him?

His brain and his cock battled for supremacy.

Then she touched the bead of pre-cum that glistened on the tip, swirled his lubrication around the head with her fingers.

No contest. His cock won.

Groaning, he grabbed the foil as Crystal wrapped her fingers around his cock, made a few hesitant up-and-down strokes. It jumped and swelled in her hand. Her brown eyes widened.

"Okay, babe, that's it." He ripped open the foil and, fumbling like a teenager, rolled the condom onto hot flesh that felt as hard as a fencepost.

In an eye blink he flipped her on her back and covered her with his super-heated body, muscled thighs between hers, cock nudging the entrance to that sweet pussy he wanted to fuck until the sun came up a couple of months from now. He captured her expectant gaze. "You want it, you got it."

And thrust home. Deep into a warm, tight cavern that wrapped around him, tugged him, squeezed him. "Jesus." He touched his forehead to hers. He had to take a deep breath, to lie absolutely still, so he wouldn't come right then and there. "You feel like heaven."

She made a low moan. He raised himself on his elbows. "Am I too heavy?"

In response, she slid her palms down to his ass cheeks and pressed him even closer to her, raised her hips tentatively, inviting him to move his.

He needed no further invitation. This time, he promised himself, he'd give her what a woman as responsive as her should have—a long, leisurely fuck, holding back her climax...and his—until they both were slick with sweat and anticipation and need. Levering himself onto his elbows, he withdrew his cock slowly until only the head remained, then just as slowly slid it back in as deep into her softness as it would go.

Hearing his name whispered on a shuddering sigh almost made him pump into her, hard and fast.

Almost.

Deliberately he took a deep breath and repeated the sequence even more slowly, causing a hitch in Crystal's breathing. Their gazes locked. She looked so vulnerable and trusting as she trembled beneath him, Soren found himself wanting to protect her, to treat her like a priceless treasure.

Then she grabbed his ass with a vengeance while lifting her hips, trying to alter his rhythm.

A deep chuckle escaped him. "Oh no, you don't." He pinned her to the mattress by simply allowing his full weight to rest on her. Swinging her arms over her head, he immobilized them by holding both wrists in one massive hand. "It's my way or the highway."

In slow motion he advanced and retreated, advanced and retreated, until sweat beaded his forehead and she was squirming and bucking under him, her head tossing from side to side.

He dipped his head and captured a rosy, engorged nipple with his teeth.

"Soren!" Her hips shot up a foot off the bed and she convulsed around his cock, primitive sounds emanating from deep in her throat. Hell. He'd wanted to bring her to the brink and then slow down until she begged him to fuck her hard and quick, but she'd been way ahead of him. Perversely he thought, *okay, sweetheart, you got the easy one. This time, I'll make you beg*.

Her hot, tight pussy still rippling around him encouraged Soren to pump his hips faster. Made him suddenly wonder why the hell it had seemed so important for him to try to withhold her climax when it felt so good to see her eyes go blind with passion, to hear the little whimpers she was still making as he increased his tempo. God, she felt so good, so tight, it would only take a few more strokes to—

A sound like glass shattering stopped him mid-stroke. "Jesus! What was that?"

Underneath him, Crystal tensed, her eyes wide. "Is someone trying to break in?"

Suddenly clearheaded, Soren levered himself off her, automatically resurrecting the downstairs floor plan in his mind. Five floor-to-ceiling windows looked out over the backyard, three from the living room, and one each from the kitchen and dining area. It could have been any one of them. "Stay here." He rolled off the bed and onto the floor. His bare feet curled into the deep pile of her carpet, reminding him of his nude state.

"Shit. My clothes. They're all over the kitchen."

Crystal scrambled off the bed and darted to a dresser. Pulling out a bottom drawer, she dug into it and said, "Here. Use this. It was my Dad's. I keep it to remember him by."

She held out a green-and-black plaid woolen bathrobe that showed light wear around the collar. Wordlessly he donned it—it fit snugly but covered everything—wrapped the sash tightly, happy to not feel exposed and vulnerable against an unknown menace. As he crept down the steps, he remembered the condom that hadn't received any of his cum. Since the adrenaline rush from the breaking glass had wilted his cock, he easily shucked it off and stuffed it into a side pocket, cursing his macho need to draw out his lovemaking until she begged for release. Instead, she'd gotten a good pop and it was his balls that were aching.

At the bottom platform he forced his attention to the problem at hand. Held his breath. Listened.

Nothing.

When he'd earlier swooped Crystal up in his arms and marched to the bath, he remembered, he hadn't stopped to turn off any lights in the living area. That light spilled over into the hallway, dimming to shadows at the bottom of the stairs. Soren noticed a Chinese-looking umbrella stand in the hall. It held a couple of umbrellas and what looked like a cane.

Senses on high alert for an intruder, he crept to the stand. His hand closed on a thick, heavily knobbed cane. Silently he lifted it out and, holding it to his shoulder in a two-fisted grip, with the hefty knob as the business end, moved carefully toward the light. He'd broken up any number of fights at his pub with a baseball bat. He hoped the shaft of the cane wouldn't break if he had to use it on whoever might still be inside.

At the door to the garage he saw the deadbolt in its place and the chain still in its slot. Good. One less place for someone to hide.

Standing at the archway of the living-dining room, he saw that the blackness of the night made mirrors of the four windows he could see. The empty living room reflected back at him. No one hid underneath the round dining table.

Adrenaline sharpened every one of Soren's senses. He could hear the hum of the electric clock on the stove. Some sort of frogs croaked intermittently — and loudly — outside.

No wonder. The kitchen window was shattered, he saw as he gingerly edged up to the half-wall separating the work area from the living area. Glass shards lay strewn across the tile floor and on their discarded clothing. Otherwise, the kitchen was empty.

Relief flooded him. His grip on the cane relaxed.

Until he heard a sound behind him. Whirling around, his arms cocked to swing his makeshift weapon, Soren saw the flash of a gun.

"Are they gone?" Crystal's voice was a mere whisper.

"God, you shouldn't creep up on a body like that. I almost swung at you!"

"I didn't want them to hurt you."

Soren's heart settled down from blocking his throat to where it belonged, inside his chest. Only then did he notice she'd slipped into some jeans, a sweatshirt and sneakers. "What are you doing with a gun?"

"It's a water gun. Keeps the stray cats from digging in my garden." Tucking the toy into her back pocket, she came up behind him. And gasped. "Oh, no!" She darted into the kitchen, pieces of glass crunching under her sneakers.

"Be careful," he said, a little too sharply. "Don't cut yourself."

She stooped down to where his loafers lay. Lifted them, turned them over and shook out the glass pieces. Came back to him. "Here."

"Thanks," he said quietly, chagrined that he'd snapped at her for thinking of him. Slipping his bare feet into the loafers, he joined her in the kitchen. "Look. There's what did the damage." He walked to an object at the base of the corner cabinet, stooped for a closer look, decided not to pick it up. "We should call the police. Looks like someone sent you a message."

He looked around for switches then started turning lights off. "Someone might be watching," he explained. "Let's get out of sight." *And out of range*, he thought but didn't say.

He grabbed her hand, eyes darting from window to window as he pulled her back into the hallway and to the stairwell. "Where's your phone?" he whispered.

"We don't need the police. It's probably just a teenage prank."

Soren put his hands on her shoulders and turned her to face him. Light from a streetlamp glimmered dimly through the hall window and made her eyes look dark and huge. "There was a piece of paper wrapped around a rock the size of a baseball. That's more than a prank. It shows premeditation."

"No, really. There's a couple of rowdy teens down the street. I don't want to get them into trouble."

The lightbulb went off in Soren's head. She was a rich society girl. He was a bartender. It was okay for her to walk on the wild side where her friends couldn't see her, but God forbid someone should think she would actually invite a lowlife into her home. "You're ashamed to have anyone see me here." His voice was flat, emotionless. "I'll get my clothes and just fade away into the night. But don't worry. I'll hang around outside until the cops get here to make sure whoever tossed that rock doesn't come smashing through the hole he made."

With that, he shrugged off the hand she'd placed on his arm, ignoring the fleeting look of hurt in her expressive eyes, and stalked back into the darkened living room. He remembered exactly where each piece of his clothing lay on the kitchen floor. Snatching his jeans and shirt, he shook them vigorously to dislodge any shards then strode to the hallway so he could shuck his shoes and get into his jeans. And the hell with his boxers. Let her explain *them* to the cops.

Women. He'd lived fine without them up to last week, but no, he had to go like a lamb to slaughter and offer himself up to auction, never mind that it was for a good cause. What the *hell* had he been thinking?

So she was slumming. So what? She was a good lay, once he got over the guilt that he'd taken her cherry.

He was pissed about that too. Why on God's green earth she'd ever chosen him to be her first, he'd never be able to guess. She'd acted like he was hers for the taking. And him, like a dumb schmuck thinking with his cock, he'd played right into her hands. But a lowly bartender in her home at three in the morning? Uh-uh, that wouldn't do for Miss Rich Bitch and her high society reputation.

Still, he had enough male in him to want to protect her. He'd slip out the front door, make a quiet circuit around the house and find a vantage point to keep watch over the shattered window.

"Here." Crystal's timid voice came from the stairwell as she crept down the steps. Her eyes held a wariness so at odds with the warmth he'd seen in them not so long ago.

Okay, so he had to shift gears. What was that saying about women changing their minds? With little grace, he took the phone she thrust at him, dialed 9-1-1 and tersely explained their situation. When the dispatcher said a unit would be there within fifteen minutes, he dialed another number.

The sleepy voice mumbled a hello. Soren barked, "Got an emergency. I need a big piece of plywood, something to cover a shattered window. About three feet by seven. How fast can you get here?"

"Where's here?"

"Uh, wait." He turned to Crystal. "What's the address?"

She told him.

"Okay, how do you get here from Route 611?"

Crystal reached for the phone. Without preamble, she gave explicit directions, then said thank you and goodbye. She looked up at him. "And thank you too. Who's our white knight?"

"My brother."

Chapter Six

ॐ

"I still don't understand. Who would want to do this?" Crystal felt the back of her throat tighten. She'd changed her mind about teenagers after she'd seen the ugly message. The police had come and gone, taking with them the rock and the paper, promising to check them for fingerprints, although they'd treated it as a teenage prank, too. She tried to get a grip while she poured herself another cup of coffee.

"A jealous boyfriend?" Soren speculated.

"No. That's quite impossible."

"Why is it impossible?" He looked at her with such an intense gaze that she had to lower her face to her cup and take a too-hot sip.

"I haven't dated much."

"That's hard to believe."

Her chin lifted. "Why? Because I'm a rich society girl?"

A look that might have been disbelief flitted briefly across Soren's face. "Because you're such a looker, you're nice and you're fun. I can't believe men aren't lining up three deep to take you out."

She fingered the ever-present crystal at her throat. "I'm just too busy. I have my consulting work, my charities. I spend a lot of time looking after my grandmother." She wasn't about to tell him she'd been waiting—the crystal had been waiting—all these years for him to enter her life, so she hadn't been interested in fleeting relationships with men.

"Seems to me there can only be one interpretation of that message."

Crystal shuddered. *Whore*, the message said, in headline-size letters cut from a newspaper and pasted on a sheet ripped from a student notebook.

"Someone took exception to my spending the night with you," Soren continued relentlessly. "Sounds like someone thought he had you to himself."

She turned a troubled gaze to him. "But I don't *know* anyone who feels that way. I'm telling you, I rarely date."

"What about your job? Give me an example of your working day."

She shrugged. "It varies. I go to estate sales. Sometimes to auctions where several estates are lumped together. I know most of the auctioneers and antique-store owners in a wide radius. Either my circle of acquaintances—mostly Grandma's friends—ask me to keep an eye out for a specific piece or I find a sleeper that no one else is bidding on, so I buy it on spec. I can't think of anyone who's ever been overly friendly."

"Boyfriends from college?"

"No. No one I spent a lot of time with."

"Okay. You buy and sell antiques for others. Give me a for instance. Tell me how you went about your last purchase."

"I found a terrific two-piece cherry corner cupboard at an auction that went for a fourth of its value. I bought it with no buyer in mind and took it to Time Treasures. The owner, Jack Healy, has a standing offer to buy anything I come across, because he trusts my judgment. He pays me a thirty percent commission and then sells it for up to twice his cost."

"Tell me about Healy."

"He's owned that shop for about twenty years. He's, oh, I'd say mid-fifties. Really nice guy. Very knowledgeable. High-quality merchandise, stands behind everything he sells."

"How do you get the stuff to him?"

"I usually ask Augie to help me. He has muscle and time, and a beat-up truck that he doesn't mind getting dirty on rutted farmland or dirt roads. I think he does grunt work to get his father upset."

"Is that the father-son pair I met at Rowena's home?"

"Yes."

"Either of them ever put the make on you?"

She frowned at the thought of the young man who had done just that in his truck, but dismissed it as simply a combination of opportunity and testosterone. She couldn't see Augie making the effort to stalk her in the middle of the night.

"Crystal? You'd never make a good poker player. Which one of them bothered you?"

"It was nothing."

"Let me put it another way. Would you spend the day alone with either of them looking for treasures at an abandoned farmhouse?"

"Well…Augie did try to kiss me after we dropped off the corner cupboard, but I think it was just a spur-of-the-moment thing. You know, male hormones running amok."

"He ever try anything like that before?"

"Never. I wouldn't have asked him to help if he had."

"What about the older man? Trey, was it?"

"To hear Augie tell it, Trey's interested in my grandmother."

"Fortune hunter?"

"No. They're old money. Trey owns a fairly large estate. I think they're merely of like minds."

The growl of a heavy engine in the driveway sent a shaft of unease through Crystal. Until she remembered. Soren's brother. Plywood. She glanced at the clock. Four-ten in the morning. She had to admire the family loyalty of the Thorvalds.

Soren was already off his chair and striding to the front door. She followed him, but stayed on the porch as the two men wrestled a piece of plywood out of the truck bed and disappeared around the side of the garage.

Crystal turned on the outside patio lights then decided on a way to thank them properly.

By the time they sized and nailed the plywood to the window frame and clomped into the kitchen, she had nuked some bacon slices, made a fresh pot of coffee, set the table for three, and stashed a pile of freshly made French toast in the warming oven.

Soren introduced them. She reached out a hand to a taller, earthier version of Soren. "I can't tell you how much I appreciate your coming here in the middle of the night."

Magnus shook her hand with, she noticed, nicked and callused fingers. "He's my brother. He needed my help."

"As did I. Please. Sit down and have a cup of coffee."

"That I will. Thanks."

She filled an earth-toned mug and set it before him then set the warm plate of French toast on the table. She was gratified to see Soren's eyes light up. She wondered how often the bachelor who ate lunch and dinner at the pub made himself a hot breakfast.

As she poured warm maple syrup into a small pitcher and set it alongside the toast, Magnus looked up at her and said, "You're the lady in the newspaper picture?"

Heat bloomed in her face. "Yes."

Magnus gave his brother a sly look. "Amazing. Two cataclysmic events occurring on the same evening."

She cocked her head, a quizzical expression on her face.

"Not only did Soren wear a tie to the auction," Magnus explained, "but he also did something totally out of character." He raised his mug in a toast. "Here's to the woman who got Soren to make a memorable exit."

Soren's ears turned red. "I thought she was grandstanding."

"So you outdid her."

Saying nothing, Soren studiously cut his French toast into small pieces.

While they ate, conversation revolved around the incident, Magnus asking similar questions to what the police had. When Magnus had polished off four slices of French toast and two cups of coffee, he politely thanked her and stood up to leave. She stood as well, thanking him again for coming to her rescue in the middle of the night.

"Mags, could I hitch a ride?"

Crystal's attention had been focused on Magnus' goodbye. She saw him do a double take at his brother's question. Heck, she felt the same way. How could Soren simply leave? Didn't he want to finish what had been interrupted?

Magnus cleared his throat, obviously trying to read the situation and come up with a suitable response.

"This was our Buy a Bachelor Dinner night," Soren said, looking uncomfortable. "Crystal picked me up at Thor's Hammer. And, uh, after all she's been through tonight—" his ears turned red again, "I mean, the police and all, she's probably tired. She shouldn't have to cart me around at the crack of dawn."

After a long pause, during which time Crystal bit down on her tongue to keep from jumping into the silence, Magnus said, "All right. I'll wait for you outside."

Determined not to be a clinging vine, Crystal ignored the man who came to stand next to her. She began stacking the dirty plates and cups.

"Look, I'm not good at this man-woman thing," he said.

She picked up the stack and brought them to the kitchen sink. He followed her. Rubbed a hand on the back of his neck. Cleared his throat.

She would *not* make it easy for him. She would *not*.

"I, uh, I'll call you, okay?"

"Sure. Whatever." She changed her mantra. *I will not cry.*

It seemed he stood behind her for a long time, but it was probably no more than a minute. Finally she heard his footsteps stomp across the now-swept kitchen floor and down the hall. The door closed behind him with a soft click.

Crystal comforted herself by remembering that her grandmother had only said the crystal would tell her when she *met* The One. She didn't say bringing him around to the same point of view would be simple.

* * * * *

"You're an ass, you know that?"

Soren sunk down deeper into the truck seat. "You're probably right."

"She's a beautiful woman. Had kind of a rosy glow, a satisfied look, so I guess you slept with her, which was why you were still there at two-thirty when the rock came sailing in." Magnus took his right hand off the steering wheel and raised it, palm up, to forestall a denial. "Look, I'm not fishing for juicy details. I'm happy that you finally found a woman you wanted to snuggle up to. It's just, Jesus, Soren, you have the sensitivity of a backhoe. I hope you at least kissed her goodnight. The whole time I was there, you hardly looked at her. Don't tell me you were so embarrassed to be caught in the act, so to speak, that you didn't even want to talk to her in my presence."

"Hell, it was just supposed to be Buy the Bachelor a Dinner. No fuss, no entanglements. Put in my time for charity and be done with it. I sure as hell didn't expect to end up in her bed."

"And now you're afraid she's going to get her claws into you."

Soren gnawed on the inside of his cheek. "Well, yeah."

"And you don't want to get hurt. Like Dad did."

"You didn't hear them."

91

Pulling into the Thor's Hammer parking lot, Magnus cut him a glance. "Hear who?"

"Dad yelling. Mom crying."

Magnus cut the engine. "When was this?"

"Couple of weeks after my ninth birthday. I think you were at the studio with Grandpa Knut. Mom was in the kitchen crying. I heard her from upstairs, but before I got to her, Dad walked in. Then they started fighting."

"About what?"

It was a long time before Soren answered. "I don't know."

He did know. He just couldn't bring himself to talk about it. Because if he did, it would change everything.

* * * * *

A refined woman like her, being carted out of the auction room like a sack of potatoes was bad enough. But now, she goes and sleeps with him? He couldn't believe she brought that pre-civilized bully home with her and then actually invited him upstairs.

Torturing himself with images of his precious Madonna stripped naked on a bed, he imagined her spread-eagled in sacrifice to the baser instincts of that hooligan. He should have interrupted them earlier. Should have blasted through the window right after the rock, should have come prepared with a weapon.

He'd give her one more chance. If she repented, if she came to him willingly, he might forgive her. If not…he'd have to punish her. Soon.

Chapter Seven

ೲ

"Wait a minute, Mags. Where the hell are you going?" Relegated to the back seat of the BMW, Soren grabbed for the door handle. "No way we're having your bachelor party in that house. Stop the car and let me out."

Magnus flicked a glance over his shoulder at his brother as he drove down an impressive Belgian-block driveway on the most exclusive street in Devon. About a dozen high-end cars lined both sides. "This is the right address."

Sitting in the shotgun seat, Rolf chimed in. "Kat gave us directions, so we're sure."

"What the hell's going on?" Soren fiddled with the lock as the car glided to a smooth stop. "Damn door won't open."

"Childproof locks," Magnus said mildly. "You won't be able to get out until someone opens the door from the outside."

Soren glared at Rolf. "You're in on it too."

The youngest brother shrugged. "I'm just along for the booze and the broads."

"Ah, the welcoming committee awaits." Ignoring Soren's blue-streak cussing, Magnus stopped the car at the well-lit portico, pocketed the keys and headed toward the steps.

"I'll get your door in just a minute," said Rolf as he opened his own door.

"I'm not getting out. What kind of stupid stunt are you trying to pull?"

"Relax. It's only a birthday party. And you're *very* cozy with the guest of honor, so what's your problem?" Rolf turned his back to the car and started speaking to— Soren groaned. To Kat. And coming up alongside her was—

Rowena D'Angelo. Crystal's grandmother. It had to be Crystal's birthday.

"It's a setup, dammit." His glance bounced around the car. He felt iron bars close around him. Damn, he'd look like an idiot climbing over the seat to escape through the driver's door. And then do what? Run back down the driveway in the dark? He'd look all the more like an idiot.

Magnus and Kat were getting married in less than two weeks, and Soren had truly believed they were going to a bachelor party for Mags tonight—he even had a gag gift secreted in his jeans pocket. Instead, he'd been snookered. Hell, they couldn't let him proceed at his own pace to date or not to date Crystal. Just because he'd already slept with her made it certain, in his brothers' eyes, that they'd follow Mags and Kat down the aisle.

Oh, he'd get back at them. Both of them. Next time Rolf posed nude for Kat's art class, he'd splat his brother's brass balls with toxic paint. And Mags, well, there was always some mischief he could do in his woodworker's studio. Or put sawdust in the honeymooners' bed.

Kat opened his door, smiling serenely as though she wasn't in on the joke. "Come on out, Soren. No moping in the back seat."

Giving Kat a surly glare as an answer, he climbed out, only to face Rowena.

"So nice to see you again," the older woman said. "I'm always happy to have three handsome young men at a party." She held out her arm as though expecting him to escort her.

Gracelessly Soren took her elbow, resigned to another evening of dancing to someone else's tune. Then Kat took his other arm. Mags and Rolf fell into place behind them. He felt as though he was being herded into a prison. Or to a firing squad.

A butler-type man with snooty demeanor and a black suit opened the massive front door as they approached. Soren handed Rowena over the threshold, felt the firm palms of both brothers on his back as they nudged him inside as well.

The tight-knit group swept Soren down the spacious center hall, past the study where he'd first met Rowena, and into some kind of garden room, a huge, airy space with bushy trees in oversize pots reaching toward an atrium-type ceiling fifteen feet or so high. Fat cushions on wicker sofas and peacock chairs splashed primary colors around the room.

A quick glance told Soren the room held twenty or so adults of all ages. No birthday cake was visible, nor ostentatious display of wrapped gifts, he noted with a frisson of relief. There'd be hell to pay if he had to explain the glow-in-the-dark French tickler condoms he'd wrapped in a brown paper bag for Magnus' bachelor party.

Rowena had been introducing him to a pair of guests when he spotted her. Crystal. With an older man not much taller than she, their heads close together as though they were cooing sweet nothings to each other. Crystal looked into the man's eyes, smiling, and something in Soren's gut twisted.

Hell. What was it to him? It was her birthday, after all. The man had probably just given her a present. He looked prosperous, muscular and fit in dark slacks and light polo shirt. His dark hair was thick, with touches of gray at the temples. Soren pointedly turned back to the vacuous woman he'd just been introduced to, whose name he'd already forgotten, and feigned an interest in her comments about ficus trees, whatever they were.

He felt a delicate hand on his forearm. "Hi, you must be one of the Thorvalds," said a melodious voice. "I'm Deirdra. I've known the guest of honor since fourth grade."

Soren turned to see a knockout brunette about five-foot-eight, wearing snug jeans and a well filled-out yellow sweater with tiny sleeves. Her amber eyes scrutinized him so thoroughly, he wondered if a tick had landed on his forehead.

"You're Soren, right?"

He nodded curtly. He was out of his element with small talk, unless he was at Thor's Hammer, where the long mahogany bar would shield him from such close contact with females.

"I thought so. Kat and Magnus are making goo-goo eyes at each other, and Rolf has the dark hair. So you must be The One."

"Uh, yeah, that's me, I guess." The one, what? Left over? Left out? Pick your pick, he thought morosely.

"I'm surprised to see a bartender without something to drink in his hand."

"How do you know what—" Well, of course Crystal would probably have told her friend what he did for a living.

"Come on, let's fix that." She grabbed his biceps and tugged him to a corner where Soren hadn't noticed a bar had been set up. "Nice muscles, by the way. What's your poison? I'll have another gin and tonic, tall glass, please."

Soren watched the gray-haired bartender's well-practiced movements as he rubbed a lime wedge over a glass rim, squeezed its juice over ice, then poured gin and mixer simultaneously, with a flourish. Soren fished out his wallet and a business card. "Any time you want a job, give me a call."

The man's face crinkled into deep lines as he smiled. "Thanks, but I'm retired. Just do this as a favor to Rowena. What can I get you?"

"Dark beer, if you have it."

As the man rattled off several choices cooling on ice, Soren decided he'd stay right there, talking shop, until it was time to go home. He gave his back to Deirdra.

But she was apparently tenacious. Or on the prowl. "You look like an athlete. What sports do you play?"

From his peripheral vision Soren noted she'd plunked her elbows on the stand-up bar, just like he'd done. "I don't. No time. I work long hours."

"So those muscles are from tossing beer kegs around?"

"Excuse me." Soren took his beer and, brushing past the young woman, went in search of Magnus, ready to tear his head off. For this he took a night off from work? To be exposed to trite pickup lines? Shit.

A shrill, two-fingered whistle stifled the murmur of conversation. "Gather around, everyone," Rowena called.

Guests sauntered to the long interior wall, where Rowena stood near a folding screen with four or five louvered panels.

Soren hovered at the periphery of the group, nursing his beer. Then frowned when he noticed that the older man he'd seen Crystal with earlier was still with her, creating a path for her to reach her grandmother's side. As she approached, Soren noted that she wore a swingy skirt and matching sleeveless blouse printed with red flowers on a dark background, her curly hair pinned haphazardly on top of her head. She gave the man a hard embrace, her eyes bright and cheeks flushed. From kissing him?

So what? Soren told himself yet again as he took a backward step into the shadows.

Rowena grandly surveyed her audience. "We're all here to celebrate a milestone in Crystal's life." She turned to the honoree. "Your outrageous grandmother has an outrageous gift for you."

A man in front of Soren nudged his neighbor and, in a loud aside, said, "Yeah, outrageous is right. Rowena is Auntie Mame with a cunt." They both laughed.

Soren stifled the urge to defend Rowena's name. What was she to him, anyway?

Raising her voice for all to hear, Rowena continued, "A gift to open your eyes—indeed, all your senses. For the past thirty years you've lived a rather sheltered life, of your own volition. It's time you kicked up your heels—and your skirts—and sampled what's out there. You've heard me make reference to the Platinum Society."

Soren shifted uneasily. He knew all about the Platinum Society, thanks to Kat being on their board and Magnus having weathered some difficult moments at the Society before they'd pledged themselves to each other.

"You've always been skeptical that there was a club that catered to the sybaritic among us, even though I've described it many times." Rowena spread her arms to encompass the guests. "Most of the people here are members. I'm happy to say that the board has authorized me to present you with your own membership."

She pulled a platinum bracelet out of a pocket of her long skirt and held it up to a smattering of applause, then opened the clasp and affixed it to Crystal's wrist.

"So." She clapped her hands twice, like a magician. "Let the fun begin!"

Loud, pulsating music—stripper music—blasted out of hidden speakers. Spotlights flared at the opposite corner from the bar, illuminating a stage that was revealed as two men removed the folding screens. Three well-built young men in tight black pants boogied their way onto the stage to a hard-driving beat, unbuttoning white dress shirts as they played to an audience that started cheering and clapping.

Soren swore. Rolf was one of the strippers.

Damn, it wasn't enough that he'd heard endless stories of how Rolf dazzled Kat's art classes with his nude poses over the past six months, his pecker swollen and pointing directly at one or another of the eager students. Now he would be subjected to seeing it too? He began to back away from the group. And bumped into the sour-faced butler.

"Madam has instructed me to be sure every guest stays for the entertainment," he said.

"Yeah, well, watching male strippers isn't my style."

"Madam would be very disappointed in you."

"Sorry. She'll just have to be disappointed." He tried to sidestep the butler, but the man adroitly anticipated every move

Soren made as he tried to reach the sliding pocket doors that led to the hallway and freedom.

"And the guest of honor?" The butler raised a snooty eyebrow.

"Crystal? What about her?"

"Do you wish to disappoint her too?"

"She doesn't even know I'm here."

The smug look made Soren want to rearrange the man's face with a fist. Especially since catcalls and whistles were now emanating from the stage area.

"*Mademoiselle.*" The butler tilted his head in a slight bow.

"Soren. Thank you for coming."

He turned slowly, noting the cautious tone of Crystal's voice. They hadn't spoken since the rock-throwing incident the previous week when he'd accused her of slumming. Then he'd compounded it by bumming a ride from Magnus. Who had told him, Soren remembered ruefully, that he'd acted like an ass.

No wonder she looked so hesitant, as if afraid he'd bite her head off if she touched him. So what was he supposed to do, apologize again? And say what? Sorry I took your cherry? Sorry I left without thanking you?

Suddenly he felt boxed in, Crystal on one side, the butler on the other. He swung back around and took the three steps needed to reach the pocket doors, tucked his fingers in the slots, and yanked.

"Locked. But don't worry, sir. In case of fire, I'm stationed right here with the key. Or you could exit onto the patio from any of the French doors."

"Come on, let's get closer to the stage." With a slight hesitation he almost didn't notice, Crystal took hold of his left hand and tugged. Her flushed cheeks were the same shade as the flowers on her dress, like a field of red-orange poppies growing wild. As he took a step to follow her, her beautiful brown eyes went heavy lidded, like they were when he'd carried her to her bed the other night.

Soren shook his head. He didn't need that vision. He would not let his cock trap him into something he wasn't ready for.

She pulled him through the crowd, which was tossing out raunchy asides to the performers. "Grandma said something to me that really made sense. She said that since I'm just starting to try out my wings, I shouldn't make a commitment to anyone. In fact," Crystal squared her shoulders, as if she expected him to contradict her, "she lined up these three gorgeous guys so I can, as she says, sample their wares."

Soren tensed. He wasn't sure he liked the idea of Crystal making out, maybe screwing, any or all of the guys on stage. Especially not Rolf. Or that older man she'd been so cozy with, for that matter. Or, he realized, the young guy he'd met in Rowena's study who Crystal said had forced his attentions on her in her truck. Augie, he thought his name was. At least Augie was leering at Deirdra at the moment, and not Crystal.

"On the other hand…" Crystal tentatively settled an arm around Soren's waist and watched the men on stage. They now had removed their black pants as well as their shirts and shoes and were swiveling their hips clad only in Speedo-skinny trunks. "She says I might want to consider a *ménage a trois* with you and one of the men on stage. Would you like to try that?"

"Your *grandmother* tells you things like that?"

"Oh, she's always saying outrageous things trying to shock me." She cocked her head and looked at him, her face an intriguing mixture of coquette and naïf. "Does the idea of a *ménage a trois* bother you?"

"You…with two…*men*?" The last word came out no better than a squeak.

No way. No how. Soren couldn't wrap his mind around that idea. Not her. Crystal was still so innocent. For Pete's sake, she'd just had sex for the first time the other night. With him, he reminded himself. He'd taken her cherry. Still, she had all but demanded it.

"Or with me and another woman, if that's your pleasure. I notice that you met Deirdra. She's beautiful, don't you think?"

She was pulling his chain. She had to be. She'd smoked something, or snorted something, or had too much to drink. But hell, she meant nothing to him. Nothing. Let her do whatever she wanted, with whomever she wanted. "It's none of my business."

Crystal turned fully, leveled an intense gaze at him. "So the fact that we made love doesn't—"

One of the dancers—the tallest, most muscular, and to Soren's eye the ugliest—jumped off the stage and swept Crystal into his massive arms. He swung around and handed her to the other stranger, who set her on her feet on the stage. By God, if Rolf did something with Crystal in full view of two dozen adults, he'd—

But no. Rolf was flaunting his barely covered dick to the grandmother, who had somehow also gotten up on stage, and she was rocking her hips in a suggestive way to the insistent beat of the music. *Auntie Mame with a cunt*, he remembered a guest saying.

The big goon went after Deirdra and sent her up the stage as well, then jumped back up to join them. To Soren's horror, the women all began disrobing, Crystal unbuttoning her blouse and her friend slipping her T-shirt over her head. Rowena simply undid some buttons at her shoulders and her entire shift slid to the floor.

A disconnected part of Soren's brain noted that, for a septuagenarian, the grandmother had a terrific figure, lean, firm, with well-toned skin, the finest money could buy, he thought cynically.

Then his gaze flicked back to Crystal. Her face was even more flushed, she was laughing, her eyes sparkled, and she had just stepped out of the skirt, which lay in a puddle of red flowers on the stage floor. She was covered, barely, by what he fervently hoped was a bikini bathing suit and not underwear. Dammit, it looked like she enjoyed being an exhibitionist! He was torn between jumping up there himself to cover her with his shirt, and getting down and dirty — and naked — along with her.

Something registered in his peripheral vision. More skin. The other guests began flinging shirts, tops, skirts, slacks, every which way, and it looked like Rowena was their ringleader, encouraging them to get more comfortable. Meaning, more naked.

Suddenly a bank of lights flared outside. Soren blinked. Behind the wall of French doors the butler had mentioned earlier, a spacious flagstone patio led to an expanse of blue-green shimmer. Water. Lit from below.

Rolf lifted Rowena into his arms. The ugly stripper swept Crystal up and the third one took Deirdra. As if it had been choreographed and rehearsed, the three men with their armfuls marched down the stage steps and out one of the French doors.

"Suits optional," Rowena shouted. "Everyone into the pool!"

Chapter Eight

ଛ

Even though the old woman had told them all to wear swimsuits under their party clothing, he hadn't been prepared for this...this...orgy, the frenzy of ripping off clothes and lewd comments. How could she do this to him? She'd been so sweet and innocent, and suddenly she'd become a tramp. Moving her hips obscenely up there on stage, her breasts barely contained in those tiny swatches of cloth that passed for a bra, her creamy skin sheened with a glow of perspiration and arousal as she reveled in having all eyes on her.

He couldn't give her the painting now. Not after she'd prostituted herself before all those undeserving, ogling men. He'd pictured it time and time again. How he'd invite her to the special place he'd set up for her. How her eyes would light up when she first realized what he'd done, after she'd studied the way he'd had the artist superimpose her own face on that of the Madonna in all her purity, her white and blue robes swirling about her, the delicate feet crushing the snake, spawn of Satan, in the Garden of Eden.

Perhaps there was still hope for her. Perhaps he could convince her of the error of her ways. If he could just get her alone for a few weeks...

Yes. That's what he'd do. He'd make it so she had to depend on him for every little thing she needed. Food, water, light, sleep. She'd bathe when he said she could, she'd hold her bladder until he allowed her release. He'd cleanse her of all trace of obscenity. And then he'd have his pure Madonna forever.

* * * * *

"Come here, you witch."

Kat gave a short *whoop* and dodged Magnus' hand as he tried to catch her. She'd shed her bra, daring him to skinny-dip along with those already frolicking buck-naked in Rowena's heated, Olympic-size pool. Taking a breath, she dove to the deep end, gliding beneath various hairy and sleek legs bobbing above her. She surfaced, swung her fiery red hair out of her face, and reached for the edge to hoist herself up.

And felt a strong hand grip one ankle, another hand on her calf, then Magnus was walking his hands up her body from behind. She felt the friction of his chest hair as he slid his slick, wet torso up her naked back.

"Those tits are for my eyes only," he growled in her ear just before he scraped her earlobe with his teeth. His huge hands cupped her breasts possessively, capturing her hard nipples between the knuckles of his index and middle fingers and squeezing gently. "Guess I'll just have to keep them covered until everyone's out of the pool."

She arched her back, thrusting her ass into his groin area. His very formidable groin area. Oh, she'd love to rip off his swimsuit and get that thick, heavy cock into her right this minute. She was teaching Magnus to be more playful, more open with his emotions and his urges in public.

And he was learning even now. "Don't move."

Releasing her breasts, he dipped below the surface of the pool, his mouth leisurely following the contour of her spine until he reached the top of her crack. With one yank he tugged her bikini bottom down to her ankles, then worked it over her feet. Just the idea of Magnus stripping her naked in a crowded pool gave her libido a jump-start. As if she needed an excuse to get horny with him.

Magnus surfaced again, and with a quick movement lifted her hands off the pool's edge, where she'd been obediently treading water, and spun her around. He curled her arms around his neck and positioned her legs around his waist. The scrape of fabric against her shin brought a fleeting frown to her face. Why was he still wearing a swimsuit?

"Hang on to me," he ordered. With one hand on the pool's edge to stabilize them, he reached between their bodies and yanked out a formidable handful of hot male flesh from his suit. With no foreplay he rammed his cock upward into her waiting pussy. His mouth captured her involuntary cry at the suddenness, at the *daring* — for him — of Magnus' action.

A long moment of utter stillness ticked by during which his lips remained pressed against hers, his cock deep and unmoving in her pussy. Kat knew he was teasing her, silently imposing his will on her. She also suspected that if she rocked her hips, urged him in any way to continue fucking her, that he'd withdraw. He was doing his best to accommodate her exhibitionist tendencies within his own comfort level — his level being one that kept his swimsuit on in public — and she loved him all the more for it.

Still, she couldn't resist rhythmically squeezing her Kegel muscles around him, teasing him in return.

"Witch," he murmured against her mouth. He withdrew his cock until only the tip remained inside her, locked his intense gaze to hers. "Don't move unless I tell you to."

She loved this side of him, the domineering lover who would play her like a harp, plucking, riffling, sending her headlong toward a climax only to dampen the vibration of the strings then send another arpeggio spiraling through her body.

Slowly he pushed his throbbing cock back inside her pussy. One hand controlling her hip, the other holding on to the pool's edge, he established an excruciatingly unhurried rhythm until she was biting her tongue to keep from moaning. Her breasts flattened against his chest as she squeezed her arms more tightly around his neck, clutched his waist with her legs. Her teeth bit into the side of his neck. The sounds of other voices, the playful splashing of water around them, faded away until there was only the two of them, cocooned by their love and their lust.

"Take a deep breath and look at me," Magnus whispered then let go of his anchor to immovable land. Warm water closed over their heads and, gazes locked and still joined intimately together, they drifted to the bottom of the pool. He grabbed both her hips in an iron grip and began to pump his hips violently, ramming his cock deep into her, again and again. Kat bucked against him, her passion at last allowed free rein. She felt the tension within her spiraling out of control and she let it come, the ripples turning into waves and then into an atomic explosion all the more powerful for its silence.

When her conscious mind returned, she realized Magnus had shoved them up from the bottom of the pool with his powerful legs. Then realized, too, that he was still deeply imbedded in her, hard and hot and throbbing.

They breached the surface and she took a great, deep breath. Arms and legs still entwined around him, she ventured, "Mags? Why didn't—"

"Shh." He grabbed for the pool's edge to hold them shoulders-deep in the water, then began strewing tiny kisses over her face. "That one was for you."

He allowed his rock-hard cock to slip out of her, and even in the warmth of the heated water she could feel the scalding heat of his flesh as it skimmed hers. "You stay here. I'll find your bottom before it gets caught in the filters."

And he dove back down, gingerly working his suit up over his hard-on.

Kat could only marvel, again, at his control.

* * * * *

"Come on," Crystal said as she dragged Soren around knots of guests nibbling at canapés on the flagstone patio. Her hair was still wet from having been tossed into the pool. A fluffy towel rode lightly on her shoulders and draped over her yellow bra. "Grandma keeps spare suits in the cabana."

Having not heard a word from Soren since Magnus drove him home from her house four days ago, Crystal realized she would have to be more proactive regarding her future. Her crystal had selected a gorgeous man for her, but he was skittish, almost gun-shy, with women. She'd noticed how he ignored the beautiful Deirdra. But. He certainly wasn't a woman-*hater*, not after the way he made her feel so delicious all over, the considerate way he made love to her after that first time when he'd taken her with so much less finesse. Something in his past, a woman no doubt, had hurt him deeply. That conviction made her want to heal him.

So she gave him her most winning smile. "Don't be a party pooper. It's my birthday."

"It's not that I'm a party pooper. I just don't like surprises."

Crystal stopped at the open louvered doors, deliciously aware that she was nearly naked while Soren was covered from neck to toes in jeans and a light-blue polo shirt that highlighted the brilliant blue of his eyes. "How could you have been surprised? Grandma told me she invited all three of you Thorvalds. And everyone else certainly came prepared with a swimsuit."

Soren's eyes narrowed. "She may have told you she did, but apparently she forgot to call me. Since she apparently knows Kat from the Platinum Society, she may have just issued a blanket invitation to bring her fiancé and his brothers. Until Mags actually pulled into the driveway, I thought we were going to his bachelor party."

"You did?" Taken aback, Crystal let her eyes skim over the guests illuminated by myriad Japanese lanterns, looking for Rowena. She wouldn't put it past her. After all, her grandmother had given her the crystal and knew how it had almost scalded her skin when she'd first seen Soren at the bachelor auction.

Still, it was underhanded of her to surprise Soren like that. "I'll talk to her," she promised. "Wait. Shouldn't your brothers have mentioned— Oh, I get it. They didn't want you to know. You'd have backed out, wouldn't you?" Yes, he was definitely skittish. "Guess they know you pretty well."

Soren just glared at her.

"Meanwhile, you'll feel more comfortable if you take your clothes off."

Heat spread up her throat and bloomed on her cheeks at the searing look in his eyes. "I mean, get into swim trunks," she managed. "That way you won't stand out."

She felt her blush deepening at her Freudian slip. She remembered all too well how much a certain part of him stood out when he was naked in her bedroom. "I mean…"

Turning her head away from his intense gaze, she nudged him inside the cabana, with its wicker chairs in a small grouping and kitchenette against one wall, and walked to a tall, narrow cabinet painted white. "Just…let me find you a suit."

"I don't get it." Soren stood near the entrance, as if needing to be near an escape hatch. "One day you're a virgin…" he stumbled over the word "…and a week later you act like an experienced woman of the world. Suggesting a *ménage a trois*. Traipsing around on stage with male strippers. Tossing off double entendres. Wearing a tiny bikini that has every guy's tongue hanging out."

A smile spread across Crystal's face. "Really? Is yours?"

"Yes. Stop distracting me. Were you just playing a role of innocent babe in the woods when we—" he cleared his throat, "the first time we—"

"Made love? Yes, I was a virgin the first time we made love. But I wasn't an innocent babe in the woods. I have a healthy knowledge of sexual matters. I've kissed my share of frogs and fumbled through some anatomy lessons in the dark. When we met, I knew I wanted you to be my first, and I was thrilled that you wanted me too."

She tossed him a pair of size 34 royal blue trunks with its hangtag still on it. "Here. If it fits, there's a pair of scissors on the counter to cut off the tag."

Deliberately she slid the towel off her shoulders, flinging it on one of the chairs as she walked toward him, her breasts gently swaying under the yellow triangles of lined cotton. "Do you need help?"

Soren stood his ground, one large hand holding the trunks. In the reflected light from the shimmering water, his eyes glowed a piercing blue. She could see his Adam's apple move as he swallowed.

She reached for his belt buckle.

He tossed the trunks aside and grabbed her wrists. "I can handle it," he rasped. "Get out of here."

The tenor of the party, her new Platinum Society membership with all its possibilities, and what she'd seen and heard in and around the pool, had shifted Crystal's sex drive into higher gear. Here she was in a darkened room with the man she intended to marry. The champagne she'd drunk had made her feel bold. She set into action the plan she'd just devised.

"These doors lock from the inside," she said, indicating a simple thumb-latch, and blithely sauntered out of the cabana. "I'll be waiting for you."

She walked away a few steps then heard the gratifying sound of the latch clicking into place. Before she lost her nerve, she rounded the corner of the structure and snuck into the utility shed housing the pump and other pool equipment. Silently she turned the knob on the inner door that opened up at the edge of the kitchenette.

It took a moment for her eyes to adjust to the darkness. But more to the point, she followed his mumbling and the rustle of denim as Soren slid out of his jeans. The slivers of light through the louvers showed him in profile while she, Crystal was sure, was invisible against the darkness of the room. She unhooked her bra and set it down gently onto the back of a chair, then crept forward.

She could tell the minute he realized he wasn't alone. Having just bent over to put a leg through his trunks, he shot upright. "Who's there?"

"It's me. I decided not to wait," she said, snaking her arms around his waist and hanging on tightly, for she knew he'd try to pry her loose. She rubbed her bare breasts against his chest hair. Her nipples hardened instantly and she shivered at the feel of him, the muscle and sinew and skin that was Soren Thorvald.

"Jesus, Crystal. There's people outside!" He grabbed her arms, as she'd expected, but couldn't seem to decide what to do next, whether to push her away or press her tighter to him.

She pressed even closer to him and rose on tiptoe, capturing his thick cock between their bodies. The heat of him almost melted her bikini bottom, to say nothing of her insides. Juices pooled at her crotch. "Most of the people outside are doing the same thing. Besides, it's my birthday and I wanted to do something totally daring."

"But your grandmother—"

"Is a member of the Platinum Society." She ran her palms down his back until they reached his firm ass cheeks. She cupped them, marveling at their firmness, then pulled his hips forward to grind against hers.

"Crystal, we can't—"

Her mouth found his. She kissed him with less expertise than she had advertised, but it didn't matter. His own innate skill took over the kiss. He stroked the seam of her mouth with his tongue. Like a flower she opened for him, and he thrust it inside, tasting, stroking, exploring. His arms encircled her, pressing her body flush against him, shoulders to thighs. His cock rubbed against her bare belly, scorching her.

"We've got to stop," he choked out.

"I know. Just one more kiss." She dropped to her knees, her palms sliding down his hips and thighs. She feathered eager but unschooled kisses on his cock. It throbbed against her face, thick and hot and heavy.

Did she dare do more? Yes, she wanted to—needed to. She wrapped the fingers of one hand around the most blatantly male part of him to hold him in place. Her other hand kneaded the firm flesh of his ass cheek. Her tongue darted out to taste him, small, shy licks on the thick ridge circling the head. Slightly salty, incredibly smooth, scorching hot. The primitive groan

110

escaping his throat emboldened her. She opened her mouth and drew him in a couple inches, feeling with her tongue the vein standing out against the rigid length of him.

His hands tunneled under her hair at the nape, holding her head in place. His musky, masculine scent filled her. She drew her cheeks in, clamping the insides of her mouth against him as though she were sucking a Popsicle.

With a guttural sound, he leaned down, thrust his hands under her armpits and yanked her to her feet. "Don't."

"Oh dear, did I hurt you? I'm sorry, I've never done — "

Her voice faded as he released her, standing silent and rigid, hands fisted, eyes tightly closed as if he couldn't stand looking at her. Grateful for the relative darkness, Crystal felt her face flame. She'd certainly showed him what a country bumpkin she really was when it came to sexual matters.

Crystal spun on her bare feet, stubbed her toe on the chair when she grabbed her bra from where she'd dropped it. Without knocking anything over, she managed to find the door to the utility room. In that small space, she fumbled with the clasp, cracking her funny bone against the wall, but managed to jiggle her breasts into the cups. With a last deep breath, she walked out into the cool, clear night.

Alone. And dumbstruck.

How could she have done something so wanton? She couldn't really use the excuse of too much champagne. One or two glassfuls, that was all she'd consumed. Nor was the herd mentality to blame. She was old enough to be master of her own fate, never mind that all around her, people were pairing off and seeking dark corners.

She'd thrown herself at Soren because she knew he was The One. But the crystal only had so much magic to it. Until he felt the same way, it wouldn't do to scare him off by being so blatant.

Cautiously she sought out her grandmother, afraid she'd discover Rowena doing a horizontal dance with Trey or one of the other men attending tonight. She was relieved to see her in the great room, wearing a thigh-length, red striped terrycloth robe as she spoke to one of the clean-up staff. Crystal sat down to wait.

* * * * *

Inside the cabana, Soren also sat down. More like collapsed, he thought ruefully.

So far he'd managed to cover his rampaging cock with his briefs, but he felt like a freight train had run over him then backed up and done it again. Was he a damn fool for stopping her? Hell, she'd been all over him—again, acting like a practiced courtesan in between moments of innocence. Jesus. When she'd kissed his cock so artlessly, he thought he'd explode right then and there. But hell, when she started sucking on him, he wanted nothing so much as to ram it all the way down her throat. And those tits, soft and firm at the same time, rubbing against his chest, the glorious handfuls of her ass cheeks—a man could only stand so much teasing before he wanted to fuck her brains out. That he couldn't do, not with a bunch of strangers within earshot who could burst in on them at any time. And especially not to Crystal, who was, dammit, special.

But wait. She'd *apologized* to him. Christ, did she think he'd pulled her off because she'd *hurt* him? Did she think he found her inexperience distasteful? Should he apologize to *her*?

Damn. What if she told Rowena what he'd done? They could get a restraining order against him.

No, they wouldn't. Rowena was a Platinum Society member, and she'd encouraged Crystal to follow in her footsteps. Besides, Crystal had come on to him with her big brown eyes and her double entendres. He'd lived without a woman for most of his life. His sex life was practically nonexistent. He could live without this particular woman.

But damn, she was so bubbly, so full of life. God knew, his life was about as exciting as watching beer ferment. She'd brought a ray of sunshine into it. He could use her to get his rocks off and then walk away before things got sticky. He didn't have to give his heart away the way his father had done only to find out the feeling wasn't mutual. He'd never let himself go down that route, putting someone so far up on a pedestal that when she got off it, you lost the will to live.

With a baffled shake of his head, Soren stood up to slip into his jeans. It was time to think about logistics. If he knew his brothers, Mags went home with Kat, and as sure as midnight is dark, Rolf scored with one of the women there and wouldn't want a tagalong. He figured it was late enough that the snooty butler wouldn't object to calling him a cab.

*****

"Really, Rowena, don't you think you're letting things get out of hand?" Portable heaters scattered around the patio kept the cool April night at bay, but his hand trembled as he lifted the coffee cup to his lips. The pool had been heated, and after a swim so he wouldn't stand out as a party pooper, he'd donned one of the terrycloth robes laid out for the guests' use and hovered near the buffet table.

"Not at all." She squeezed his biceps in what he deemed a too-familiar gesture. "I thought it was time I introduced you to the idea of the Platinum Society. You're mature, strong, handsome. Just the kind of new blood we need. I'd be glad to sponsor you for membership. The initiation fee and dues are steep, but I'm sure it wouldn't be a hardship for you."

"It's not the fees." He had to reach hard to control his anger. "People are coupling like rabbits, even in the pool. I'm thinking of..." His voice softened. "Crystal. She's so innocent. How can you expose her to all that's going on in plain view?"

"She's thirty years old, dear heart. It was time to push her out of her comfort zone. Did she look embarrassed up there on stage with those gorgeous young men? Hell, no. It's obvious she has her grandmother's appreciation of the opposite sex." She scrutinized him thoroughly, making him glad he'd covered his solid, muscular body with the robe.

Deliberately he set down his coffee cup and reached for a mini-éclair he didn't want, trying to control the outrage that threatened to overwhelm him. The old bat had taken his pure Madonna and made her into a whoring Mary Magdalene. When he finally had Crystal ensconced in her special, secure place, he'd punish the salacious grandmother for what she'd done to his sweet, innocent angel.

Chapter Nine

ജ

"Okay. You were down on your knees in front of Soren. Tell me exactly what he said," Kat Donaldson demanded. The three women sat around Deirdra's breakfast table over homemade scones and strong coffee, and Kat's manner was part sex therapist, part voyeur, and all encouraging.

Having met Kat at the birthday party, Crystal had been delighted to discover that the woman was acquainted with her best friend — Kat's art gallery was on the same block as Deirdra's New Age shop. When she heard Kat was soon to be Soren's sister-in-law, Crystal had jumped at Deirdra's suggestion that the three women put their heads together to brainstorm next steps.

Still, she felt a moment of panic at admitting just how raunchy she'd been in the cabana.

As if reading her mind, Kat lifted her arm and indicated the platinum bracelet on her wrist that matched the one her grandmother had given her at the party. "You do know that the Society is all about finding and nurturing your own sexuality, don't you?"

Crystal nodded shyly.

"And you seemed to have no trouble shaking those gorgeous titties up on stage."

Fire crept up Crystal's throat and into her cheeks. "I don't know where that urge came from."

"It came from inside you. I can assure you, you won't embarrass me with anything you say. After all, I'm on the board of directors of the Society. And, I was a butterfly, flitting from man to man. Until I met Magnus. He convinced me he was the only one for me when he handcuffed me to the ceiling at a cocktail party, stripped me down to my thong, kissed and finger-fucked me in front of dozens of people until I was babbling."

She paused dramatically, sipped coffee from a china cup. "Then the son of a bitch stalks out of the room and leaves me this close—" she held up her hand, indicating a sliver of width between thumb and forefinger, "to an orgasm."

Crystal's mouth dropped open. She slid an astonished glance to Deirdra, who had the same reaction. "Then what happened?"

"That's when I realized I didn't want anyone else to fuck me. Only Magnus." She patted Crystal's forearm. "So believe me, darlin', nothing you say will shock me."

Crystal cleared her throat. "Well." She lifted her own cup, more to gather her thoughts than for the taste of Bucks County Coffee Company's finest ground. "I...uh, I went down on my knees and, uh, I touched him. There."

"It's okay, you can say it. You touched his cock."

"Um, yes. His cock. I didn't get a chance to, you know, examine it before, when we were in the Jacuzzi or in bed." Her face felt like flame. "It jumped when I kissed it. It was hot and hard and—never mind. You know what it's like. He moaned, and I felt such a thrill that I could make him do that, that I had such power over him. So I dared to put my mouth around it. Around his cock."

She didn't look up, but she saw Kat nod in satisfaction at her use of the descriptive word. "He grabbed my head with both hands, as though he was afraid I'd run away." She barked out a short laugh. "As if I'd want to. Anyway, I pulled my cheeks together and started sucking, you know, like he was a lollipop."

This time Crystal did take a sip of coffee. Her throat was dry just thinking about the size, the flavor of Soren's cock, the vein throbbing on one side of it, the scent of him. She set the cup down with a clatter. "That's when he yanked me away from him and said 'Don't'. I thought I'd hurt him, or did it wrong. I'd never had a man's cock in my mouth before. Right up until that moment, I thought he was enjoying it. The playing with his cock. But…"

Kat was silent, so Crystal continued in a rush, "When I realized what a country bumpkin I showed myself to be, I grabbed the top of my swimsuit and rushed out of there before I made myself look even more of a fool."

"Let me get this straight. You and Soren were in the darkened cabana. People were outside, either in the pool or behind the bushes, pairing off to make love. You initiated the love-play, not him." Kat mulled that over a minute. "Knowing Soren, I'd say he stopped because he didn't want to fuck you in such a public place. He's a very private man, our Soren. He hasn't had much experience with women, to hear Magnus tell it. Something in his past turned him off. Something deeper than just a relationship gone sour."

She reached over to squeeze Crystal's upper arm. "Honey, there isn't a man alive who would turn away from getting his cock sucked by a beautiful woman. There's no such thing as doing it wrong. Even a guy without a lot of experience would just tell you how to do it to set him off. You didn't hurt him, believe me. Guaran-damn-teed, if you two were in bed, he'd ask you to suck harder. He'd even tell you to use your teeth. No way would he stop you." Kat stopped to sip her coffee then continued.

"Magnus told me later that Soren thought they were taking him to Mags' stag party, because they didn't think he'd willingly go to Rowena's for a birthday party. So," she concluded, "he was uptight enough to worry about what people would think. And you should cut him some slack."

Crystal stroked the pendant hanging around her neck. It almost hummed — she could feel traces of vibration against her fingers. "That sounds logical."

"Tomorrow is Magnus' night to be a bouncer at Thor's Hammer. I think we three should go there for the jazz. Saturday nights they have a combo. It'll be packed. And," Kat looked in turn at the two women at the breakfast table with her, "three beautiful women without escorts ought to bring a lot of bees to the honey, don't you think? Let Soren chew on *that* while he's filling beer mugs."

* * * * *

By eleven o'clock, they were three deep at the bar, Soren noted with satisfaction. Youngish crowd, drawn by the magnet of the Dougall Trio. A pianist with a deep, vibrant voice like Al Hibbler, a reed man who was equally proficient on clarinet and alto or soprano saxophone, and a funky bass fiddler known to go on riffs that had patrons shutting up to goggle at him. To say nothing of how danceable their mellow old standards were. The postage-stamp dance floor was packed for every number.

Beside him, Trang worked with smooth economy, flashing her smile at everyone, making the guys happy to wait for one of twelve beers on tap. At the far corner, Old Man Peck was keeping up with the two waitresses' tableside orders. A light haze of smoke hung over the room, the air kept breathable by powerful exhaust fans in the ceiling. For himself, he'd be happy when the new no-smoking-in-bars law took effect, even though his business might suffer.

The kitchen had closed an hour earlier, the chef and his assistants cleaned up and gone. Only coffee was available now, along with the ubiquitous peanuts no self-respecting bar would be without.

All in all, Soren mused as he built a Guinness in a chilled mug, he was right where he wanted to be, master of all he surveyed. He was done with birthday parties, swimming pools and dark-eyed gypsies who wove magic spells around him. For a virgin, she'd certainly been all over him. God! He'd never felt anything so good as when her lips clamped around his cock. It had taken every ounce of self-possession to pull her away, or he'd have fucked her mouth until he came deep inside her throat with a roar that would have been heard on the other side of the pool.

Shit! He jumped as foam surged over the hand holding the mug under the spout. And wasn't that the first time *that* ever happened. He hoped Trang didn't notice how much his mind had wandered, or he'd be in for a bushel of razzing. Casually he set the mug down and wiped his hand on the towel hanging off his belt, then topped off the Guinness more carefully and served it to the patron.

From a corner of his eye he saw Magnus talking to Table Six, far enough from the combo so as not to invite busted eardrums, yet close to the dance floor. His bouncer skills hadn't been needed yet tonight. These particular musicians apparently kept the patrons from being too rowdy. He frowned as Mags took hold of one of the men's arms and "helped" him up. Soren wondered if the man was flagged, or maybe he'd made one too many lewd comments and someone complained. Whatever, the three men finally got up as Coral approached the group carrying three shot glasses on a tray.

Soren blinked. He could have sworn he lip-read Magnus saying "On the house". The three guys grabbed their liquor and sidled away. Coral quickly bussed the now-empty table and Mags put down a placard. A "Reserved" sign? Since when did Thor's Hammer offer such amenities?

He didn't have time to ponder. Trang caught his eye, cocked her head toward Peck. Soren nodded, shifted his attention to include Trang's patrons while she helped fill a large table order.

In the sudden flurry of order-filling, he almost missed them, the three women strolling in who had captured the interest of, seemingly, every man on a stool or standing behind one. A tall, fiery redhead cut a swath through the pack of warm bodies—Kat, he realized. *So that's why Mags reserved the table.* She was followed by the woman who tried to pick him up at Rowena's party, whose unusual name escaped him. The last one in the parade—

The soapy mug slid out of his hand and bounced against the wooden pallet that covered the bartending floor. With a muffled curse he stooped to retrieve it then set it behind him on the ledge where the liquors were stored in lighted glass shelves. He'd check it out for cracks later.

Crystal. Here, in Thor's Hammer. Face rosy with excitement, sparkle in her eyes, be-bopping her way to the table to the bouncy rhythm of "Fly Me To The Moon". Christ, every man's gaze went to her swaying hips. Soren made a fist under the counter. He'd as soon knock their teeth out as let them leer at her.

"Okay, boss, I'm back." Trang nudged him, pulling Soren out of his stupor. He gave her a short nod of acknowledgement then plunged his hands into the soapy water under the counter. No skin off his nose. It was a free country. He just hoped Mags didn't expect Table Six to be "on the house" the rest of the evening.

Dammit, he thought a short time later. *Bees to honey* was the first thought that came to him when he looked up to see Table Six surrounded by guys. Craning his neck, he saw Crystal on the dance floor, snuggling up to an overly muscled guy to the tune of "Cry Me A River". *I'll cry him a river with my fist*, he thought fiercely.

For a moment Soren was relieved when the man relinquished her and Crystal sat back down at the table. Deirdra, that was her name, Deirdra got up to dance with someone and two guys fought for the right to sit in the vacated chair at Crystal's side. Undaunted, the loser pulled a chair from another table and wedged himself between them, casually throwing an arm across the back of her chair. Soren gritted his teeth. *MYOB*, he chanted inside his head like a mantra. *Mind Your Own Business.*

Her sweet laugh floated through the din and wrapped itself around him. Damn, it sounded like she was having fun. He had no right to be fuming at that. He didn't want any entanglements, right? Especially since she was the happily-ever-after kind, the kind you walked down the aisle with. He wanted no part of it.

Still, his cock swelled at the way her face softened when their eyes met through the smoky haze. She held his gaze for a moment, eyelashes at half-mast, even though someone was tapping her on the shoulder, clamoring for her attention.

The moment ended when Trang nudged him again, pointing with her chin at three empty mugs waiting to be filled.

It hit him so hard he staggered backward until his butt came into contact with the rear counter. *They're doing this on purpose.* It had to be Kat's doing. Soren vividly remembered the time Rolf brought Kat here, teaching her to shoot pool while Magnus seethed with unacknowledged jealousy. History repeating itself.

Well, it wouldn't work. Soren wasn't Mags. He'd be damned if he'd let such a blatant ploy sucker him into anything. He didn't even *like* women.

Still, he found himself glancing at the bar clock, wanting to make the time go faster, so he could send out a "last call for drinks" and get all those hangers-on out of Crystal's orbit and out the door.

The minutes dragged by. Crystal danced damn near every dance. At least they weren't all with the same guy. If that were the case, Soren would be escorting the man outside with the aid of his trusty baseball bat.

About an hour before closing, Mags sauntered up to the far end of the bar where no stools were allowed due to fire code regulations. Soren automatically filled a tall glass with ice and seltzer water, his drink of choice when he was bouncing.

"Thanks." Magnus downed half the seltzer, set the glass on the mahogany bar. "What's that evil eye for?"

Soren tamped down his ire. "Seems like a quiet night tonight."

Magnus nodded. "The band keeps the rowdies down."

"Good." Soren removed the towel from his belt loop and tucked it on the rack. "Take my station for ten minutes, will you?"

Without waiting for an acknowledgement, Soren ducked under the counter, fully expecting—*knowing*—Mags would comply. He refused to look at the smirk on his brother's face as he shoved his way through the crowd.

"Excuse me, I believe this is our dance."

Crystal's chocolate-brown eyes lit up like Fourth of July sparklers when her gaze connected with Soren's. She made a rueful little moue of regret to the redheaded clown who'd damn well better get his hand off her ass in a hurry, or else he'd—

"Yes, it is." She lifted her arms to him, and Soren's heart did a funny jump as the trio segued into "Smoke Gets In Your Eyes."

With no preliminaries, he swept her into a brutal embrace, pressing her tight to the erection he'd been battling all night. His right hand slid down from her bare waist to her sweet ass under the same low-slung jeans she'd worn to dinner at Chica's. His left hand pulled her arm close to his chest and set her palm against his heart. He wondered if she felt it beat as loud as it sounded to him, *ka-BOOM, ka-BOOM,* pulsing through his veins.

"You smell so good," he murmured, burying his face in the riot of dark curls she'd left free and flowing. He wasn't an especially good dancer, but he shuffled his feet in time to the music and to hell with anyone not calling it dancing.

"You smell like beer, smoke and Soren." She sighed against his neck and arched her back. "Intoxicating."

His cock jerked against the cotton boxers under too-tight jeans. "You're a tease," he growled.

She pulled back as far as she could within his embrace, and raised an uncertain gaze to him. "What do you mean?"

"Shoving your sweet tits so tight against me and breathing on my neck. And the other night. Taking my cock in your mouth and then running away."

Abruptly Crystal stopped moving her feet. He almost stepped on them.

"You're the one who told me to stop," she said through clenched teeth.

"So why did you run away?"

"I thought I hurt you. Either that or you thought I was from some backwater town, some rube who didn't know what she was doing. Which I didn't, by the way, it was all instinct. You were standing there with a pained look on your face, your eyes squinched shut like you didn't want to see me, what else was I to think?"

Heat flared from his eyes. Crystal felt the scorch of it from her aching nipples down to her damp crotch. He bent his head forward and rubbed his lips against hers, slowly, oh so slowly. Eagerly she lifted up on tiptoes to deepen the contact. "Now who's teasing?" she complained.

Soren released the hand that had been pressing hers to his heart and brought it up to tunnel his fingers through her curls. Holding her head rigid, he thrust his tongue into her eager mouth. She relished the way his vision had narrowed down to him and her, mouths fused in wet heat, bodies as close as a pearl in its oyster, with the other dancers, the music, the smoke fading away until they were in a private cocoon of lust.

Someone bumped into them. Crystal staggered back at the impact, their bodies torn from each other. Soren took a shaky step forward before stabilizing them. She realized the trio had shifted to a bouncy thing, a hot jazz beat, and people around them were doing a jitterbug, a twist, and all kinds of other dances where partners were flung around.

"Go." Soren pushed her off the dance floor. "The ladies' room is over there. Wait for me in the hallway."

Crystal wobbled a bit as he relinquished his fierce hold on her, but managed to follow directions. Through an archway she could see three doors, two with appropriate silhouettes of stick figures in pants or skirts, the third with a "No Access" sign.

Once in the hallway, she leaned against a wall, trying to catch her breath. She hadn't sat down for at least an hour. She enjoyed dancing, truly she did. If only the guys didn't hold her like an octopus, their arms and legs brushing suggestively all over her. She'd ordered a Tom Collins, she remembered that, an old-fashioned drink in a tall glass that she planned to sip over the course of at least an hour. She probably had two sips from that, no more. She'd love to have a glass of ice water. She'd love to use the john. But she didn't want to miss Soren.

"Crystal." Her name on Soren's lips was almost a whisper. "I had to get the keys."

He walked past her to the door that said "No Access," inserted a key and unlocked it. "Come here," he growled, pulling her into a cavern-dark space and slamming the door behind them.

Only then did he flick a switch. Crystal had to blink in the sudden glare of fluorescent lights illuminating a long, narrow storage area with shelves along the long wall, with no more than two feet of room to access the boxes lining the shelves.

"Christ, I can't get enough of you." He nudged Crystal so her back was flush against the wall and swooped down on her with his hot mouth. His tongue was everywhere, thrusting hot and hard, touching her teeth, exploring the roof of her mouth. And his hands, oh, his hands burned her skin as he shoved the bra above her breasts, scrunched the cropped sweater up to her armpits. He dipped his head and captured a hard nipple in his mouth, sucking, sucking as though he was showing her how to suck his cock, deep, hot and frantic.

Crystal dug her fingers into his blond hair, arched her back to offer even more of herself to him. She wanted everything at once, his mouth on hers, soul-kissing her, but also his mouth right where it was, pulling and tugging on her nipple that streaked darts of pure erotic heat down to the aching nub between her legs, one hand tweaking her other nipple between his fingers. She wanted his cock inside her, thrusting hard, his body heavy and hot on hers, pinning her, fucking her…

"Shit." He withdrew his hands, his mouth, and she almost whimpered at the loss. "Give me a minute," he rasped.

He turned to the door and snapped the lock. Eeek! She'd been in such a frenzy to get her hands, her mouth on him, that anyone could have walked in and found them indecently occupied. Then realized that this must have been how he'd felt in the cabana, and understood. He'd been protecting her, even at the expense of what Kat had called "blue balls".

Before she had time to take a breath, he spun her around to face away from him. His hands snaked around her waist from behind and he snapped open her jeans, yanked the zipper down and ripped the pants down to her knees.

Holding her immobile with the flat of his palm against her belly, he swept a large box marked "cocktail napkins" off a shelf at waist level and nudged her closer to the empty space. "Bend down. Lean on your elbows." He followed his directive with a hand to the back of her neck, forcing her to comply.

Crystal felt a sharp thrill of erotic fear—she didn't know quite what to expect. Here she was, naked from shoulder blades to knees, in a locked room with a hungry alpha male, her exposed breasts swaying freely, her butt thrust high in the air as she put her weight on her forearms and elbows, unable to escape with the denim holding her knees immobile. And Soren was acting like a sex maniac, his hands now pulling on her nipples, now grabbing handfuls of flesh on her hips, his mouth ranging all over her back, her hips, his tongue licking the dark crevice between her ass cheeks and down to her swollen labia. She made a small sound of frustration when he withdrew his hands, but relaxed at the sound of a foil packet being ripped open.

Seconds later he grabbed her hips again and drove into her from behind, seating himself as deep as she could take him in a single mighty thrust. And stayed there, his chest expanding and contracting against her back like a blacksmith's bellows.

Oh God, she didn't want him to stop. How could she let him know? Would he think her too wanton? "Soren, please."

"I want you so much, I can't think straight." His rough voice thrilled as it scraped over her tingling nerve endings. She moved her hips experimentally. He withdrew his cock almost to the tip, then plunged back in, setting up a harsh and fast rhythm that had her gyrating her hips frantically, wanting him to scald every inch of her with his burning heat.

The daring of their situation fueled her need. She understood now why Kat wanted Magnus to fuck her in the swimming pool. The danger of discovery, the clandestine location, their private island amid a sea of testosterone and pheromones, heightened Crystal's passion. She bucked against him, felt her inner muscles begin to spasm around his cock.

A groan started from the deepest, most feral part of her and surged up her throat, erupting into incoherent syllables of want and need. Only the tiniest part of her mind was still rational enough to hear the insistent knocking, and that sliver of sanity thanked heaven the door was locked.

"Soren? You in there?"

The climax overtook her like an avalanche, and she felt Soren's hand against her mouth, silencing her cries, but her orgasm was so powerful, her teeth sank into the knuckles of his index finger as she fought to control the sound level emanating from this wild woman who acted nothing like the Crystal she'd been.

"Damn you, Magnus," Soren growled under his breath as he fought the urge to keep pumping into Crystal until he too could find release. It was the most difficult thing he'd ever done, but after a moment, he stilled his movements.

"We need a magnum of house vodka."

I'll give you a magnum, right up your ass, he thought savagely as he forced oxygen into his lungs and loosened his hold on Crystal's mouth and hip. Sweat beads rolled down his temple. A moment later he was able to stand more or less upright and rasp out, "Be right there."

Damn, but his balls ached. He felt like the subject of an X-rated reality show. The last thing in the world he wanted to do right now was pull out. When the fuck would he be able to come inside of Crystal's tight, welcoming pussy? Jesus, he was sick and tired of wasting condoms.

Then his sanity returned. He had his cock inside a woman who, until she met him, had been a virgin, in a public place where he might as well have turned on a blinking neon sign saying "We're fucking like rabbits," and all he could think of was himself? What kind of man was he?

With a Herculean effort and more regret than he wanted to admit, he took a step back and allowed his throbbing cock to slip out of her welcoming heat. Like a living thing, it bobbed and dipped, scraping the tender, sensitized skin against the zipper. He'd have laughed if it hadn't stung. He, who hadn't cared enough to have more than a handful of women in his lifetime, had been too sex-crazed to even pull his own jeans down, but had yanked his dick out through the zipper opening like a john in a crude porn movie.

Gingerly tucking his raging hard-on inside his jeans, condom and all, he bent forward and began pulling Crystal's jeans up her gorgeous thighs and over her ripe, sweet ass. It jarred him for a moment that he couldn't find panties underneath the denim then wondered, did she come here tonight commando, without underwear?

Shit! Had she expected to do the nasty with one of the bozos she danced with? He closed his eyes against the pain that such a vision conjured up. He'd kill any man who tried to fuck her. Or at least rearrange his face and send him to the emergency room.

When he opened his eyes again, Crystal had turned around, her mouth soft and pouty, her eyes warm and glowing, like she'd just had mind-bending sex. Her jeans were zipped and snapped, her top smoothed over her luscious breasts.

"I'm sorry," she said, rising on tiptoe and kissing one side of his mouth then the other. "You'd better get your vodka and go before things get even more awkward."

He brushed a tendril of hair away from her cheek. "Are you okay?"

Her smile dazzled. "I'm terrific. But I think maybe you're not?"

Wondering if he'd be able to walk back to the bar without wincing, he said, "I'll be fine. Here. Take these." He handed her the key ring by the appropriate key and said, "Wait here five minutes after I leave. Lock the door behind you then go to the ladies room. I'll ask Mags to send Kat to see if you need help. I don't want to put you in the position of being speculated about if we're seen leaving together."

With that, he grabbed a bottle, flicked off the lights and slipped through the smallest crack in the door that his wide shoulders permitted. He waited until he heard the lock snick before taking a deep breath and mentally arming himself against the gantlet he was sure was coming.

* * * * *

"Crystal? It's Kat. Open the door."

Watching her new friend tonight like an attentive mother hen, Kat had been delighted to see Soren's unrestrained, single-minded jealousy erupt on the dance floor. And kissing her in public! *Way to go, Crystal!* Mister Cool and Unemotional was well and truly hooked.

"Crystal," she said more forcefully. "Let me in."

Slowly the door to the supply closet opened.

"Are you all right?"

"Oh. Kat. Come—"

Kat pushed through the opening and quickly closed the door behind her.

"—in," Crystal finished unnecessarily.

"Did he hurt you? Soren can be rough around the edges."

"Hurt me? What makes you think Soren would hurt me?" Her gaze didn't quite meet Kat's. "We, um, only had the one dance then he went, um, back to the bar."

"Crystal, sweetie, you're talking to a pro here. That man would have fucked you on the dance floor if he thought he wouldn't be ripped apart by all those eager would-be suitors. Yeah, he went back to the bar. But as soon as he opened a cabinet and put something in his pocket, he went back into the hallway."

She tucked a stray lock of hair behind Crystal's ear. "And it took him fifteen minutes to come back out. Must be the hair," she mused. "Yours curls wildly the way mine does. Obviously it's a trigger point for those rough, tough Thorvald brothers."

As she'd hoped, Crystal gave a weak chuckle at the attempted humor and lifted her eyes to look at Kat. "Fifteen minutes? It felt like an eye blink. Soren didn't even—"

Her cheeks bloomed with two big red spots that delighted Kat. "Good. I thought so. He walked like an aging cowpoke who'd been on a cattle drive for two months. Let him work for his orgasms."

"Oh Kat, you're a riot. But why did Magnus—"

"Believe me, sweetie, I was pissed when I saw him leave his station and march down to the hallway. As soon as I saw him come back, I jumped on him for interrupting you. Of course, he'd already figured it out too. Said he was really reluctant to knock, but it was kind of a no-win situation for Mags. Three customers were tossing back Russian Kamikazes—the drink calls for three ounces of vodka—and he'd run out of the house vodka. It was either get a fresh bottle and incur Soren's wrath or give the guys the expensive stuff at no extra charge and incur Soren's wrath."

A reluctant smile tugged at Crystal's mouth. "Yeah, I can see his point of view."

"Now listen up. Just before I came in, Soren did the 'last call for drinks' thing. So here's what we're going to do."

Kat spoke and Crystal listened, wide-eyed.

"You think it will work?" Crystal asked when the plan was laid out.

"You bet your sweet ass it will. Go to it."

Chapter Ten

"You're grouchier than usual, boss."

Soren gave Trang a scowl eye. He'd managed to make a detour to the men's room to shuck off the used yet unused condom, but his cock and balls were still pelting him with major distress signals. And wouldn't Trang be tickled to hear *that* from her grouchy boss. "Damn drinkers are going to make me lose my liquor license if they don't hustle their asses out the door in ten minutes. Some of them look like they're settling in for the night. Tell Mags to roust Booths Two and Three. Or better yet, send Coral to bus their tables and give them a nudge."

"Right." Trang chewed on her lower lip a moment, no doubt gauging how far she could push him, then without another word turned and hailed the waitress.

He knew he should start reconciling the till. He should be taking liquor inventory. He should be filling the heavy-duty glass-washer. Instead, Soren ducked under the counter and weaved his way through the tables trying not to look like he was looking for someone. Damn, Table Six had been bussed and wiped dry. Its former occupants, all three females, had disappeared. How could Crystal have just walked out on him and left him feeling like a sailor on his first shore leave in a year who was dumped on a deserted island?

If she'd left the bar with one of those yahoos—

Don't make it any worse than it is, dammit.

After a complete circuit of the tables and booths, he had to accept that she'd left Thor's Hammer. He hoped she'd at least gotten into her car safely. And alone.

Damn, that's why he steered clear of women. How could he have forgotten how his mother had played his father for a fool?

Kitchen. Maybe Mags hid her in the kitchen so she wouldn't have to fend off a guy on the make who wouldn't take no for an answer. He was headed in that direction when Trang caught his attention.

"Phone," she mouthed, holding up the receiver.

Crystal.

You idiot, why would she call? If she wanted him, why wouldn't she just wait for him? Or maybe some broad kicked Rolf out and he needed help getting home. Then he snorted. Rolf kicked out of a woman's bed? *Get real.*

With a sigh, he wended his way to the still-noisy bar. Trang gave him an "I don't know who it is" shrug. He took the phone from her outstretched hand. "Thorvald."

"Hi, there. I'm waiting for you."

His cock jumped to attention at the breathy sound of Crystal's voice. He turned to the wall, cupped a hand to his free ear to drown out the cacophony behind him. "Where?"

A giggle made him wonder how much she'd had to drink. "Upstairs."

"What?" He squelched the instinctive need to turn his head upward, as if he could see through the beams and the ceiling. "How did—never mind. Don't move."

He slammed the receiver back into the cradle. "Where's Magnus?"

"Right behind you. I just locked up the pool room."

"She give you the keys?"

Without needing an explanation to Soren's verbal shorthand, Magnus nodded and reached into his jeans pocket for the ring of master keys Crystal had passed on to him.

"No, hang on to them. You lock up tonight, buddy. I've got to get out of here."

Magnus watched as his preoccupied brother hustled through the swinging kitchen doors and out of sight of the bar.

He wondered if anyone else had noticed the bite marks on Soren's index finger.

A smile broke over his face. Kat was right. Soren was going down for the count.

* * * * *

She couldn't believe she was doing this. Kat had made it sound so simple. But Kat was the daring one, not her.

Soren's reaction had quickened her heartbeat when she called the bar from her cell phone. *Don't move*, he'd said. Heck, she couldn't stand still. Kat had been explicit that she not wait in the office at the top of the stairs, but to go all the way into his apartment. She'd even given her the five-digit combination for the push-button lock. Magnus was supposed to be the only other person who knew the combination, but Kat apparently had her ways of wheedling a secret or two out of him.

As Crystal discovered, the upstairs office suite included an employee lounge of sorts—a small room with a sofa and chair and a private half bath, so any of the staff coming up for a break would find her if she waited there. The point, Kat had impressed on her, had been to keep her visit private from the staff so Mister Cool and Unemotional—she giggled at Kat's nickname for Soren—didn't get teased about finally falling off his high horse. And no one would know if she spent the night up here, since they'd come in Deirdra's car.

Wide-eyed, she let her glance roam around his space. An eave ran the length of the second floor, with a two-windows-wide dormer lifting the ceiling over a large kitchen and another enlarging an almost empty living room. The huge space contained nothing but an arcing floor lamp shining on an oversize sofa in navy blue corduroy, and a small TV perched on a table topped by a spectacular slab of highly polished oak.

At the far, shadowed end stood another closed door, but Crystal dared not peek inside. That could only have been his bedroom, and she didn't want to be *too* forward. She had firmly nixed Kat's idea that Soren find her naked and warm between his sheets.

Although she fervently hoped that's where she'd end up. She shivered in anticipation just thinking about how he felt as he'd entered her from behind, as frantic to get to her as she was to receive him. And the way he'd kissed her on the dance floor, staking his claim in front of his brother and everyone else, thrilled her down to her plum-painted toenails. The crystal had been right. Soren was The One. If he hadn't figured it out yet, he would tonight.

She sat on the sofa, testing it. With plump seat and back cushions, it was deep enough for two to snuggle or spoon while watching the tube, the fabric an intriguing combination of smooth and rough under her palm, long enough to accommodate his six-foot-plus height.

The door at the bottom of the stairs creaked open, slammed shut. A bolt slid home with a metallic *clank*. The determined thud of large feet on the carpeted floor of the office—

He's here. How should she act? Demure? Kittenish? Sultry?

Nervous. Hearing the clicks of the push-button lock on the living room door, she suddenly had second thoughts. Would he think she was too brazen? Would he kick her out?

"Crystal." The word came out as rough as the unfinished edges of the slab of oak in front of her. In two long strides he came to her as she half turned on the sofa. He grabbed her by the upper arms and, pulling her to her feet, swept her into a crushing embrace. Her breasts were flattened against his chest as one arm held her tight at her back. The other cupped her butt, pressing the heat of his bulge into her belly. All she could do was worm her arms around his waist and bury her face in the crook between his neck and shoulder.

"When you disappeared, I thought you were just stringing me along, wanting me to think you went home with one of those yahoos who were pawing you." He loosened his hold a fraction, as if just realizing he was squeezing her like an anaconda, and dipped his head to kiss her temple. "God, I want to fuck you all the time." Stepping back, he released her and plowed his fingers through already-mussed blond hair, as if it wasn't the first time in the past few minutes that he'd made the nervous gesture.

"Hell, that was crude. I don't know how to say pretty things."

She allowed all her desire and love to show in her eyes as she lifted her gaze to him. "I want you too, Soren." She stood on tiptoe and kissed him lightly on the mouth. "And this time, we have all night."

Pushing him lightly away, she added, "So make sure you locked all the doors."

"Locks. Oh, yeah." Turning to the door between office and apartment, he pushed buttons at random to disengage the combination. Then turned back to her.

And just looked.

His gaze devoured her, so intense it sent tingles to her mouth, to her breasts, to the warm, wet spot between her legs, and all the way down to her toes that curled inside her wedge-heeled slides.

She opened her arms to him in invitation. He stepped forward, knelt before her. Placed his large hands on her hips, tenderly touched his lips to the navel above the low-rise waistband of her jeans then placed equally tender kisses all around the exposed skin of her waist and hips that he could reach.

Crystal bent down, tucked her hands around his neck, rested her cheek on the crown of his head. "You smell like cigarette smoke."

Immediately he let go of her and stood up, barely missing her chin with his thick skull as she ducked out of his way. "I can't help it. Comes with the territory."

"It's not a criticism. I was trying to..." She let her gaze bounce around, suddenly unsure whether to continue.

Do it!

She cleared her throat. "I was trying to make a suggestion. If you'll let me, I can wash your hair...in the shower..."

"Oh." His Adam's apple bobbed visibly. "Yeah. Great idea. Yeah. The shower."

He grabbed her hand and started tugging her through the vast, shadowed living room to the door in the far wall that she'd noticed earlier. Then stopped, searched her face with sober eyes. "Are you sure?"

She fingered the crystal dangling between her breasts. It was warm and, she could swear, vibrated with a low hum. "Very sure."

"Crystal." He cradled her face with his large hands. "I'm sorry about what happened in the storeroom. I acted like a madman. You deserve to be treated like—"

"Don't you dare apologize. It was wonderful." Her eyes sparkled as they drank in the emotions she saw in his—desire, self-loathing, insecurity. "I've read about, um, quickies in public places. The excitement. The daring. Like thumbing your nose at society. God knows, I've wanted to give the world the finger for years, but it was drummed into me that a socialite doesn't stoop to emulating the hoi polloi. I feel like I'm coming out of exile."

He was rough around the edges, but he was so innately protective of her, she was charmed. She turned pointedly to the closed door. "Now, where were we?"

"Right. Shower." He took her hand in his and, swinging the door open, led her through. An automatic switch lit a bedside table lamp with a soft glow. "Sometimes I'm pretty bushed when I finish up at three a.m.," he explained. "After I smacked into the bathroom door the second time in the dark, I installed it as a safety measure."

Sublimely conscious of his hand still holding hers, Crystal wondered if he thought she truly cared why the light went on, or if his babbling was an unconscious mechanism to distance himself in case she hurt him in some fashion.

As if she could.

He let go of her hand to touch a wall switch and the bathroom came to life under a row of lights over the sink counter. Tucked inside another double-windowed dormer, the room was as spacious as his kitchen. But it was the shower that caught Crystal's eye, a decadent, walk-in space big enough for two, tiled in random shades of blue, with a ledge seat on one side.

"Soren?" Her voice was soft and, she hoped, seductive.

When he turned, Soren looked like a little boy uncertain whether to expect a reward or a reprimand. She forced herself not to look down at it, but in her peripheral vision she could see the massive bulge pushing against the zipper of his jeans.

"Where's your shampoo?"

That seemed to break the spell. He took the one step that separated them, cupped her jaw tenderly with his large hands, and looked deeply into her eyes. "You're sure?"

"Soren Thorvald," she said, finally exasperated enough to act, "I appreciate your chivalry, but I'm not made of glass." She grabbed two handfuls of his blue polo shirt and tugged the material out of his jeans. "Will you get in the shower so we can get rid of the smell of smoke?"

Let him think the smoky smell bothered her, if that's what it took to get him naked. She smiled as he suddenly caught up with the idea of *naked* and *we* and ripped off his clothing, kicking everything to one side. He turned on the shower flow full-force and stepped into the stream, letting the water cascade from his head down.

Crystal disrobed more slowly, licking her lower lip unconsciously as she followed the trail of water clinging, sliding down that magnificent, well-honed body. He stood motionless under the stream, his penis rampant in anticipation, eyes burning into her as she took the half-dozen steps to join him within the tiled enclosure.

"Can you hand me the soap?" she asked, her voice thready with desire.

Without taking his eyes off her, Soren reached to the tiled pocket and found the soap by touch. Wordlessly he handed it to her.

"You're going to have to pay attention to what I say."

"I'm listening," he rasped.

"I don't want you to do anything except *feel*." She began soaping her hands, the fresh pine scent mingling with the smell of smoke and man. "You don't think, you don't rationalize, you don't argue. You just let things *happen*. Do you understand?"

His assent was a cross between a grunt and a groan. He raised one hand to stabilize himself against the side of the shower, obviously—she hoped—anticipating a knee-weakening experience.

Crystal didn't keep him waiting. Handing the bar of soap back to Soren, she began to soap him around his waist. His eyes widened but he kept silent. He probably thought she would start with his hair and work her way down.

She had other plans.

Making smooth, sudsy circles, she washed around his hipbones, his navel, then narrowed her focus to the line of hair leading down to the thick, dark blond nest of wiry curls between his thighs.

Intent on her mission, Crystal smiled to herself when he involuntarily thrust his hips forward. *Yes*, she thought. *Coming right up.* When she had thoroughly washed his pubic curls, she said, "Soap," and reached her hand up. A little more teasing wasn't amiss in this situation, was it?

The soap plopped in her hand, and he cupped her fingers around it to be sure she didn't drop it.

Crystal made a big production out of making more suds, then handed the soap back to him without looking up. She bent down, ready for the *pièce de résistance*. This close, his cock was magnificent. The head was a fierce, dark red. Purple veins stood out sharply against the paler red of a long, thick shaft. She took a deep breath and swirled one hand around its girth then moved it back and forth gently.

"Crystal—" His voice was strained. He clamped both hands around her head.

"No," she said mildly. "I asked you to just *feel*. Remember? Please don't interrupt my concentration."

Soren took a deep, shuddering breath, but let go of her and locked his knees.

Now she slid both hands, rhythmically, one after the other, from the base of his cock all the way to the tip, squeezing gently as she encountered the mushroom-shaped head. She could feel it throbbing, pulsing. The knowledge that *she* could make him react like this was an aphrodisiac.

One hand still stroking his cock, she let the other wander down to his balls, which had contracted hard and tight up against the base of his cock. She lathered and stroked both cock and balls, until he called out her name hoarsely.

"Turn." She grabbed his hips and set word to action. Water splashed against his groin, the foamy water sliding down his muscular legs as Crystal moved his genitals this way and that to take advantage of the warm spray.

With the lather gone, his cock glistened. Droplets beaded on his slick skin. She couldn't wait another minute to feel all that manhood in her mouth. This time it wasn't tentative. Heedless of the water spraying the back of her head, she opened her mouth and closed it around the head of his glorious cock.

Directives be damned, Soren thought. No way could he stand still with paradise right before him. He grabbed handfuls of her wet curly hair and held her tight against him. Dear God, he'd never had a sensation like the feel of her warm, wet mouth enclosing him, squeezing him, milking him. He threw his head back and did what she'd ordered—he didn't think, didn't argue, didn't rationalize. He just—

"Jesus Christ!" It felt as though she'd siphoned his cum all the way from the bottom of his feet, zapping it like lightning up through his legs and into his cock, exploding into her mouth in a series of hot, pulsing jets that buckled his knees and forced all the air out of his lungs until he was reduced to making primitive, incoherent noises and fighting to stay upright.

It seemed an eternity later that he was able to put two words together into a lucid sentence. "Crystal." Make that *one* word.

"Soren? Are you okay?" To his sensitized ear, her voice sounded like the soft breath of a spring breeze after a tornado had ripped through his brain. "Was it…all right?"

The cobwebs floated away. Jesus! Did she think that because he didn't say anything, that he didn't like it? He flashed on the scene in the cabana, when she thought she'd somehow done it wrong, that she'd hurt him.

Hell, no! It was as right as thunder following lightning. Whispering her name, he bent forward and tucked his hands under her arms, gently lifting her to her feet. She slithered so that her breasts rubbed against him all the way up, especially as it pertained to his cock. Somehow she'd managed to capture it between those soft, full tits, stroking it already into semi-hardness.

Standing on tiptoe, she kissed his throat, his jaw. "Okay. Now that we've gotten the easy one out of the way—"

"What?"

"—let me wash your hair and we'll go on to Part Two. Sit down."

Dumbly he sat on the shower ledge. What did she— "Crystal. What did you mean, the easy one?"

Humming as she squirted a generic brand of shampoo onto his hair, she replied, "This one was for you."

"But you didn't have to—"

"Yes I did," she ran right over his protest. "The first time we made love, remember? On the kitchen counter? You had to pull out because you didn't have a condom? The second time, after you bathed me in the Jacuzzi and we did all kinds of things on the bathroom floor and in my bed, you got interrupted by glass breaking. Then in the cabana you were afraid to come in case someone heard. And let's not forget that little session in the liquor closet tonight. So much *coitus interruptus* can't be healthy for a man."

She began making finger circles on his scalp, working the shampoo into a lather. He'd never felt anything so good. Well, so good on his head. Because she'd sure given his cock a doozy of a good feeling a few minutes ago.

"This time, I wanted to make sure we got your orgasm out of the way so you could concentrate on giving me mine. That is, mine, plural."

A surprised laugh erupted from deep within Soren. "You're too much. Come here."

He moved her to stand between his outspread knees and tongued her nipple. "Look how ripe it is. Like a raspberry." He sucked on it, gently. "There's such a contrast. Your breast is so white, so soft. And the nipple is hard as an acorn. Then there's all those little pebbles surrounding it."

"The areola." Her voice hitched. Crystal stopped massaging his scalp.

"Hey, if it makes you stop what you're doing, I'll have to stop sucking on your tits."

In response, she lifted one heavy breast with her soapy hand and offered it to his mouth. "We have all night," she said, a little breathlessly. "We can take turns."

And so they did.

* * * * *

"The bitch!" He grabbed the boning knife from the knife holder on the counter and stalked out of the kitchen. "She never came home!"

Last night he'd watched from his special vantage point as a late-model convertible holding two women stopped in front of

Crystal's home and drove off with her inside. He'd scurried around to follow them at a discreet distance—the creamy color stood out easily in the darkness—until they pulled into a parking lot on a main street two towns down. He'd driven past then made a U-turn in time to see them enter the bar.

When he deemed it safe, he pulled into the lot to reconnoiter. A door near the back marked "Employee Entrance" would bear watching. He returned to the street and parked where he could see both the entrances.

One look at how the tall redhead walked—or rather, swaggered—told him she was a real troublemaker, like she thought she had every man at her beck and call. *That* kind of woman could destroy Crystal's innocence. The other one, a longtime friend of hers, he'd seen many times. Her moral qualities had seemed a match for Crystal.

Except maybe not.

Because some time during the evening, Crystal had apparently left the bar with someone—and it was neither of the women she came with. The driver went home alone in her convertible. The redhead left with a hulk of a man who looked like he could bench press a truck, probably the owner or manager, since they left through the employee entrance long after closing time. He'd waited an extra half hour after that to be sure Crystal hadn't lingered then furtively walked around back to look for another exit.

Two cars, a midsize truck and a huge SUV still occupied the lot. All the result of drivers having too much to drink? He glanced at the dormer windows on the second floor. Did someone live there? Probably not. No curtains or draperies covered the windows, just blinds closed up tight, although light seeped through the edges in the front window. Security lights, no doubt. Probably a storage area for liquor.

He leaned over the fence to check out whatever part of the back wall he could see behind the dumpster. Then swore. A fire exit. Had someone who worked there allowed her to slip out that way? With whom? To do what?

Thinking about it drove him crazy.

He stalked downstairs to the special place he'd set up for his beloved and pulled the key off the hidden nail hanging high on a floor joist. Was she with the man who'd been in her bedroom that night, when he'd had to distract them by tossing the rock through her window? He'd hated to inconvenience her that way, but dire situations called for dire solutions.

And it had worked. The usurper had not been back.

He unlocked the door to the special room now, stepped in and turned on the light. With its white-painted walls and ceiling, deep-pile white carpet, white velvet loveseat, the room glowed. One corner held a white-painted iron bedstead with a white satin coverlet. The only color in the room came from the painting holding pride of place on a side wall, highlighted under a spotlight. Almost life-size, the Madonna on canvas radiated purity, with her white robes and pale skin against a backdrop of deep blue sky. Three drops of vivid red blood from the pierced heart of her dripped down her virgin breast. Her pale, delicate feet stood triumphantly atop the head of a fat green snake whose red tongue flicked impotently at nothing.

Unlike most paintings of the sort, instead of raising her arms to the heavens, she stretched them out to the viewer — to him alone.

But it was the face that interested him. The face of his beloved that he'd had the artist superimpose on the Madonna, perfectly capturing her heart-shaped face, those fathomless dark brown eyes that looked directly at him, the untamed curls cascading down her slender shoulders. Her full, ripe mouth was as red as the drops of blood.

He stared at her for a long time, stared at the picture of innocence that should have been his, praying for her forgiveness. Then he raised the arm with the knife again and again, viciously slashing at the face of his heart.

Chapter Eleven

❧

Crystal raised her arms over her head and stretched like a lazy, satisfied cat who'd had her fill of cream. *Scarlett O'Hara,* she thought, *I bet I look as smug as she did the morning after Rhett Butler carried her up that sweeping staircase.* The smile on her face could only be called decadent. The ache between her legs felt like a badge of…oh, maybe an Eagle Scout badge for trying out a half-dozen Kama Sutra positions—and succeeding with each of them.

Kat had strongly advised her to take a nap yesterday afternoon. She was glad she'd listened. With a lassitude engendered by terrific sex and multiple orgasms, Crystal let her gaze wander around the bedroom. It too was a vast, loftlike space. Its only furnishings were a nightstand and a comfortable king-size bed, its navy blue duvet pulled haphazardly around her. Built-in drawers were tucked under the eaves. Early morning light filtered in through the dormer blinds, illuminating bare walls. No tchotchkes strewn about, no family photos, no artwork. No personal touches.

Soren Thorvald must be a lonely man.

Not anymore, she vowed silently. She fingered the ever-present crystal around her neck. He was hurting, deep down inside the soul that he closed off to the world. She wondered how far his brothers had been able to penetrate. She hoped she could help him heal.

The bedroom door opened. Soren strolled in, wearing blue boxer shorts and carrying two mugs.

"Coffee." She fairly drooled at the delicious smell. "You're my hero."

"It's black and strong and hot. Do you use additives?"

She gave him a thorough, teasing scrutiny, lingering over the bulge in his shorts. "Are you carrying any sugar in that pocket?"

Under the soft cotton his cock jumped as though she'd caressed him. And in a way, she had. With her eyes. Because just seeing him made her want him again.

She sat up and let the sheet drop down around her waist. The bulge grew a bit as his eyes caressed her naked breasts. And yes, she felt the zing of it, from his eyes to her nipples and down to her suddenly damp pussy.

Soren rounded the bed and set both mugs on the nightstand then opened the blinds to slits to gaze out the window. "I rarely see morning," he mused.

On impulse, she scrambled out of bed, sidled up next to him and slid an arm around his waist. "I love sunrises. Sometimes the colors beat anything an artist tries to put on canvas."

To her surprise and delight, Soren slung an arm across her shoulder. It felt so right to be next to him this way, hip to hip, thigh to thigh, their night of phenomenal sex and morning coffee perfuming the bedroom air, as they watched a few small clouds turn pink then gold.

"Sugar," she said.

"Yeah?" he responded absently.

Crystal's laugh tinkled like glass chimes. "Yes, you're like sugar, Soren, but what I really wanted to do was remind you that I take sugar in my coffee. Two packets."

He dipped his head and gave her a soft kiss.

"Hey! You've already had your coffee! I can taste it." She set her hands on her hips in mock outrage. "You don't play fair."

"I don't? Just wait."

Turning, he lifted her by her waist, walked to the bed, tossed her onto the mattress and followed her down. He covered her with his warm, muscular body and began kissing his way down her neck, her shoulder, her—

"Stop!" Around a giggle, she managed, "Please, sir, may I have my coffee?"

He scuttled down further and captured a rosy nipple in his mouth. "Woman, you have a one-track mind."

"The pot calling the kettle black," she retorted.

Undaunted, he grasped her other nipple between thumb and forefinger and tweaked it. She arched her back. "Soren!"

"Hmm?" His teeth lightly scraped the first nipple as he pulled on the other. He bunched them together and laved both nipples with his tongue, tried to stuff both of them in his mouth at the same time. "I need to taste you. All of you."

His name on her lips came out like a sigh. Coffee could wait.

Slowly, thoroughly, Soren proceeded to taste her skin with his tongue, taking little nips with his teeth as he inexorably marked a path to her pussy. "This is what I want," he murmured as he pulled her engorged lips apart. "I want to taste that hard little bud right—" he swiped her clit with his tongue, "here."

Her hips shot off the mattress and she cried out. She grasped handfuls of his hair and tried to pull him up. She wanted—needed—his cock inside her *right now*!

"Please," she begged.

"Please, what?" He paid single-minded devotion to her slit, now lapping his tongue from back to front, now stabbing that hot weapon as deep inside her pussy as a tongue could go.

"I want you, Soren. Inside me. Please!"

He stuck his tongue a millimeter deeper into her pussy. "Like that?"

"Your cock, Soren, I want your cock inside me!"

"Can't. Not hard enough. Besides, you taste too good." He substituted two fingers for his tongue and gently thrust them in and out of her weeping pussy then turned his tongue, his teeth, to her clit.

As turned on as she was at this unexpected, playful side of Soren, Crystal couldn't stand being without his cock a single minute longer. If he wasn't hard enough, by golly, she could do something about it. She wormed a leg under his chest, and with all her strength, shoved up with her knee to overturn him onto the mattress.

Then pounced on him. Or, more specifically, on the magnificent cock that thrust out thick and proud through the opening of his boxers as he landed on his back. She latched onto him with her mouth, drawing her cheeks inward to milk him, to taste him, to feel him throb with the power of his untamed hunger.

As if to one-up her, Soren grabbed her hips, pivoted her so her pussy was positioned directly over his face, and pulled her down to meet his mouth.

Crystal felt an unbelievable jolt of pleasure, of triumph. This was the sixty-nine position she'd been hoping they'd try. How *right* it felt! Her mouth filled with the swollen length of his rock-hard cock, while his mouth sucked and lapped at her labia, his tongue intermittently thrusting deep inside. Her breasts flattened against his hard lower torso. His chest hair tickled her belly. She half-rose on her elbows and knees to allow her hips to move in faster and faster counterpoint to his rhythm.

Moisture seeped more heavily from her slit. She ground her pelvis into Soren's face, feeling the delicious tension inside her build, build, until there was only his throbbing cock in her mouth, her drenched pussy grinding into him, the intensely sensitive bud of her clit rasping against his morning stubble until she thought she'd go mad with sensation.

Colors more precious than a sunrise exploded behind her closed eyelids, every hue of the rainbow winking and shining like a turning kaleidoscope, and she gasped for air around his cock, not willing to let it slip from her mouth at this most precious of all moments, the instant when she gave up all control, all will, to her Soren.

* * * * *

"Soren?" she said lazily.

"Later. I can't get my brain in gear."

Crystal lay on her side, one arm and one leg draped over Soren, her head resting on his chest as she listened to the heavy thump-thump of his heart beneath her ear. His strong arms held her securely to his sweat-sheened body under the sheet he'd pulled loosely over their waists.

"About that coffee…"

He picked up her hand and brought it to his mouth, kissed her palm. "Obviously one of us didn't just have the best sex of her life, since all you can think about is coffee."

"Oooh, you're mean." She pulled her hand from his and gave him a halfhearted slap on his biceps. After his mouth brought her to climax, Soren had put on a condom and ridden her hard and long, bringing them both to heights unimaginable just a few short weeks ago. Her pussy throbbed deliciously from the unaccustomed exercise, and it had taken a long time for her pulse rate to return to normal.

But now, now it was time for coffee.

"What would it take to get your brain in gear? Pancakes? Omelets? Home fries?"

Soren turned his head to squint at the bedside clock. The digital numbers glowed green. Nine-seventeen. "Sorry, the kitchen staff don't arrive for a couple of hours yet."

She pushed her way out of his embrace and sat up, her bare breasts thrusting up and out as she shoved her wild hair out of her eyes. "Soren Thorvald, I am offering to cook breakfast for you. Provided, that is, that there's something in that kitchen besides stale coffee."

"Hey, I made that coffee fresh this morning."

Leaning forward to better read the clock face, she made an unladylike snort. "That 'fresh' coffee is over three hours old. And if it's still plugged in, it probably tastes like mud." Then she sat back, her eyes widening. "Oh my god, three hours. Soren, did we really spend three hours…?"

She giggled. Unconsciously her hand sought the crystal around her neck. She ducked her head, marginally embarrassed but unaccountably happy at her eagerness to make love with this man.

Yanking the sheet down to his knees, she sat back on her heels and let her eyes rove down the sleek, muscular length of him. "Want to go for four hours?"

"Woman, have mercy! You're going to kill me."

"Not if you let me make you breakfast," she said pragmatically.

Soren raised his arms and stacked his hands under his head. "On one condition."

She gave him a wary look. "What's that?"

A smug smile spread across his face. "You have to do it stark naked."

* * * * *

He didn't think she'd actually do it. But when she'd marched out of the bedroom in her birthday suit with her chin high and her glorious tits bouncing, he felt the need to watch her every move like a lecher.

And what moves they were.

Bending from the waist to peer into the bottom shelf of the fridge, showing him the perfect heart of her ass, as she searched for a carton of eggs.

Jiggling her lush breasts as she fork-mixed eggs and milk.

Reaching up to a high counter for plates, lifting her breasts in the process. It was enough to make him come up behind her and grab those soft, milk-white globes.

149

"I hope this isn't your good china," she said, juggling the two cheap plates he'd picked up at the Goodwill store. Since he didn't entertain in his apartment, he hadn't seen the need for china.

The plates clattered as she dropped them onto the counter then leaned back into him. Or more specifically, into another hard-on. He couldn't remember ever being so horny. Hell, he couldn't ever remember feeling so satisfied.

"Mmm," she said, leaning into him and rubbing that delectable ass against his johnson. "Equal opportunity nudity. I like that."

"You know, we could christen my counter too." He tweaked her nipples, nuzzled the nape of her neck.

"Hold that thought. Let me flip the omelet."

He sighed and stepped back with a mock grumble. "Geez, give a woman the run of a kitchen and she's handing out orders like a drill sergeant."

"You're lucky you're eating anything at all. Your cupboard would give Mother Hubbard competition."

"I usually eat downstairs."

She turned, spatula in hand. "I'm sorry, I didn't mean to—"

That comment had come out almost like a snarl. He backpedaled. "It's all right. Just thank your lucky stars I didn't have bacon. The grease could have spattered onto that sweet belly of yours."

A grin flashed on her face. "I like to think I'd be smart enough to ask for an apron—or at least a shirt of yours to protect against such a catastrophe."

The thought of seeing Crystal wearing one of his shirts made him go weak in the knees. He shook the vision away. "Let's eat before it gets cold."

She gave him an odd look then asked, "Where would you like to sit?"

That brought him up short. He had no dining room table, no counter with stools. *Face it, Soren, you live in a cave, for all that it's on the second floor.* For the first time in as long as he could remember, he wished he had more than the bare minimum needed for survival in his living quarters.

* * * * *

"So where would you like to go?"

Soren helped Crystal negotiate the step up into the cab of his pickup truck, handed her the overnight case she'd admitted she'd stowed in Deirdra's car when they went to Thor's Hammer, then got behind the wheel. They had eaten their omelets while standing at the counter near the sink. "All the better to wash the dishes," she'd quipped, obviously trying to make him feel he wasn't such an ogre after all.

Then he'd done something that had him still shaking his head in disbelief. He'd called Trang and told her he wasn't coming in today, that she'd be in charge of the pub and to call the temp bartender if she thought it necessary. Trang hadn't asked any questions, but he could hear them in the silent pauses as she waited for him to explain.

Which he hadn't.

It was none of their business. Hell, when was the last time he'd taken a day off? Wasn't a successful businessman entitled to a vacation now and again?

Crystal gave him a sidelong glance as she buckled her seat belt. "You'll take me anywhere I want to go?"

"Uh, yeah, as long it isn't to California or Oregon. Not today, anyway."

She studied him a moment, as if to gauge his sincerity. Then rummaged in her bag for her cell phone. Soren listened as she explained to someone that a mutual friend had suggested she call, then made arrangements to come by. She ended the call and slipped the phone back into her tote. "This woman wants to sell some family pieces. Said she's been waiting for my call. It's a beautiful day for a drive, and it isn't far. And if we come to an agreement on terms, maybe we can take it right to Jack Healy's shop — he'll buy anything I bring him — and I won't have to ask Augie to help me."

"Augie? Oh yeah, the spoiled rich kid who tried to force you. He should only hope he doesn't run into me in some dark alleyway."

Her heart skipped into overdrive. Soren probably didn't even know he was jealous. Crystal fought a smile and gave him directions to Tedi Giordano's farmhouse.

A short while later they pulled up in front of a weathered farmhouse in dire need of paint, both on its windowsills and on bead-board siding that, Crystal thought, might be original to the house.

Mrs. Giordano turned out to be a short, arthritic woman with a fine network of wrinkles crisscrossing her face and snow-white hair cut to just cover her ears. Leaning on a walker, she took Crystal's business card, stuck it in the pocket of her housedress after glancing at it, and invited them in. "As you can see, I can't get around much, so I only use the first floor. The grandkids brought down everything I need. Just go on upstairs and make an offer on anything that strikes your fancy."

The three bedrooms were denuded of any evidence of habitation. Bare mattresses lay on the beds, drawers were half opened on dressers, closet doors stood open. In a way, it was sad seeing the end of what used to be a family home. Mostly Crystal got called to a home full of life with only a single piece to be sold in the interest of space.

Still, a fine cherry dresser with chamfered corners and French feet looked to be original. She pulled out drawers, studied their dovetailing, asked Soren to move it so she could check out the patina on the back. "This one," she said at last.

She also chose a tall, slender bookcase made of poplar. After a discussion during which she politely declined an offer of tea, Crystal wrote out a check and Soren wrestled the dresser base — she carried each of the four drawers down one at a time — and bookcase into the truck.

Once on their way, she directed him to Time Treasures, calling Jack Healy on her cell phone as they rode. He met them at the back door of the shop. Crystal introduced the two men, who eyed each other as if rivals in a contest.

Or maybe she was seeing things. The two men made short work of moving the furniture, with little wasted motion.

"As usual, my dear, your eye is impeccable," Jack told her as he studied the pieces.

"They are lovely, aren't they." Crystal gave an almost imperceptible nod to Soren, his signal, again, to wander outside while they discussed business. "I wish I could have seen what she had in the downstairs rooms."

"You must indulge me this time, Crystal. We need to toast your success."

Crystal bit back her annoyance at this delay. She wanted to spend the rest of the day with Soren, since she realized how rarely he took a day off. But, she remembered, she'd begged off the last time.

She mustered a smile. "Fine. A short one."

"I'm honored." He nodded then turned to his desk where he'd already laid out the Lalique glasses and a bottle of sherry on a silver tray. He poured an inch in each glass and handed one to her. "To the most important woman in my life."

"To a great relationship," she corrected then realized she should have said "great *working* relationship" in case he harbored other intentions.

"I'm happy to say that the two-piece corner cupboard you found has already sold."

This time her smile was genuine. "Congratulations. I knew it would go fast."

His look was so intent that Crystal realized she hadn't yet tasted the sherry. She brought the glass to her lips and took a small sip. "This is excellent, Jack. You have such wonderful taste. I'll write up a detailed bill for you tonight."

"Yes, please do. If you bring it tomorrow, I can write you a check immediately."

"Oh, that won't be necessary. We can do this all by mail."

When he stiffened, she realized her *faux pas*. He probably thought she was rubbing it in that she didn't need his money. "It all depends on my schedule," she added hurriedly.

"Crystal…"

Something in the tone of his voice alerted her. "What's wrong?"

"Nothing. I just wanted to ask you about this…gift…Rowena gave you at your birthday party. What is this Platinum Society that has accepted you into membership?"

"From what I gather, she shouldn't have announced it if some people at the party weren't members. It's some kind of exclusive club that caters to, as Grandma said, the sybaritic among us." She chortled. "I can just see me reclining on a divan and saying, 'Beulah, peel me a grape.' I think that was a line from a Mae West movie."

His expression didn't change, but it seemed to Crystal that Jack's entire body tensed.

"And those dancers who stripped and made lewd moves on the stage. Was that the kind of sybaritic Rowena was referring to?"

"Oh, lighten up. They were just doing the Chippendale strut."

"And it was acceptable for them to pull you up on stage and force you to disrobe in front of an audience?"

"Jack, I was wearing my swimsuit. It was just Grandma's quirky way to get everyone into the pool. It was a *party*, for heaven's sake."

"But there were so many who took off all their—"

Just then Soren stepped through the back door. His gaze dropped to the glass Crystal held in her hand. "I take it the business part is done?"

"Oh. Yes. Yes, it is." She set down the glass on the silver tray. "Thank you, Jack. It's always a pleasure doing business with you. I'll get the bill to you right away. I'm glad the corner cupboard sold," she added as an afterthought.

Jack Healy stared after them as they went out the back door. That man had been at the party. In fact, he distinctly remembered seeing both of them disappear into the cabana. But then Crystal walked back out.

He hadn't seen where she went, but the man stayed inside for a suspiciously long while. Had there been another entrance?

The way there had been another entrance at the back of that bar?

This was bad. This was very, very bad.

He'd have to teach her a lesson.

Soon.

Chapter Twelve

 හ

"This is really nice. I never knew this was here." Soren stood in the center of the footbridge over the Delaware River north of New Hope and gazed at the wide swath of water in late-afternoon light, shimmering as it flowed south at a leisurely pace, the border between Pennsylvania and New Jersey. Compared to the port of Philadelphia, the water this far upstream was clean, the banks covered with greening trees and shrubs as opposed to houses or industry.

They'd stopped at a drive-in for burgers and coffee, eating as they headed north on Route 32 at Crystal's direction. He'd parked the truck at the side of the road opposite an old-fashioned general store and they'd hiked the half mile.

"I used to come here more often than I do now. I learned to canoe in this river."

"Did you." Leaning on his elbows at the railing, Soren turned his head a bit to see the expression on Crystal's face. Her voice had a wistful quality to it that he hadn't heard before. He could understand why. Out here in the middle of the river, away from the noise of civilization and close to the serenity of nature, you could think about things on a visceral level. Could hear that little voice inside you that said maybe you didn't have to be gun-shy around women. That maybe they weren't all like his mother. That maybe a man could take a chance and open himself up to a certain kind of woman.

Crystal's voice intruded on his musing. Good thing. It wasn't like him to be maudlin. "My parents loved this area. Paddling through the Delaware Water Gap, I felt like I was one of the early explorers. I was six when I took my first dunking at

Foul Rift rapids." She was running her hands lightly over the railing, but she seemed to be in another time, another place.

"Of course, at that age I was outfitted in a hard hat and a bright orange life jacket, even though I already knew how to swim." She squinted into the distance and fell silent.

A soft breeze ruffled her curls. Water gurgled as it parted and flowed around the stone buttresses. Soren let the silence build. He didn't think he had the social skills to coax information out of her. He wasn't even sure he wanted to know any more, to get emotionally invested in her and her family. There was still a part of him that needed to hang back and keep a relationship on a surface level, giving and taking the sex, but not the vulnerability. Things were going too fast for his comfort level.

"Then they met a couple at the country club who introduced them to hot-air ballooning. I was twelve when the four of them went down after a freak lightning bolt hit the bag." Her voice cracked. "None of them survived."

A different kind of silence ensued. The breeze whistled between the cables holding up the bridge. He could hear her deep breaths, as if she were trying to stay calm and unaffected. A couple of kids on the far bank raised their voices in excited chatter. A bird swooped down from the sky and flew under the span.

Finally he cleared his throat. He didn't know what made the words come out. "My father killed himself."

Her sharp intake of breath made him stand up, take a step away from her. "She drove him to it. My mother."

He thrust his hands into his jeans pockets, turned southward to watch the water flow away from him on its inexorable path to the ocean. "They ruled it an accident, but to this day, I believe he aimed his car at that abutment. He didn't want her lying, cheating self anywhere near him, but he couldn't live without her."

Abruptly, he turned on his heel and strode back to the near bank. "Wonder if that general store has something cold to drink."

Crystal had to almost run to catch up to him. Had she been able to foresee this turn of events, she would gladly have gone anyplace but here. She thought they had established some kind of rapport after a dozen or so orgasms between them, after spending the night in each other's arms, after the camaraderie of a nude breakfast and the fun of antiquing.

She reached his side just as he stalked up the three chipped concrete steps leading to a planked porch and a screen door that squeaked when he yanked it open. Inside was a feast of nostalgia, a store that was part deli, part jeweler's, part bookstore, with old-fashioned bric-a-brac, postcards, gewgaws, shawls and other handmade items. A hand pump stood at a deep sink. A shaggy dog lolled near a potbellied stove. An array of penny candy enticed from behind a glass case.

But Crystal dismissed the urge to explore with barely a glance at the offerings. The object of her concern studied the contents of a refrigerator case then withdrew a brown, longneck bottle of ginger beer. She reached around him for a cream soda, in the process placing her palm on his back in silent, if fleeting, support.

She felt the ripple of tension in his muscles, but he didn't pull away. "Want to sit outside and drink these?" With her chin she indicated a wooden picnic table under a weeping willow just turning a delicate yellow-green.

He nodded once then paid the middle-aged man behind the deli counter, who rang up the sale on an antique cash register that made a hell of a jingle.

Outside, Soren sat on the tabletop, feet on the bench, arms resting on his thighs, the bottle hanging between his fingers. A red-breasted robin hopped through a thin layer of mulch around an azalea, cocked its head then started jabbing its beak into the ground. Soren seemed to take an inordinate interest in the bird's pecking.

Crystal sat beside him, for the moment silent as she pondered how to reach him. After a swallow of cream soda, she said, "How old were you?"

"Nine."

"Oh, wow."

"Nine when he kicked her out. Took him several years to go out of his mind."

"Why did he…never mind. I shouldn't ask."

"She had an affair. Broke the family apart."

"That's awful. My parents…" Crystal stopped, wondering if what she'd been about to say wasn't pouring salt on his still-festering wound. "…seemed happy," she tempered her statement. "They didn't fight or anything in front of me."

"I wish I'd never overheard them. I don't want to know what I know."

Crystal waited. If he could get whatever it was off his chest, maybe he could start healing. Because the hurt, she could see, went deep down into the depths of his soul.

The robin flitted away without having found a meal. Soren watched him fly out of sight then lifted the bottle to his lips. He took a long series of gulps. Crystal wondered how he could drink something so pungent without coughing. To her, it tasted like the shredded pieces of fresh ginger still lived inside the bottle.

"She wanted a divorce. Wanted to follow someone to Fairbanks."

"Oh no." Instinctively Crystal touched her hand to Soren's forearm. How terrible that she wouldn't want her children. And how much worse for Soren to live with such knowledge.

"Pop said over his dead body then kicked her out."

"What happened to her?"

Soren was silent a long time. "Don't know. I never heard from her again."

There was more, but Soren couldn't talk about it right now. Maybe he never would.

Chapter Thirteen

෯

The mood was subdued on their ride home, the quiet punctuated by Crystal's occasional "turn here" or "about five miles down Route 30" as she directed him to her home. It had taken him a moment to backtrack in his mind as to why he was going there. She'd come to Thor's Hammer last night in her friend's car, and had been with him since then. Her own car was parked at her home, a place he'd been to only once, in the dark, when she'd brought him over after their "dinner with a bachelor".

Christ, that seemed like a lifetime ago. The woman was messing with his mind. He'd never revealed what he'd overheard to anyone, not even Magnus. He didn't *want* to get close to her. He didn't want to get close to *any* woman. Soren had learned his lesson at age nine—love hurts.

He'd be dipped in sheepshit before he'd let a woman get close enough to hurt him.

And this one was damn near there already. Under his skin. Inside his mind.

Well, she'd gone as far as she ever would. From now on she was history. He'd see to it.

Finally he pulled the truck in front of her home. In the late afternoon light he saw tidy flower beds with yellow and red flowers swaying in the breeze, tulips, he thought. The house looked like a Cape Cod without dormers in front, although he knew the back roof was raised and the second floor accommodated two large bedrooms and a spacious bath.

A bath with a Jacuzzi that fit two.

Shit. *Don't go there.*

"Thanks for…everything, Soren." Her chocolate brown eyes were somber on his. "I appreciate your helping me with the antiques. And the, um, well, everything. You've had a long day, all that driving. I have some homemade lasagna in the fridge, if you'd like to stay for dinner."

Christ, had she planned this whole thing as an ambush? The "way to a man's heart" business? "Don't worry about me. I'll pick up something at the pub. I'd better be getting back. Trang's never had the responsibility of the whole place for an entire day before."

A fleeting look of…hurt?…passed over her face, but so quickly he thought he imagined it.

"Sure. I understand." She reached out as if to touch the hand that rested on the steering wheel then withdrew it when the muscles in his arm tensed. "Thanks again." She gave him a patently false smile. "See you soon."

Then opened the door and got out. He didn't watch her walk up to the cozy porch or enter the house.

Still, he sat curbside, engine idling, for a long moment, his hands gripping the steering wheel until he noticed how white his knuckles were. Then gunned the motor and laid a track of rubber on the asphalt as he sped away from the temptation to bury himself deep within her warm body and find oblivion for a few minutes.

* * * * *

Crystal stood in her front hallway, stunned. Of course she hadn't expected violins and orchids with a Shakespearean fare-thee-well, but the callous way he'd dumped her made her feel like a floozy who'd been paid to perform sexual acts.

Okay. Fine. He was hurting, that much was obvious. And he wasn't accustomed to baring his soul, of showing—feeling—emotion. He'd built a Berlin Wall around himself and it was up to her to dismantle it.

She reached for the crystal dangling at her throat. No wonder it chose him, she thought. He needed someone who cared, really cared, for him. She would just have to prove to him that she did.

Making love with Soren had been magical. How perfectly his body had fit into hers, how strong and hard his muscles, how tender his kisses. Well, sometimes. At other times, how hot and insatiable he'd been, devouring her mouth, her breasts, her pussy. And most of all, how he filled her, whether slow and gentle or fast and frantic, how they'd held each other's gaze as their orgasms exploded in tandem.

He could be warm, loving, funny, quirky when he forgot about that wall.

"I'm not done with you, Soren Thorvald," she declared. "Not by a long shot."

* * * * *

"What's the stare for?"

Soren's chef, bald and outgoing Milton Semonik, stopped stirring his famous pot of chili as he watched his boss enter the kitchen through the employee entrance. "What are you doing here? You're supposed to be off tonight."

"Since when do you make the rules?"

Milton shrugged his shoulders. "I only know what Trang told me."

"What she says isn't gospel. One would think the boss could do pretty much what he wanted."

"Yep. You'd think so."

Soren narrowed his eyes, but Milton studiously turned his attention to his stirring.

"How's business today?"

"Second pot. First one's about gone." Milton lifted a bit of the spicy mixture to his mouth on a wooden spoon, blew softly to cool it then tasted it. "Mmm. Just about ready for the evening crowd." He looked up. "Want me to dish you up some?"

Soren warred within himself. Chili—again—instead of homemade lasagna? "Nah, not hungry yet. I'll catch some later." Without asking himself why he didn't take a bowl of it upstairs, he strode through the swinging doors and out into the bar area.

"What are you doing here?"

"What's this, an echo?" Soren glanced around the room by habit then glared at Trang, who, it seemed to him, had everything under her competent control.

"You're supposed to be—"

"Yeah, yeah, I know. Can't the boss change his mind? Hell, everyone else around here does."

"Well, aren't you in rare form. Now we know why it's been three years since you've taken a day off."

Soren worked a jaw muscle as he scanned the tables and booths. Nothing amiss.

"Because you come back from your 'vacation'…" she made quotation marks in the air with her fingers, "growling like a bear just out of hibernation."

"And your point would be…?"

Trang calmly wiped down a nonexistent spot on the bar's surface. "Maybe you need more…vacation."

She was studiously avoiding his gaze, but she had a kind of smirk at the edges of her mouth. Even Coral, bussing Table Four, glanced his way and gave him a leer. Christ, did everyone in the place know he'd gotten laid last night?

And this morning and several times in between.

"Hey, boss, feeling better this evening?" Ellen, the other table waitress, chimed in.

That did it. "I see everything is under control," he said testily. "I think I'll go upstairs and…and read a good book. Call me on the house phone if there's a problem."

He strode out of the bar, ignoring the dropped jaws and speculative stares, and plowed through the kitchen to reach the inside stairs to the second floor. One of these days, he swore to himself, he'd get an outside entrance to the apartment so he wouldn't have to endure all the wise-ass remarks.

As soon as he'd punched in the combination and opened the door to his living room, her scent assailed him. Like flowers and oranges. Shit. In three long strides he reached the bank of windows in the dormer and opened each one. Sure, April nights were cool, but he'd be damned if he'd wallow in her scent. Hell, it probably even clung to his skin.

Right. Scrub it off, that's what he had to do. Walking through to the bedroom, he pulled off his polo shirt, unzipped his jeans...

And stopped dead.

His bed. The unmade bed, with its rumpled sheet and blanket long since shoved to the floor, where they'd made love over and over and —

No! They didn't make love. They'd just had sex.

Plenty of sex. Mind-bending, soul-searing, once-in-a-lifetime sex.

But they hadn't made love.

Not once.

Savagely he stripped the sheets and stuffed them into the washer he'd installed in the bath hallway, poured detergent in then set the controls to wash away all trace of her. Hopping out of his jeans, he kicked them aside then hit the shower.

God almighty, the shower. Where she'd gone down on her knees and soaped him until he was ready to burst then took his aching cock into that sweet, soft mouth of hers and...

And made him feel like the king of the mountain.

Ruthlessly he turned the faucet to cold and stepped under the frigid spray, trying to put Crystal D'Angelo out of his mind.

It wouldn't take long. He'd forget her by tomorrow. He wanted to forget her. Had to forget her.

Because love hurts.

* * * * *

Dispiritedly, Crystal stepped out of a shower as hot as she could stand it and reached for a pair of warm, fluffy towels. She'd worked out a number of possible scenarios to approach Soren again as she stood under the relaxing spray, but discarded them all. She wasn't a vamp. She wasn't devious. What she was, was tenacious. Some inspiration would come, she was sure of it. He hadn't seen the last of her.

She towel-dried her freshly shampooed hair, combed the knots out of it, and clipped barrettes to keep the unruly curls away from her face. After drying her body and hanging up the damp towels, she strolled nude into her bedroom and posed in front of the cheval mirror.

Her breasts were adequate, she judged as she lifted them to feel their heft. Maybe a little too full, too ripe. Her hips curved in the right places, and her waist was tiny. She turned to catch a glimpse of her derrière. Maybe a little too round. But she had good legs. Not long like a runway model's, but shapely and proportionate to her five-foot, three-inch body.

She stroked her clit absently. He certainly hadn't taken exception to her sexual response. She'd been eager, hungry for his touch, and had surprised even herself with her passionate nature.

No, it wasn't her body that had turned Soren off, she was sure. It was his own mind. His pain.

With a sigh she opened a dresser drawer and withdrew an extra-large sweatshirt that said "Librarians are novel lovers". She had bought it years ago during a fund-raising event for the Bryn Mawr Library. Under it she pulled on a pair of frayed blue tights. This was her "feel-good" attire, like the little boy in the

Sunday cartoons who clung to his blanket. Within this cotton and wool she felt cuddled, wrapped in warmth, safe.

She took the stairs down to the first floor and rummaged in the fridge. She'd made a lasagna the day before, hoping that she and Soren would eventually end up here in her kitchen after a day of lovemaking and sharing.

Well, two out of three was good, wasn't it?

* * * * *

The man pumped his fist into the air. *Yes!* He'd gotten here in time. He adjusted the camera's zoom lens to its full 400-millimeter setting as he watched her drop the towel and come into view in the center room on the second floor, the one with the full-length windows opening onto a balcony.

Her bedroom.

She stood before a mirror in all her naked splendor and posed for him, thrusting those exquisite breasts upward and outward so that they almost filled the lens as he clicked. As she touched them, the dusky nipples stood hard at attention, teasing him, filling his cock with lust. He frowned at that. He'd have to punish her for making him have such impure thoughts.

Nudging the camera downward on its beanbag base, he focused on the dark brown curls that nestled where her thighs came together. This was where he would have to punish her, pull her legs wide apart and tie her knees to the restraints at the sides of the bed, and flail her slit until it wept for him. For she had taken a lover. She was no longer pure. He would have to whip the badness out of her.

She reached between her legs, touching and stroking herself at the slit that was his and his alone. How dare she! When he had her to himself, he would teach her how to be pure. He would never allow her to please herself. She would have to beg him to do so. And she would learn that the only way she could find relief would be at his hands — with the whip.

The grandmother was key. She doted on the old woman. All he had to do was capture Rowena D'Angelo and Crystal would rush to her rescue.

And he would save her. Forever.

* * * * *

Crystal stared morosely at the lasagna. She'd made way too much for one person. She should divide it into portions and store them in the freezer. But not just yet.

She wanted to keep the illusion—that Soren would join her—alive for a little while.

Shoving the oblong pan back into the fridge, she took out the brie, a pear, and an opened bottle of Chianti that she'd used for the marinara sauce. She arranged them on a small lacquered tray along with a deep-bowled wine glass and settled down on the sofa in the living room.

This was shaping up to be a good-book kind of night. Time to start that new Jaid Black she'd been wanting to read. Or, instead of erotic romance, maybe she'd be better off with something interesting and heart-pounding, like Ninety-Nine Ways to Prepare Squid.

At her entertainment unit she set the CD player for some vintage Sinatra, the one where he sang only sad songs like "Only the Lonely" and "One for the Road". She certainly didn't feel like a Franz Lehár operetta tonight.

She knifed off a tip of brie, spread it on a pear slice, tucked her fuzzy-slippered feet under her and nibbled on the hors d'oeuvre. Laying her head against the back cushion, she closed her eyes and ordered herself to concentrate on the juxtaposition of taste and feel on the tongue, the creamy-smooth cheese, the juicy, ripe fruit.

No good. She kept imagining the creamy-smooth skin of his cock as it slid in and out of her mouth, the juicy ripeness of her slit as it lubricated her passage for him.

Face it, girl. You're hooked. You want this man.

She touched the bump that her crystal made under the sweatshirt. Grandma was so right. Soren was the man for her. Only Soren.

All right, girl, get off that one-track mind. "A kick-ass heroine, that's what I need," she declared as she shoved off the sofa and went in search of a J.D. Robb or a Suzanne Brockmann.

The doorbell rang while she was rummaging through her to-be-read pile stashed in her downstairs guestroom whose window faced the front porch. Silently she moved to the window and cracked open the blinds with one finger, squinting in the dusk at the tall figure standing in silhouette.

Soren!

Oh God, she looked a mess. No makeup, her ratty tights frayed along the edges, her hair shooting every which way because she'd let it dry naturally —

So what? If they were fated to be together for the rest of their lives, he'd be bound to see her at her worst once in a while. If he couldn't take it, she'd better find out early, hadn't she?

Regardless of how he might or might not react, her heart was making funny little loop-de-loops in her chest as she came down the hall, flicked on the porch light and unlocked the door. *Be cool. Don't fawn all over him,* she repeated to herself.

"Hi," she said, proud that the word came out without squeaking.

"I told you, I'm no good at this thing." Soren flicked his hand back and forth between them. "You know, man-woman stuff. But I, uh, lasagna? You made it?"

Her smile blossomed. "I did. It's a killer recipe, if I do say so myself."

"I'm willing to risk dying. I'm partial to lasagna. Especially when it doesn't come frozen from a cardboard carton. Even though she was Nordic down to the blonde pigtail wrapped around her head, my grandmother put together a lasagna that made me a fan for life."

"Uh-oh, I hope I can measure up. Come in and let's see how I rate." She stepped back to invite him into the hall, drinking in the sight of him with her eyes. The snug jeans, the dark blue button-down shirt under a leather bomber jacket. His five-o'clock shadow noticeably absent. *Yes!*

He followed her in, closed and locked the door behind him. *Oh, you rate*, he thought as he imagined the gentle sway of her sweet ass under that shapeless sweatshirt as she walked through the living room. Dammit, but he still didn't know what dumb impulse brought him here when he'd had to run the gantlet of the kitchen staff a second time when he went back out, hair wet and slicked back, freshly shaved, everyone probably speculating that he wanted to get laid again.

No, it was more than that. He wanted to be with Crystal, that was all. Whatever happened after, would happen.

He stepped into the kitchen just as she was bending down to slide the pan into the oven. The stretchy blue material covering her bottom cradled her ass like a second skin, making the demarcation of the two halves distinct and making his mouth water. He'd known, loved the feel of that soft cushion of muscle and fat in his hands, the silky smoothness of her naked skin against his. He wondered if she'd ever…if he'd be too big to fit…

He forced thoughts of ass-fucking out of his mind as she stood up and reached into another cupboard, bringing out a wine glass.

"It'll take at least a half hour for it to warm up. I just set out a bottle of Chianti and some cheese. We can nibble on stuff in the living room while we wait."

"You look different."

She stiffened. "I don't mean you look bad," he rushed on. "It's just, you look, I don't know, like a teenager or something. Your skin is so pure and shiny. I mean it looks so healthy, so…vital, I guess." His gaze dropped down to her chest and read aloud the legend silk-screened onto it. "Librarians are novel lovers." He smiled and could feel the corners of his eyes crinkle. He didn't often smile that broadly. "I didn't know you were a librarian. And look at how you blush. I've never seen anything so pretty as a blush. Your blush, that is." He stroked her cheek, felt the heat of blood spreading through her capillaries.

"Crystal." While his fingertips touched her cheek, he bent his head and gently kissed each corner of her soft, trembling mouth. "You're an amazing woman."

He looked into the brown depths of her wide-open eyes and felt himself falling.

* * * * *

"Bitch! The bitch! How could she do this!"

He thought she'd gotten rid of that big hulk who was hanging around her. But from the looks of things, it was getting out of hand. He'd have to do something sooner rather than later.

He packed up his surveillance equipment, climbed down from his vantage point in the forest outside her backyard and began to execute Plan B.

Chapter Fourteen

ღ

"You were right. That lasagna was awesome."

Crystal leaned back in the spindle-back chair. "Must have been. You had three helpings," she teased.

"And you just…threw some spices in a jar with oil and stuff and…and it tasted like something that should have Paul Newman's face on the label."

"Oh, you mean the salad dressing?" She gave a self-deprecating shrug. "I never do the same thing twice. I like to experiment."

Soren raised a thick blond eyebrow. "Is that right?"

Another blush began to make its way up her cheeks. "In fact," she said, rising from the table and picking up both their dirty plates, "I've been mulling over an idea about another experiment." She rinsed the dishes and stashed them in the dishwasher. "Are you game?"

"Don't tell me. You're going to throw together some chocolate, butter and cognac—and presto! Dessert!"

Her laugh wrapped around him. She had such verve, such an optimistic way of looking at things, as though everything was a happy adventure. "Not quite, but it could certainly turn out that way."

"Okay, I'll bite. What kind of experiment?"

She turned to face him, her hips resting against the counter. "I've created a new kind of poker. Can I interest you in a game?"

"If you dare. I've been known to win a pot or two."

"Okay. Clear the table and I'll a find a poker deck."

"Marked cards?" He smirked as he gathered the salad bowl and lasagna pan and brought them to the counter.

"No way." With a flourish, she opened a drawer and produced a deck still wrapped in cellophane. "You open them, and test them for bumps or nicks, or whatever it is that card sharks use to feel for aces."

When the table was cleared and wiped down, he unwrapped the deck and with an expert grace riffle-shuffled the cards a number of times.

"Mmm, I'm impressed," she said, eyes sparkling as she slipped into the other chair.

He slapped the deck face down on the table. "Cut."

She did then stacked the bottom half on the top, leaving her hand on the pile. "Here's how this game is played. Six cards up. No draw. Winner gets to make a mild demand of the other, like 'Pour me some more wine', or 'One little kiss, no hands'. Mild," she repeated.

Taking the cut deck in her hands, Crystal proceeded to deal one card at a time to each, carefully placing the subsequent cards to cover at least half the previous one. When she had laid out six each, Soren swept his into a pile.

"No! Leave them the way I set them."

"I just wanted to put my two aces together to be sure you knew they beat your king-high," he said with a Groucho Marx leer.

"You didn't need to set them in sequence in order to see you had two aces," she argued as she returned them to their original arrangement. "Anyway, I'm not finished with how this game is played. After the first hand, the other partner removes the first three cards of each dealt hand, and adds three more from the deck. So you have to leave them exactly the way they were dealt. No bluffing, no discarding."

"Okay, I understand. You're afraid you can't compete with my strategy and you're counting on chance to win. So," he said, cutting off her objection and making a big show of studying her hand, "looks like I won this one. Agreed?"

"Yes."

"Good. My request is that you get rid of that baggy sweatshirt."

"You can't do that! I said 'a mild demand', not 'strip poker'."

"But I asked you in a very mild tone of voice, did I not?" he asked mildly.

He could see the flush building up in her cheeks again. God, he loved to make her blush. And her face was so transparent, he could almost read the emotions crossing it, that this was really what she'd wanted to happen, only not so soon.

Soren played a trump card. "You did say you like to experiment, did you not?"

Her cheeks got even redder. *Caught ya.*

"Fine." Without ceremony she crossed her arms at her waist, pulled up the hem of the sweatshirt and ripped it up over her head.

A fist punched into Soren's gut. She wasn't wearing a bra.

"And I believe it's my deal," she said with a great deal of aplomb, considering.

"You dealt last hand."

"Sorry, didn't I tell you? Loser gets to deal the next hand." Ignoring his raised eyebrow, she removed the bottom three cards from each, taking both his aces and leaving her king. Then dealt him a pair of treys and herself a pair of fours.

"I win," she said matter-of-factly. "I want you to come here and kiss me. Mouth only, no hands, no other touching. Soft and sweet and melting."

"The woman knows what she wants." He stood and bent over her as she lifted her face to him. "My pleasure."

But he bent down past her face, his mouth landing softly on her right breast.

"No, I meant kiss my mouth!" She lifted her hand to push away his head.

Ignoring her protests, he captured the nipple between his lips, softly running his mouth back and forth over the dusky rose tip that hardened under his gentle onslaught. It was exquisite torture to keep his tongue behind his teeth, but he complied with the letter of her request to be sweet and melting and mouth-only until he felt his cock pressing against his jeans.

"Okay, enough," she gasped, and he allowed her desultory shove to move him backwards.

"It's my deal," he said as he sat back down in his seat.

He dealt himself a pair of queens, but when he counted the hearts in her hand, he held his breath to see how much she knew about poker.

"I believe that's called a flush." She smiled sweetly at him. "I would like you to remove your jeans."

He threw her a look of mock horror. "I can't do that, I still have my shoes and socks on."

A shrug. "Whatever you have to do to comply with my request."

Again he stood then toed off his boots. With great deliberation he unsnapped the waistband. It gave him a tickle of satisfaction to see her tongue creep out and lick her lower lip as she watched him gently work the zipper down past his hard cock and slough off the denim.

Jeez, if she kept looking at the way the ridge of his cock poked at the silk of his boxers, she'd get more than—

"Okay, it's your deal," she said, suddenly prim.

Soren tamped down a smile. She was not unaffected for all her posed nonchalance.

His pair of jacks was bested by her three sixes. "See that tray with the bottles?" she said. "Please pour after-dinner drinks for us. I'd like a Kahlua, and I think you should have a cognac, since you mentioned it before."

Deliberately he brushed his silk-imprisoned cock across her upper arm as he followed her directive. On his way back, he leaned over her naked shoulder, pressing his cock—which by now had found the opening and poked its head out—into her warm skin, and placed her tiny glass in front of her. Then sat down, as nonchalant as she. Sheer pretense, he thought, for them both. He lifted his glass in silent toast then sipped.

She wet her lips against the coffee-flavored liqueur then dealt. This time neither of them had a good hand. Both had king-high. But he had a queen and her next highest card was only a ten.

Giving her a predatory smile, he said, "I request that you come here and sheathe my cock with your sweet pussy."

Her eyes widened. "I can't do that, you have to ask for..."

He could see the wheels of her mind saying, *I made him take off his jeans while he still had shoes on, so he had to take off his shoes. So now I have to take off my tights in order to —*

His cock took a leap upward at the thought.

"Soren Thorvald, you're evil," she said as she shimmied out of her tights, her naked breasts jiggling provocatively as she moved. She came around to him and made as if to put her leg across his lap.

"Uh-uh, you're still wearing panties."

"Doesn't matter," she said smugly. "I can still follow your directive." Pulling the crotch of her cotton panties to one side, she positioned herself so those glorious tits of hers brushed against his face then reached down and put her fingers around his cock. He damn near jumped out of his chair.

"Steady," she murmured. "I'm just trying to make sure I aim right."

Then she slid slowly down his shaft until he was buried right up to the hilt, and he cursed the fact that he still wore those damn boxers. He wanted to feel her sweet skin on his, pubic hair against pubic hair, her thighs rubbing against his hips instead of having the silk between them.

She rested her entire weight on the point of contact and looked him in the eye. A small smile played at the corners of her mouth. "Do. Not. Touch. Me."

He hadn't even realized he'd placed his hands on her hips.

"Sorry, Soren, but you didn't say anything about anything except sheathing your cock with…my sweet pussy, I believe were your words."

She rocked her hips back and forth with precise movements, lifted herself and sank down onto his hard cock a few times, then lifted herself all the way to her feet and strolled back to her chair, readjusting the crotch of those damned panties before she sat. "My deal," she said, her breath coming just a little too fast.

Soren couldn't help it. He unbuttoned his sleeves and rolled them up. It was much too hot in here. In fact, he could feel sweat on his forehead. He pulled up the tail of his blue shirt and wiped his face.

"Whose deal is it?"

He smiled at her question. Having declared it was her deal just a minute ago, she was obviously as addled as he was, and it served her right. It was a damnably devilish game, and she was enjoying every inch…er, every second of it.

The hell with it. He couldn't remember either, so he simply nudged the pack toward her. "Yours."

Nipping her lower lip with her teeth, Crystal concentrated on the cards she'd exposed. Her own read four-five-six-seven — rats, she needed one more for a straight. She had nothing. She wanted the opportunity to get those navy blue boxer shorts off so she could see the full glory of his cock, to see how long they could restrain themselves, but he seemed to have better luck. He had a pair of eights.

She raised her lashes halfway, so he wouldn't see how eager she was to hear his next "request". "You win again."

"This time," he stood as he spoke, "I want to pour my cognac on your slit and lap it up without those panties you're wearing, so they don't get wet or in my way. I suggest you lie on your back, knees up, legs spread apart so I can access the spot." He ripped his shirt off, buttons popping, and pulled it off his shoulders, folding it into a kind of pillow. "And your sweet ass will lie on this so I won't make a spot on the carpet when I pour."

He set down the "pillow" on the rug in the living room—he was enough of a gentleman to want her to be more comfortable than lying naked on the kitchen floor—and shucked off his socks. "Well? I'm waiting to collect my winnings."

Crystal's throat went dry. He stood like a colossus, one hand around the snifter to warm the cognac, feet spread apart, his magnificent cock thrusting thick and heavy through the opening in his boxers, tantalizing her even more than if he'd been entirely nude. She grabbed for her Kahlua and upended the liquid into her mouth, swirling it around with her tongue to moisten her inner cheeks, her tongue.

Then with thumbs in the elastic, she slid her cotton panties to the floor and stepped out. She took a deep breath, her breasts thrusting out, walked to his folded shirt, and sat down on it gracefully, knees together. Swallowed hard. Watched his cock twitch and jump as he stood otherwise motionless. Leaned back on her elbows until her back rested on the carpet.

"Keep going," he growled.

This was the hard part. Even though she knew he'd seen her most intimate areas close up, she was expected to deliberately expose herself to him in a decision of free will rather than in the heat of the moment.

The crystal nestling between her breasts heated, infusing her with warmth. This was Soren. Her Soren. The One. Allowing her love to shine in her eyes, she slid her feet apart just to the point of discomfort.

Soren sank to his knees between them with a reverent curse. His hand trembled as he lifted the snifter and dribbled a few drops on the slit that she knew was already well moistened.

He bent forward and worshipped her with his tongue, lapping, sucking, nibbling on her labia with his teeth.

She lifted her hips to his face, encouraging him. He poured a few more drops, suckled with more force, his tongue delving into her vagina with long, slow thrusts. Exposing the hard bud of her clit with his fingers, he took a sip of the aged brandy and bent down to bathe the sensitive nubbin with the fiery liquid and his hot mouth.

All thoughts of games, of cards, fled. Crystal's every synapse zeroed in on him, on his talented mouth, his strong hands now lifting her bottom to him, on the exquisite sensations spiraling higher and higher, tighter and tighter inside her, until she grabbed handfuls of his hair and repeated his name over and over until she was breathless and gasping and rocking and, finally, mindless with the spasms washing throughout her limp and boneless body.

She gave a soft protest when he slid his hands away from her hips, but dammit, he had to in order to reach his jeans and the condoms he'd stowed in his pocket. Stripping the damn shorts off, he ripped open the foil and covered himself with no wasted motion, then plunged hard and deep into her sweet pussy, which, thank you God, was still convulsing as it welcomed him into her delectable softness.

Take it slow, make it last, he told himself, but she had already wrapped her legs around his waist, her eyes open and devouring him, her fingernails digging into his shoulders, encouraging him to go faster, harder, deeper, and he did. Oh God, he couldn't get deep enough, couldn't get enough of this woman who'd gotten under his skin and had come to mean so much to him.

"Stop!" He couldn't believe he said that. But... "This way. I've got to get in deeper."

He pulled out, flipped her unceremoniously onto her belly, then raised her hips and plunged into her again from behind. "Yes! Dear God, yes!" He felt himself getting even harder, if that was possible, felt his cock reach deep inside, touching her very soul as he hammered into her, his balls tight against his cock, and slapping into the straining curve of her ass cheeks with every stroke. Her juices flowed with every outstroke, coating him and running down her legs, her pungent fragrance imprinting itself into his DNA.

Seeing his engorged cock slide in and out of her pussy drove him into even more of a frenzy. His! She was his, he was her first and, he swore, the only man she would ever fuck. He could hear her throaty moans, encouraging him, asking, begging him for more. And more he'd give her, until he'd given her everything he had.

He reached around her hip and found her clit, that hard, responsive bud that had blossomed under his mouth, and pinched it, squeezed it until she cried for more, harder, and he wished he had four hands, two cocks, to give her everything she wanted all at the same time, her mouth, her nipples, her cunt, clit, asshole, every orifice filled with him, only him, until—

"Aaaaghhh!" He grabbed her hips in one final death grip and shot his cum in spurt after ragged spurt into her, convulsively pumping, bruising her with the force of his orgasm, until he half collapsed onto her back, his arms coming around her belly in a loose embrace, only vaguely aware that her own tension had subsided. Wryly he realized that his own climax had been so intense, he hadn't known, hadn't felt hers.

Still imbedded, half-hard, in her, he contrived to get both of them onto the floor on their sides, his arm under her neck for a pillow of sorts, his body making a protective arc around her. His free hand lazily followed the contour of her waist, hip, thigh, and back up again, feeling the sheen of sweat under his fingertips. He couldn't stop touching her.

After what seemed like a long time, she leaned back into him. "Did you get the license plate of that steamroller?"

He barked out a laugh at the unexpected humor. "You bet. It was S-O-R-E-N-1."

She turned her head to capture his gaze. "Yes. You are. Number one."

"You'd better make that 'One And Only'," he growled.

"Mmm. Sounds good to me." She made a move to turn around to him.

"Wait. Hold on. Let me get this first." Belatedly he realized he'd shot so much cum that millions of sperm were probably holed up in the condom and he'd better be damned careful with this one-of-a-kind woman.

He eased everything out. "Don't move. I'll be right back."

* * * * *

"Trey! I thought you were out of town." Rowena tucked the receiver of her portable phone between her ear and shoulder as she relaxed back onto a poolside lounge chair and watched the last feeble shades of mauve and midnight fade to the darkness of night.

"Came back early."

"Everything go all right?"

"I think I made a favorable impression. If all goes well, he'll be a lucrative client."

"Congratulations."

"So, that puts me in a mood to celebrate. Want to shoot up to the cabin tomorrow morning? We could spend a week there, looking for wildflowers in the woods."

Rowena chuckled. For months Courtland A. Quillan the Third had been making oblique references to getting her into his bed, and she'd played along. The man was almost twenty year her junior, but age had never stopped her from enjoying a man's body before. She just wondered if his son Augie's remark about going after her fortune held any validity.

Still, there was no harm in sampling. Her fortune, her will, her trust fund for Crystal, were protected with all kinds of checks and balances. If he was inaugurating a campaign to separate her from her money, she might as well enjoy the perks. He was easy to look at, kept in shape, and knew his wines and his cuisine. And hell, he *was* a member of the Platinum Club. It could be a fun week.

"Will there still be snow in the Poconos?" It was the end of April, but in higher elevations, who knew?

"Maybe on the ski slopes, but the cabin has a southern exposure. You won't need thermal underwear, if that's what you're worried about."

Rowena hesitated. She wanted to be close by if Crystal suddenly got cold feet, even though she and Soren seemed to be making progress. But maybe they didn't need any further impetus to come to the conclusion that they were meant for each other.

"I'll pick you up at eight sharp. And Rowena? Don't tell anyone. I don't want the gossips to know about my soundproof dungeon and all the handcuffs and restraining devices."

At that, she laughed. "Promises, promises."

"I'm serious."

"Okay, okay. Listen, Trey, another call's coming in. I'll be ready at eight tomorrow morning."

"You better be. I want you up there if I have to drag you by the hair."

Still smiling, Rowena punched buttons and answered the second call.

"Good evening, Rowena. I hope I'm not intruding by calling after nine."

"Not at all, Jack. I don't go to bed until midnight."

"I'm glad to hear it. I'm calling to ask you for a very big favor."

"What's up?"

"You may recall that I never gave Crystal a gift at the birthday party you hosted for her. I ordered it a month ago, and it just came in. I'm unpacking it now. I wonder if you could stop by Time Treasures and give me your expert opinion as to whether she would like it."

"I'd love to, Jack, but I'm leaving town tomorrow for a few days."

"I'm still at the shop. You just said you don't go to bed until midnight. Could you come by now? I'd really appreciate it. I don't want to wait any longer than necessary to present it to her. You know she holds a special place in my heart and I don't want her to think I ignored such a special occasion as her thirtieth birthday."

Rowena's mind raced. Surely she could spare an hour for her granddaughter. She'd pack when she returned. "Okay, I'll be there in a half hour."

"Thank you. I'll be forever in your debt."

* * * * *

At the guest bath off the downstairs hall, Soren took a washcloth off the rack, moistened it and returned to the living room.

God, she was beautiful—her wild, gypsy hair spread over the carpet, her brown eyes slumberous and sated. Her luscious breasts flattened a little, listing to the sides. Her pussy was swollen and red, her thighs shiny with her juices. The ever-present amulet sparkled at her throat.

He knelt at her side and gently stroked between her legs with the washcloth. She had not a bone of artifice in her, he thought. Every emotion she experienced showed on her face. Had anyone ever looked at him with such—

Love?

Had he been tarring every woman with the brush of his child's memory of his mother's betrayal? He'd always kept a tight rein on his emotions, and no other woman had come close to breaching his defenses. But this one stormed right over them. She'd joked about a steamroller, but its license plate should have read C-R-Y-S-T-A-L.

He wasn't ready to put a name to what he felt about her—tenderness, respect, awe. She made him happy to be with her, happy to be alive. All these years, he now realized, he'd been marking time, waiting—

For her.

Breathless, he sat back on his haunches. Good Christ, he'd need some time to assimilate this new insight. Did he want to open himself up to hurt again? His mother had taught him that he was unlovable. How long would it be before Crystal hurt him?

But maybe, just maybe…

"Penny for your thoughts," she murmured, her palm brushing up and down his thigh.

Uh-uh, he wasn't ready to talk about it. Instead, he grabbed at the first subject he could think of. "Do you ever take off that crystal thing around your neck?"

She gave him an odd smile. "Grandma gave it to me for my thirteenth birthday. I've never taken it off."

"You must think a great deal of her."

Crystal pushed herself up to a seated position on the carpet. "I'd do anything for Rowena. After my parents died, I would have been lost without her. She welcomed me into her home, into her heart. She guided me during the most vulnerable part of my life."

Taking the amulet between thumb and forefinger, Crystal stroked it absently. "She told me it was magic. That it would keep me safe until I knew what I wanted in life." Her lashes lifted until he could see deep into the soft brown depths of her eyes. "That I would know when I met the man I would give my virginity to."

Soren sat hard on his heels, the now cool washcloth forgotten in his hand. He barely kept the skepticism from his voice. "Are you trying to tell me that you picked me because of some so-called magic charm?"

Her smile was tremulous. "As soon as I saw you up on that stage, the crystal glowed against my skin with a heat I never felt before, so I knew you were The One."

He shot to his feet, towered over her seated form. "Whoa! Wait a minute. Let me get this straight. All this—" he flicked his hand back and forth between them, "you're saying it was voodoo? That you put some kind of a spell on me?"

"No, Soren, of course not! I'm just saying—"

"Yeah, right, 'the crystal made me do it'. It had nothing to do with who *I* am. You would have fucked anyone the crystal told you to."

Anger slowly seeped into every pore. She was no different from any other woman, scheming, grasping, inveigling him into intimacy and then dropping a bomb of one sort or another. He looked around for his jeans, grabbed them and stuffed his legs into them while hopping on one foot at a time. "Well, you just tell your precious grandma that her magic doesn't work on Soren Thorvald. I'm not a stupid dog you can lead along by a leash, whether it's made of leather or crystal."

She had stood up while he was dressing. Good thing, or he'd have ripped the shirt she was sitting on right out from under her treacherous ass. He snatched up the juice-stained shirt and shoved his arms into the sleeves, not bothering with whatever buttons he hadn't popped in his adolescent eagerness to get his cock into her.

More fool he.

He found his boots lying under the card table and yanked them onto his feet without even thinking about socks. Patting his jeans pockets to be sure he still had his wallet and truck keys, he stalked down the hall then spun around when she shouted his name. He felt like his eyes could zap the rug and start a fire as she ran, naked, toward him.

He wrenched open the front door, the sight of her jiggling breasts for once not affecting him.

"Soren, wait!"

Wait? Not on your life, he thought, wondering if smoke was coming out of his ears. He slammed the front door shut behind him and took the three porch steps in one long stride.

He'd never heard such a ridiculous excuse for a come-on in his life. She'd played him for a fool. His fault. He'd let down his guard and allowed her to creep into the cold cavity that passed for his heart. But an inert piece of rock telling her she'd found the right stud to do the deed? What a pile of horseshit.

A fleeting image of his brother sitting at his bar getting slowly wasted on a bottle of good whiskey flashed in Soren's mind. A woman had driven Magnus to his knees. He understood a little better now. But unlike Magnus, he wouldn't need to drink himself to oblivion. He'd just immerse himself in his work.

And woe to any employee who dared comment on his state of mind.

Chapter Fifteen

໕

Crystal collapsed onto the bottom step of the staircase as she listened to Soren's tires squeal away from her. How could she have done anything but answer truthfully when he asked her? He was her heart and soul. She would have told him anything and everything.

Elbows on her knees, she lowered her head into her palms and fought tears. Maybe she shouldn't have been so naïve as to think he'd simply accept what she'd long ago taken for granted. Darn it, the crystal *had* told her. She rubbed her fingers over the spot of skin under the amulet that had actually had a red mark the morning after the Bachelor Auction. It couldn't be wrong. The magic they shared when they made love hadn't come from the crystal. It had come from the chemistry between two people who were meant to be together.

Sure, she'd necked and petted and even had a few tepid orgasms from her own efforts, but never once had she been tempted to go all the way with any of the men who had wanted to take her to bed. But when she'd seen Soren, the attraction was immediate. Hadn't he felt the same attraction? Hadn't he made love with her like they were meant to be together? Hadn't the earth moved?

A shudder overtook her, like the feeling one got walking through a cemetery on a dark night. No wonder, she chided herself. She was still naked, and emotionally upset to boot. With a deep sigh, she forced herself to her feet and dragged herself back to the dining room table where the cards lay scattered and her ratty blue tights hung by one leg off the back of a chair.

She had pulled on her clothes and had just started straightening up the kitchen from the lasagna dinner when the phone rang. "Soren," she blurted out, her spirits shooting to the skies. Grabbing the phone, she said a breathless hello.

"It's Jack. I'm afraid I have some bad news."

Not Soren. Crystal's shoulders slumped. "What's the matter?"

"It's Rowena. She came to Time Treasures just before closing and wanted to see something I had stored in the back. She…well, she fell and twisted her ankle, I think."

"Oh, no, is she in pain?"

"You know your grandmother. She treats everything like a joke. She doesn't want me to call an ambulance."

"Put her on the phone," Crystal demanded.

"I'm afraid I can't, my dear. My cell phone isn't charged, so I'm calling from the landline in my office. She's in the storage room and the cord won't reach that far. Can you come down and knock some sense into that thick head of hers?"

"Couldn't you drive her to the emergency room?"

"She absolutely refuses. Something about saving face." Jack made what sounded like a strangled laugh into the phone. "If she was having an emergency appendectomy, she'd want to walk into the operating room on her own two feet."

Crystal puffed out a harsh breath. Yes, that sounded like her grandmother. "Okay, tell her I'm on my way."

"Pull into the alleyway," Jack directed. "It'll be closer to where she is."

"Gotcha." She disconnected and dashed upstairs for her sneakers. Grabbing her own cell phone, she checked the battery indicator. Fully charged. Good. She headed out to her car, thrusting her arms into a lightweight jacket, then speed-dialed number four, Rowena's cell phone number, in case her grandmother had that phone in her handbag.

She got the "out of service" recording. With a muted oath, she stuffed the phone into her jacket pocket and got into her Beetle.

It took almost fifteen minutes, but at last she pulled up to Time Treasures' back door, which was ajar. She shut off the ignition, slid the key into her jeans pocket, and pushed open the heavy door.

"Jack? Grandma?" As she strode into the interior of the dimly lit storeroom, she heard the door slam shut behind her. Whirling around with her hand on her heart, she saw Jack Healy come up to her. "Oh. You scared me. I thought you'd be with Grandma."

"I heard your car." He took her upper arm with a tight grip. "Come with me."

Crystal's mind registered the fact that he was agitated, his face grim. The sleeves of his white shirt were rolled to his elbows, his discreetly striped tie askew. Her heart slammed into her chest. "Is she worse?"

Jack said nothing, just relentlessly pulled her deeper into the shadows of the storeroom then pushed open a door and flicked a wall switch. "Down here."

Peering down into the yawning cavern of a stairway to the basement, Crystal pulled up short. "Oh my God, did she fall down the *steps*?"

"I didn't want to alarm you unduly," he said, nudging her through the doorway. "You might have had an accident if you drove too fast coming here. But please don't worry. She's not hurt bad, I got her into a chair. Come. See if you can talk her into getting her ankle X-rayed."

As she descended, Crystal's wary gaze took in the thick foundation wall to her right, its bumpy stonelike surface covered with a plaster finish, whitewash flaking off in damp spots. She hadn't known the property had a basement. She gripped the railing, placing her feet carefully on steep, worn stair treads that had no risers. Jack's heavy footsteps followed her down.

On hearing a sound she couldn't place, she turned to look over her shoulder and saw that the doorway behind him was dark. A niggling alarm bell began to ring in her head. *That* was what she'd heard—a lock snicking into place.

Stay calm, she ordered herself. *You're just tense because of Soren and now Grandma. You've known Jack Healy for years. Don't jump to conclusions. The door probably just had an automatic closing device and she'd merely heard the latch scraping against the faceplate.*

Reaching the bottom, she saw in front of her that a wall of the same texture as the foundation she'd noted along the steps ran for only six or eight feet before the hallway angled to a paneled wall running parallel to the stairs. It looked like the building had only a partial basement. She turned instinctively to her left, where the welcome light from a naked overhead bulb shone weakly. A door stood ajar halfway down the wall and another, closed door marked the end of the hallway not far beyond.

"In there," Jack said from behind her, nudging her toward the opening with a firm hand on her shoulder. Then, raising his voice, said, "Help has arrived, Rowena."

Only subconsciously aware of the heavy pressure of his hand, she stepped up to the doorway. "Grandma? It's Crystal. We'll get you—"

She stopped, unable to absorb the sight in front of her. White. Totally, unrelievedly white. White walls, white ceiling, white-tiled floor. White leather sofa, white side chair. A small round table covered with a white tablecloth. White candles in clear glass candelabra standing on white counters, their flames flickering with the merest hint of yellow. "What on earth...?" Her voice had dropped to a raspy whisper. The first skitterings of fear prickled her spine.

Half turning, she bumped into Jack, whose blocky frame stood between her and the doorway she'd just passed through— a door that was now closed. His eyes held an unholy glow as they caught then held her gaze as securely as his hand held her shoulder.

"Jack, this isn't funny. Where is my grandmother?"

"It was time," he said enigmatically.

She wrenched herself from his grip and spun around, her frantic glance searching for a clue to Rowena's whereabouts. The room was ell-shaped, and she took the few steps to see behind the angle. She did a double take at the sight of a bed in the far corner—a single pallet with a lacy white coverlet. Then she noticed the painting that went almost from ceiling to floor. A life-size portrait of the Virgin Mary, the only color in the room. "Oh…my…God…"

Icy shards of panic lanced through her veins when she noticed. The portrait bore her face. A face that was ripped by the slash of a knife.

"This will be your 'safe' room," Jack announced.

Her gaze snapped back to him. "Safe from whom?" she sneered then wondered if she should antagonize someone so obviously unhinged.

"From anyone who would harm you again."

"'Again'? What do you mean, 'again'? Nobody's harmed me."

"When you were nineteen. I was too young, too helpless, to prevent it the first time. That's why I made myself so strong. I will protect you with my last breath. You have my solemn vow, I won't let it happen again."

"Won't let *what* happen again? Jack, you're not making sense."

"It's okay that you blocked it out of your mind. It's a defense mechanism for something that was simply too horrible to remember. God knows, I've never been able to forget it."

"What are you talking about?" She almost yelled it. He sounded like someone who'd flown over the cuckoo's nest.

The expression on Jack's face turned from pained to rapturous. "I remember when we met. You walked into my shop with your grandmother, looking for a cheval mirror for your bedroom. You were eighteen. When I saw your dark, innocent eyes, your curly hair almost black with glints of copper in the light, I knew that I would spend the rest of my life protecting your innocence, your purity."

His gaze rested on her. "I can't tell you how joyous I felt, to find you before it happened, before you turned nineteen and that vile man—"

His face darkened, as if a black cloud passed across it. A scowl twisted his mouth downward. His eyes sparked with malice. "For twelve years I protected you, watched over you. Then *he* came into your life. Another devil, another bastard with defilement on his mind. I can't let it happen again. You must be cleansed, and I'm prepared to do everything in my power to help you. Together we will make you pure enough to continue your novitiate."

"What are you talking about?" This time it was a near whisper. Fear permeated every cell of her body. Jack Healy seemed to have turned into a madman.

"I was eleven," he said plaintively. "I was small for my age and terrified of him, but I had to try to save you. I knew what he was going to do." A tear escaped his eye. He seemed not to notice. "Instead, I…I—"

An awful sound, a mix between a sob and a keening, emerged from his throat. "I made it worse. I didn't mean to, but I-I…helped him."

"It's all right," she said softly, having not the vaguest notion what he was talking about. "I forgive you." She took one step, two, three, around his kneeling, hunched form, the door her target. "It's all right." She'd scrutinized every wall but could see no other doorway—or piece of furniture big enough—where he might have stashed Rowena, so she felt safe in trying to escape to call 9-1-1 and get help.

Or, worse, maybe the twisted-ankle story had just been a ruse to lure her here into this white room of madness.

Her hand grasped the doorknob, turned it. The door opened. *Thank God*! She took the first hurried step to freedom.

Suddenly Jack grabbed hold of her by her inner elbow. Gripping the doorjamb with her free hand and digging in her heels, she wrenched away from him. Searing pain shot through her shoulder and nearly brought her to her knees. Scrambling to stay upright, she staggered toward the stairs but only took a few steps before she was tackled from behind.

Instinctively she flung her arms out in front of her to cushion the fall and landed on her left wrist and right forearm. The shock of impact vibrating up to her injured shoulder brought tears to her eyes. Her forehead smacked against her knuckles but kept her from smashing her face onto the concrete floor.

Jack landed heavily on her legs, his hands grasping her hips in viselike pincers. "You can't run away," he raged. "You need to be cleansed. Do not run from your destiny."

Dear God, he *was* mad! Crystal managed to scramble to her knees and began crawling toward the steps, toward freedom.

But Jack had already gained his footing and lifted her by her hips until she, too, stood on wobbly legs, her back to him. He wound his arms around her chest like an octopus. She could feel his hot, heavy breath at her nape, raising the fine hairs there.

"Do not fight me, Patty."

A shudder tore through Crystal like a volcanic eruption. Who was Patty?

Slowly he began walking backwards, dragging her inexorably with him, closer and closer to the white-walled prison. "I will make you pure again. Then you will be worthy."

Crystal forced herself to speak in a normal tone. "I'm not Patty. I'm Crystal D'Angelo, and Rowena is my grandmother."

But he seemed not to hear. This time when he slammed the door behind him, he shoved her forward and she landed gracelessly on the sofa. He spun around to lock the door with a key he apparently kept on a chain around his neck.

Her phone! Please, let her phone still be there.

She tried to be casual as she slipped her hand in her jacket pocket, but winced at the pain. At least one of her fingers felt as if bones were broken when she fell.

With an effort she hid her relief as her fingers wound around the precious lifeline. But…who to call? 9-1-1? If she dialed emergency, how could she explain her predicament without Jack hearing? Could they pinpoint her location if she couldn't talk but they could hear fighting or screaming?

Soren? She'd programmed his home number into her speed-dial, but would he have gone home or to his pub? Or somewhere else entirely? The look of disgust on his face when he'd stomped out of her living room told her he wouldn't talk to her even if he did answer the phone.

But wait! If he refused to pick up and she just kept the line open, whatever transpired in this white prison would at least be recorded on his answering machine. She could give hints as to where she was being held. The sensitive tips of her fingers glossed over the buttons.

"It's time for your cleansing to begin."

Jack jerked her off the sofa by grabbing hold of both her upper arms. Crystal cried out in pain and frustration—he'd yanked her hand up before she found the correct button to depress.

"I'm sorry to hurt you. But this is the only way."

He pulled her toward the obscene painting. She turned her gaze away. She had no desire to see the object of his obsession, big as life but a travesty.

His fingers skimmed the snake writhing under the Madonna's feet. He positioned a finger on each of its eyes and pressed into its sockets. Creaking slightly on hidden hinges, the painting swung out into the room, revealing a doorway.

With another shove, he herded Crystal into a white-tiled, white-fixtured bathroom and closed the door behind him. The room was long and narrow, maybe six feet by sixteen, with a tub on one end, a shower in the other, a sink and toilet between them on the wall opposite the door.

"We will begin with the shower, then into the tub to soak out all the remaining impurities. You will please disrobe now."

"Jack, this isn't right—"

"And if you don't," he rode over her objection in a monotone as if in a trance, "I will do it for you."

Crystal felt the short hairs on the back of her neck stand up. Jack Healy was totally insane. Quickly she weighed her options. For some reason she thought he wouldn't rape her. He wanted to "cleanse" her, whatever that meant. Okay, she could stand him watching her as she bathed, if it would keep from triggering who knew what kind of craziness. He weighed close to two hundred pounds, most of it solid muscle, and she had no self-defense training. If he began to strip her, he'd find her phone.

She turned away from him, pretending to study her surroundings. Surreptitiously she slipped her hand in her jacket pocket and concentrated on the buttons. She pressed what she fervently hoped was Soren's speed-dial number then made a big production of removing her jacket, folding it, and placing it on the floor with the correct pocket facing up.

"Really, Jack, I would rather you didn't watch me get undressed."

"If it makes you more comfortable, I will turn my back until you are under the shower." He matched deed to words and stood facing the closed door.

Realizing she had to fill the silence so he wouldn't hear Soren's voice either with his voice mail message or answering the phone himself, Crystal spoke loudly as she shucked off her sneakers. "I still don't understand, Jack, why you made a special suite of rooms for me in the basement of Time Treasures. None of the rooms have windows. You know how much I love the sunshine."

"I will explain it all when the time is right."

"Can you at least tell me who Patty is?" Off came the ratty tights, which she dropped to the floor. She didn't want to put it on top of the jacket and muffle whatever sound could filter through the phone.

She could tell the question had escalated his tenseness by the set of his shoulders. To forestall an outburst, she switched gears. "Is Grandma here too? In the basement of your shop? Are you holding Rowena hostage in a separate room?" Braless, she was conscious of her breasts swaying as she bent down to dump the sweatshirt on top of the tights. "Are you planning to keep me a prisoner here in the cellar of Time Treasures?"

She was now naked except for her panties. She just couldn't take them off. It wasn't right. She took the few steps to the shower and lifted the stainless steel lever. In seconds the water was comfortably warm. She hoped she'd given Soren enough hints already, because she feared the sound of spray hitting tile would muffle further conversation. To compensate, she raised her voice.

"I'm soaping myself up, Jack. I'll be done in a minute. Keep your back to the door, okay? I'll let you know when I'm—"

In two quick steps Jack loomed over her in the shower. He grabbed her left hand, jerked it up, knocking her knuckles against the tiles. Next thing she knew, a cold band of metal surrounded her wrist, holding it immobile.

"What the—a handcuff? Jack, what are you doing? Turn me loose!"

"Did you think," he retorted, heedless of the fact that water cascaded down his shirt and trousers as he loomed over her inside the enclosure, "that you could wash away all the filth in two minutes?" He seized her other hand and yanked it up and across the shower space. With another ominous clanking of metal on metal, that wrist was imprisoned as well.

"Let me go!" Crystal yanked hard with both arms. Pain exploded all the way from her wrists to her battered and bruised shoulder, and she ground her teeth together to keep from crying out.

"You did not listen to me, Patty." He slipped a wet hand inside his trousers pocket and pulled out a small knife. She cringed at the sight.

"I will not hurt you, my dear. You have my word." Opening the blade, he slashed one side of her panties then the other, and tossed the ruined lingerie and the knife onto the floor outside the shower.

He picked up two large loofah mitts from an inside shelf, sheathed his hands and lathered them both with a bar of soap. "I watched your reprehensible behavior. It wasn't enough that you made a spectacle of yourself on the front page of the newspaper, acting wanton for all the world to see."

With both hands he began scrubbing her skin, up and down her back, around her hips, her buttocks. "No, you allowed him to take you on the kitchen counter like performers in a pornographic movie."

Crystal gasped. How had he seen—

"And in the tub, for shame!" He moved to her thighs and calves, roughly scouring her skin front and back as he crouched behind her.

Good lord, he'd spied on her! How else would he have known where they'd made love? "Jack, you're hurting me. You don't need to rub so hard."

"I have not yet begun to rub hard enough. This is the strongest soap I could find. It contains caustic lye to burn the wickedness away. It will take more than these few minutes to purify you."

As he came around to face her, swirling the soap between the loofahs to make more lather, Crystal stealthily adjusted her stance to rest on the balls of her feet, knees flexed. If he would turn j-u-s-t a little bit more, she'd slam her knee into his testicles and hope they'd shoot all the way up into his mouth.

Apparently reading her intent, he dropped the soap, swept an arm behind her knee and yanked one leg up, forcing her to hop to stay balanced and upright.

"You cannot best me, Patty. You must face your destiny." Sloughing off a loofah from his free hand, he pulled the loosened tie off his neck, flung it over a sturdy-looking grab bar positioned at waist level, and looped it under the back of her knee. Then he made another loop over the bar and tied a tight knot, leaving Crystal's leg trapped at an uncomfortably high angle and exposing her most private spot to this madman.

"Do not worry that I will ravish you, Crystal. I aim only to cleanse you." With that he knelt down before her and began to scrub vigorously, making wide swaths from her pubic bone, around the arc between her legs, and all the way up her crack to her anus. He shoved the thumbs of his loofahs inside her vagina and anus a number of times, scraping her tender flesh unbearably.

"Jack! Stop it! You're hurting me! Jack, that burns! Stop! Help me! Help!"

The horror of her predicament closed in on her and she panicked. She knew it was useless, that no one would hear her, but she couldn't stop herself. "Help, please, someone help."

He was at her breasts now, rubbing them mercilessly until her nipples felt raw and abraded. "Please," she whimpered. "It hurts. Please stop."

But he didn't.

Chapter Sixteen

ഔ

Soren sat in the cab of his truck a long time, staring at the back end of Thor's Hammer from the edge of the parking lot. He wanted to go upstairs to his cave and hibernate, maybe drink himself into oblivion, but couldn't bring himself to walk through the employee entrance and face whichever busybodies were in the kitchen.

Tomorrow. Tomorrow he'd apply for a building permit to build an outside entrance to the second floor so he wouldn't feel like he had to run a gantlet just to get home.

Hell. Why did he want to go back, anyway? He'd left the apartment earlier today because it reminded him of her. If he went back now, the same thing would happen. Maybe he should go to Magnus' studio and crash on his sofa. Maybe Mags would be spending the night at Kat's, where he belonged, and he, Soren, could wallow in his self-pity totally alone.

Or maybe he could be a man and face the music. What's a little ribbing among friends? Why get all bent out of shape from comments by well-meaning employees who were like family?

Because he was accustomed to keeping his emotions buried. Of being the aloof one, the uncaring one.

But she'd made him care. Made him feel something for her, made him hope there might be a "them". And then she'd made that ridiculous, woo-woo claim. The lesson he'd learned at age nine still held true—love hurt.

Is that why he felt like shit? Was this what love felt like? If so, Mags could have it.

Love sucked.

Still, the look in Crystal's eyes haunted him. He'd hurt *her*, not the other way around. She'd given him the kind of sex a man only dreamed of, from a body that Penthouse would pay double to photograph, and he'd walked out on her.

Soren slouched down in the cab, rested his head on the headrest and closed his eyes. He could still hear Crystal's laugh, feel her vitality, her very joy of being alive. Could see her lying on the living room rug, her hips tilted upward atop his folded shirt, her melted-chocolate eyes slumberous, her smile dreamy as she watched him smooth the washcloth over her wet pussy. His cock twitched just thinking about how good they were together.

Damn, he was one stupid son of a bitch if he let her slip away from him over a few poorly chosen words. Did it matter *why* she chose him? He should be grateful that she had.

Coming to a decision, he fired up the ignition and roared out of the parking lot. Burning up the road, he soon pulled up to her tidy Cape Cod home and killed the engine. The light near the front door illuminated the porch. The rest of the house was dark. Soren frowned. Had she gone to her grandmother's looking for some sympathy? He got out of the truck and looked through the garage window. Empty.

Damn. Okay, so he had two choices. He could sit there and wait for her to come back, or he could drive the few miles to Grandma's house.

A no-brainer. In minutes he was cursing the traffic lights on Lancaster Avenue as he passed through the business districts of suburban Main Line towns on his way to Devon. With a rueful smile, he remembered his first trip through the fancy gates and up the long driveway in the back seat of Kat's BMW, with Mags behind the wheel keeping their destination a secret in order to get him into Rowena D'Angelo's home for a birthday bash. God, that seemed so long ago.

Now he drove slowly past the darkened house and garage looking for Crystal's Beetle or, for that matter, Grandma's car. Neither was in evidence. Were they together? Had they gone for a nightcap? He glanced at his watch. Nah, it was after one in the morning and the place looked closed up tight. If Grandma was out, she'd also have left a porch light on.

Soren puffed his cheeks and blew out a long breath. Well, it was a half-assed idea anyway. He'd go home, catch some Zs and call her in the morning. Then they could have a good laugh at how he'd reacted when he'd finally come to his senses.

This time when he parked in the lot at Thor's Hammer, he squared his shoulders and strode in through the employee entrance as though he expected no flak.

And he got none, just a couple of nods of acknowledgement in the kitchen. Squelching his impulse to check the bar area, he went directly upstairs, entered the key code for his front door and walked straight through to the bedroom. He could still smell wisps of her perfume, but now it was more comforting than jarring.

He shucked off his clothes, took a quick shower and dried himself off. Damn, he was edgy, didn't want to crawl into bed yet. Slipping on an old pair of running shorts, he decided to numb his mind by watching the boob tube for a while. As he walked through the bedroom, he noticed the blinking light on the answering machine. His pulse quickened. Had she called him?

Hell, why would she? He was the one at fault. He had to make the first move. It was probably one of his brothers. Or a pub employee. No way was he in a mood to handle any more problems tonight.

Dismissing the blinking light, he strode to the living room and began randomly pushing buttons on the TV remote. A few minutes later he heard footsteps coming up the stairs. With a silent curse, Soren muted the TV. If it was Trang or Milton hoping to discuss a problem with him, he'd pretend he'd been asleep and didn't hear them. If no one had jumped him when he'd passed through the kitchen twenty minutes ago, it could wait until tomorrow. Er, morning. Still, he flinched at the hard knock.

"Soren? You alive in there?"

Magnus. What the hell was he doing here at two-fifteen in the morning?

Go away. Images flickering on the screen, he sat in the silent room, willing his brother to go back to his fiancée and leave him alone to brood.

But Magnus was as stubborn as his siblings. Scant seconds later, Soren heard the buttons being pushed on the keyless entry and the door to the apartment opened, spilling a rhomboid of light from the office into the living room.

"What the…how come you're watching TV in the dark?"

Seconds after Magnus asked the question, he flicked a switch and the floor lamp—the room's only lighting fixture—illuminated them both.

With a sigh, Soren said, "Come in, why don't you?"

"Here. Trang sends this with her compliments." Magnus handed him a large Styrofoam container. "Brewed it fresh just for you."

Soren raised an eyebrow but accepted the coffee. "Why would she be so solicitous? More to the point, why are you the delivery boy?"

"Trang called me to say you were taking a vacation day and asked could I fill in tonight at the bar. Kat told me you planned to spend the time with Crystal. Since you came back earlier than anyone expected—Milton saw you in the parking lot a few hours ago, then you left and came back—I put three and three together."

"And got what? Five?" Soren scowled at the flickering image on the TV. Someone was silently demonstrating the latest innovation in cleaning bathroom grout.

"The thought occurred to me that maybe you'd be doing what I did a few months ago. Trying to drink myself into oblivion." Mags lifted Soren's feet off the oversize sofa where he'd been stretched his full length—it was the only seating in the spacious room—and sat on the opposite end.

Sprawled with his feet on the floor, Soren stared at the wall.

"Thorvalds are thickheaded," Magnus continued, working the top off his coffee cup. "Sometimes we jump to conclusions without hearing all the facts."

Soren ripped the tab from the cup's top and took a cautious sip of the hot liquid. Strong, black, and perfectly brewed.

"You remember how furious I was to discover that Kat auctioned herself off for a weekend at her Mexican time-share. I didn't listen when she tried to tell me she'd forgotten all about it, that she had repaid the bid to the charity to get the top bidder off the hook."

Soren slid his tongue around his teeth. He remembered, all right. Magnus, whom he'd never seen drink more than two shots in an evening, had been halfway through the bottle by the time Kat found him on a barstool in Thor's Hammer.

Magnus settled his muscular frame back into the sofa cushions as though he planned to stay a while. "So. You guys have a fight or what?"

Hell. How could he come out and say it without sounding stupid? *Crystal said her magic crystal chose me.* He took a long swallow of coffee and traced a whorling pattern on the tabletop with his eyes. "Do you believe in love at first sight?"

"No shit! You and Crystal?"

"Not me," Soren said, irritated that he'd just blurted it out. "Can a woman instantly 'know'," he used his fingers to put quotation marks around the word, "that she'd met her one and only?"

"I believe," Magnus solemnly drew out the words, "that love is…unpredictable. Inconvenient. Blind to all obstacles. So, yeah, why not at first sight?"

Soren cursed under his breath.

"So what's the problem? She fell in love with you, went to bed with you, and now you're having second thoughts? If she doesn't meet your high standards in the sack, you can always teach—"

"It's not that. She…" Soren ran a large hand down his face. "She's terrific. In and out of—shit. A gentleman doesn't talk about it."

To his credit, Magnus didn't remind him that Soren had never been a gentleman. "Are you…afraid to love her?"

Soren turned his head slowly, surprised by his brother's insight. Surprised at the thought itself. "Yeah. I guess I am. I don't want history to repeat itself."

"You're thinking about Mom."

"Yeah."

They both fell silent for a time. Soren aimed the remote and the screen went blank. "I heard them the day before she left, you know. I had come into the kitchen to get a glass of milk and they were yelling at each other in the dining room. He called her a whore. She laughed in his face. He slammed her against the wall and asked her how long she—" Soren cleared his throat. "That was the first time I heard Dad use the word. He asked her how long she'd been fucking this guy."

"Ouch."

"Apparently Dad opened a love letter addressed to Mom and realized she'd been cheating on him. He slapped her around a bit. She asked for a divorce. He said over his dead body. And then, just like that, she was gone."

Magnus turned to face him. Soren noticed his brother's eyes were shiny and wondered if his looked the same. They felt pinched and wet.

"So you're afraid Crystal will eventually cheat on you."

Soren said nothing.

"Or you're afraid you'll wind up like Dad, slapping her around for real or imagined infractions."

"Imagined…? No. If the letter was what he said it was, I guess I could understand why he hit her. I hope I'd never lose control like that, but maybe he was justified."

Magnus set down his coffee cup. "I saw him hit her once." His voice was low, harsh. "She'd burned the hamburgers and he gave her a fist to the stomach. Where it wouldn't be visible to anyone else."

"You're kidding."

Magnus let out a big sigh. "Maybe she had reason to leave him."

Soren considered this. "That possibility never occurred to me. At nine years old, all I saw was that a woman did something with another man that enraged her husband and then she left him and abandoned their three children. I swore never to be so much in love that someone could have that kind of power over me."

"Does she?"

"What?"

"Does Crystal have that kind of power over you?"

Soren barked out a short laugh. "Yeah. I want her for real, Mags. I want to wake up with her beside me for the rest of my life."

"Scary, isn't it. I feel that way about Kat. And I'd sworn off women after the experience with my ex-wife." Magnus clapped a hand on his brother's shoulder. "Like I said, love can be damn inconvenient. But sometimes, it's just too big, too strong to ignore."

"Yeah. It's like an eight-hundred-pound elephant sitting on my chest."

Magnus chuckled. "I'd say that's love."

"But still—"

"Trying to weasel out of it? Lots of luck, bro."

"No, it's not that. She—hell. Don't laugh at this. That thing Crystal always wears on a chain around her neck? She told me her grandmother gave it to her on her thirteenth birthday. It's apparently some kind of voodoo charm that was supposed to tell her when she'd met 'The One'." He used his fingers again to make quotation marks around the words. "That's what Crystal called me. 'The One'. She said that when she saw me on stage at the Bachelor Dinner Auction, the crystal damn near burned her chest, so she knew I was the man she was supposed to−" he cleared his throat and rushed the rest of the words so he'd be sure to get them out, "to give her virginity to."

"Well. A woman who waits thirty years to, uh, have her first intimate experience with a man probably wouldn't want to look for excitement outside of marriage." Magnus paused before adding, "And a man who has a woman who gives that kind of commitment to a relationship isn't likely to chase her away by knocking her around."

Soren grabbed the TV remote off the table and flipped it round and round in his hands. "I guess they were both at fault. Mom and Dad, I mean. It looks a little different from the vantage point of thirty-four as opposed to when I was nine years old. I never forgave her for abandoning us. But now…"

"Yeah. Two sides to every story." After another stretch of silence, Magnus pushed himself off the sofa. "Well, it's late. I'll leave you to your pondering."

Soren stood with him. "Thanks. For everything." He ran his fingers through his hair. "Maybe you should try to get in touch with Mom. Like you said, two sides. I'd hate to think I carried a grudge all these years and it wasn't all her fault."

"I'll do that. Get some sleep, man."

"You too." He touched Magnus on the shoulder. "Give Kat a hug for me."

"It'll be my pleasure."

* * * * *

"Come now, Patty. Your bath awaits you."

Crystal opened her eyes to slits. She had squinched them shut to keep the pain at bay and the tears unshed. After uncounted minutes of scouring her skin from neck to ankles, Jack had untied her upraised leg, thankfully giving her back her balance, then went to fill the tub. Her skin felt like raw hamburger that had just been run through a meat grinder.

"I'm sorry if I hurt you. Please believe me, it's for your own good." He reached up and unhooked her right hand from the ring in the ceiling, but the manacle still ringed her wrist. She breathed a sigh of relief when her arm swung down—until the pins and needles started stabbing her nerve endings awake.

Before her sluggish brain had a chance to shift into escape mode, he had detached her other wrist and locked both rings together so her hands were bound in front of her.

"Let me help you," he said, as solicitous as a candy striper in a nursing home. He cupped both her elbows, holding his arm carefully behind her back so as not to touch the abraded flesh.

"There's Epsom salts in the water," he explained as he guided her to the tub. "It will comfort your skin while it cleanses. In you go."

Crystal hesitated, noticing that her jacket, sweatshirt and tights where still where she'd dropped them. She wondered how long her battery would last if the phone was still connected to Soren's number. She eyed her clothes longingly. But with her hands cuffed together, she wouldn't be able to cover her nakedness even if she could manage to escape. Better to follow his instructions and wait for an opportune moment.

Grasping the grab bar on the near side of the tub with her manacled hands, Crystal gingerly stepped into the tub. Relief washed over her as she found the temperature to be warm as a womb. She lowered herself into the water. The salts did indeed seem a balm to her reddened skin and she let her head fall back to rest on the rim of the tub, where he'd thoughtfully provided an air pillow held in place by suction cups. For just a moment she allowed her mind to go blank, to enjoy the silence and the peace.

The sound of metal clinking on metal woke her. How could she have fallen asleep in her predicament? Then she realized it had to be the middle of the night. Her body had simply had too much trauma.

Shivering, she jerked her arms then realized what the clinking sound was that had awakened her. The handcuffs were now linked to the grab bar. And the water had been emptied from the tub. Goose bumps blossomed on her wet skin from the chilly air.

"One more cleansing ritual tonight, Patty."

Crystal slewed her head to the sound of Jack's voice at her ear. She saw he was kneeling at the side of the tub, holding an old-fashioned hot-water bottle with a long hose and a nozzle. With his free hand he scooped up her leg and draped it over the side of the tub.

"We must rid the impurity from the inside as well."

* * * * *

After they'd gathered the empty Styrofoam cups and tossed them into the trash, Magnus left. Soren turned off the floor lamp then went to the bedroom. The blinking red light was like a fire-engine bell in his mind's eye.

"Hell. You're too wound up to sleep. You might as well listen." He walked to the phone to check the messages. Only one. Good. He pushed the "Play" button and heard the tinny voice announce, "Thursday, eleven-forty-seven p.m."

"…why you made a special suite of rooms for me in the basement of Time Treasures. None of the rooms have windows…"

Soren's brain came fully alert. That was Crystal's voice! What the hell—

"I will explain it all when the time is right."

He wasn't positive, but the voice sounded like the man he helped Crystal take the cherry dresser to. Yeah, right. Jack something. The antique storeowner. He focused all his attention on the recording.

"…in a separate room? Are you planning to keep me a prisoner here in the cellar of Time Treasures?"

Holy shit! Had Jack Healy kidnapped Crystal? Without considering that he still wore only his running shorts, Soren dashed out of the apartment and down the steps, pushed open the employee's entrance door. "Mags! Wait!"

Thank God, Mags had still been sitting behind the wheel in the parking lot, no doubt calling Kat to say he was on his way home.

"Mags! Come back! I need your help!"

When Magnus got out of his truck and walked up, Soren blurted out, "Hurry up. You gotta hear this." He dragged him back upstairs and through the open doorway.

"Listen." He pushed the "replay" button. The message started in the middle of a sentence.

"…why you made a special suite of rooms for me in the basement of Time Treasures. None of the rooms have windows. You know how much I love the sunshine."

"I will explain it all when the time is right."

Magnus made a move as if to ask whose voice it was, but Soren shushed him and pointed to the answering machine and mouthed, *Listen.*

"Can you at least tell me who Patty is?"

The brothers exchanged glances then shrugged. Neither knew a Patty.

Crystal's voice again. "Is Grandma here too? In the basement of your shop? Are you holding Rowena hostage in a separate room?" A pause. "Are you planning to keep me a prisoner here in the cellar of Time Treasures?"

Seconds ticked by with no conversation. The sound of…running water?…reached Soren's ears.

"I'm soaping myself up, Jack. I'll be done in a minute. Keep your back to the door, okay? I'll let you know when I'm—"

Soaping herself up? Soren's hackles raised to think that this Jack character was anywhere near her if she was in the shower, or even at a sink, exposing any part of her anatomy to him. He heard a series of noises, footsteps clacking on tile, metal clanging against metal, then…

"What the—a handcuff? Jack, what are you doing? Turn me loose!"

"Did you think you could wash away all the filth in two minutes?"

Shit! He wanted to jump inside the telephone and pull the son of a bitch away from her, but forced himself to listen. To think. Crystal had deliberately called him to let him know she was being held a prisoner in Time Treasures, so he concentrated on her voice, hoping to pick up whatever clues she was savvy enough to drop for him.

"Let me go!" A yelp of pain.

"You did not listen to me, Patty."

Soren cursed. If that bastard harmed her, he'd be eating his balls for lunch when Soren finished working him over.

"I will not hurt you, my dear. You have my—"

A harsh beep sounded. The recording had filled its allotted time.

He checked the bedside clock. Four-twelve a.m. "Jesus. She made that call more than four hours ago!"

"Calm down." Magnus laid a hand on Soren's shoulder. "It sounds like she's not in any immediate danger. He said he wouldn't hurt her. Go put some clothes on while I listen to it again. This time I want to focus on background noises."

While Soren dressed in jeans, dark turtleneck sweater and steel-toed lumberjack boots, they played the recording twice more.

"Either the grandmother's out cold or she's not there," Magnus decided.

"She could be, though." Soren explained his earlier trek to Rowena's home looking for Crystal's car. "Maybe he has them in separate rooms. Let's go. I don't want to take the chance that he's blowing smoke when he said he wouldn't hurt her."

"We should have a plan first."

"We'll come up with one after we reconnoiter."

"Okay. Lead the way."

Chapter Seventeen

📖

The grating of a key in the metal lock jolted Crystal awake. Fear sluiced through her as she found herself immobile. Fighting panic, she glanced at her surroundings. White on white on white.

She squeezed her eyes shut as memories slammed back into her. *Jack Healy*. A mentally unbalanced Jack Healy, calling her Patty, holding her hostage. Scraping her skin raw. Dear God, shoving a douche up her most private orifices with what he'd assured her was only soapy water. Purifying her, he'd said.

Realizing she was in a reclining chair that held her almost supine with knees slightly bent, Crystal tried to sit up but couldn't move. Her forearms were tied to the armrests, her feet bound to the footrest. She was wearing a long white terrycloth robe and white fuzzy slippers. Her heart pounded against her ribs. How could she have fallen asleep under such frightening circumstances? How long had she been out? With no windows to see whether it was sunny or dark outside, she had no way of knowing.

"How are you feeling?"

She tried to manufacture a smile as Jack Healy walked into the room. "I have to go to the bathroom."

Without acknowledging her request, Jack turned on some music. From hidden speakers Crystal heard what sounded like Gregorian chants, men's voices singing Latin in unison without accompaniment.

"Jack, this isn't funny. Don't let me embarrass myself. Untie me."

"In a minute." He turned back to the door to the hallway and locked it with the key he still wore on a leather thong around his neck. Then he opened a panel in the wall and unrolled a length of chain. One end was apparently moored to the wall. The other connected to a hinged metal circlet whose diameter was approximately the size of a neck.

Crystal swallowed hard, her eyes riveted to the circlet, as Jack loomed over her. "Don't worry. It's long enough to reach the bathroom. I'm not trying to punish you, believe me." The click as the cold metal snapped shut around her neck sounded in her ears like a gunshot.

She barely dared to breathe. The iron burden of her restraint settled on her collarbones. "Why, Jack? Why are you doing this?"

"You know why, Patty. You have to be pure to reenter the novitiate."

She bit down hard on the urge to correct him. *I'm not Patty*! Then focused on the last word. *Novitiate*. Didn't that have something to do with becoming a nun? Was that why the Gregorian chants?

"Our stepfather will never touch you again. I can assure you of that." Almost tenderly, he gathered the hair that had gotten trapped inside the heavy collar and pulled it away from her neck. "There. That should be more comfortable."

"I'll be more comfortable if you let me go to the bathroom."

"Of course." He bent down and unwrapped the bindings at her wrists, her ankles, then pulled the lever to bring the chair upright. "Up you go."

Once on her feet, Crystal had to stop a moment to stabilize herself against the corner end table. Her legs felt cramped from being in the same position for too long.

From her peripheral vision she saw the hated painting swing away from the wall to reveal the bathroom. She took careful steps until she was inside then turned back to close the door behind her.

"The door stays open. You know there are no secrets between brother and sister."

Crystal's heart pounded against her breastbone. Did he think she was his *sister*? All the years she'd known Jack Healy, he never mentioned any family.

"Go ahead and do your business," he said. "I won't look. In fact, I have some things to do. I'll be back shortly."

When she spied her clothes exactly where she'd discarded them earlier, her heart missed a beat then pounded back double-time. Would the chain allow her to reach the jacket with its cell phone? Or had Jack found it?

She used the toilet then took advantage of the noise of flushing to cover the sounds of fabric rustling. Reaching to the limit of her chain, she barely managed grab a handful of jacket and pull it toward her. She thrust her hand inside the jacket pocket. It was still there! With a trembling finger she pushed what she hoped was Soren's speed-dial button. Only then did she discard the white robe and yank on her sweatshirt and tights.

No sound emanated from the adjacent room. She hadn't heard the lock snick open or the door close. Had Jack gone? Defiantly she pulled the jacket on as well, patting the pocket to be sure the phone nestled securely in it, and walked out. "Jack?"

Her gaze bounced around the room as she made as much of a circle as she could at the end of the chain. No Jack. She pulled the phone to her ear.

"It's your dime. Talk."

Oh no, she'd gotten his voice mail again! She spoke in a rapid whisper. "Soren, please, if you're there, pick up the phone! Jack Healy's got me locked in the basement of Time Treasures. I'm in a room to the left of the stairs. There's no window and only the one entrance. He's crazy, Soren. He thinks I'm his sister Patty who needs to be purified. He probably also has Grandma, although he won't say one way or another. Please, no matter when you hear this, please come to Time Treasures and—"

Her breath hitched. "Gotta go, I hear him." She clicked off and thrust the phone back into her pocket. The chain clinking as she moved, Crystal sank onto the white sofa just before the outside door swung open and Jack walked in.

When he spied her in her own clothes, his smile turned into a frown. "I should have laid out your clothes before I left. Those rags belong in the trash. I want you to put on your habit."

He walked to the white armoire and opened the long narrow door. "Here." He removed a white…something…from a padded hanger and laid it over the arm of the sofa. "Get changed. Now. Those tight, bright things are an obscenity."

"No! I mean, no," she said more softly. "I'm thirsty. Can I have some orange juice? Or a soda? A cup of hot tea?"

He came around the sofa and stood before her. "Do as I say! If you continue to wear those secular clothes, I'll have to scrub you clean again. Do you understand me?"

Crystal gulped. Her skin still burned in places where he'd abraded it with the loofah. But more importantly, would he rip them off her if she didn't comply? *And find the phone?*

She stood up like a humble penitent, since that's what he apparently wanted to make her. "You're correct, of course. If you turn your back, I'll change."

Reaching for the costume, she took the heavy woolen pieces apart and examined them. The gown, cut in a modest A-line to her ankles, had long, wide sleeves and a placket opening in the front. Apparently it was usually slipped over the head, but the hateful chain precluded that.

With her heart pounding, she slid the jacket off her arms and let it sink to the sofa in a pile. Her breath stopped when the phone slid halfway out of the pocket. She ripped off the sweatshirt and tossed it down, trying at the same time to shove the phone behind the cushion. She shucked off her tights and hurriedly stepped into the gown and fastened the buttons.

Next she lifted a long, lined panel about eighteen inches wide with a hole in the middle, apparently the neckline, with a crudely sewn tab and Velcro closure on one side. She shuddered to think of Jack Healy's premeditation in altering the garment with the chain in mind. When she donned it, the panel hung down to her calves in front and back. A starched collar that covered her neck and shoulders snapped in the back. She drew a blank at how to secure the headgear and left it on the sofa. All the while she was conscious of the chain rattling inordinately loud in the silent room.

"That's my girl. You look radiant, Patty. We'll get you back on track."

"How long will it take? Do you plan to keep me here the whole time?"

Jack just gave her a superior look, as if she should know better than to question her brother's judgment. "I'll take these rags and burn them."

Hiding her panic, Crystal spun around. "Let me get them for you." She bent forward and shuffled the clothes around, her fingers searching for the hard plastic of the phone. *There*! She stuffed it further behind the cushion, gathered the three pieces in her hands and turned back to—

"What are you hiding?"

"Nothing! What makes you say that?" She made to sit down on top of the phone, clothes clenched in her fists.

"No! Sit down on the reclining chair. Now!"

Hesitating a moment, Crystal saw the fanatical gleam in his eye and obeyed, watching as he delved behind and between the sofa cushions with his hands. "A cell phone? Patty, have you been in touch with anyone?"

"No," she lied, jutting her chin. "I...I had, um, forgotten I had it with me until just now when it fell out of my jacket. I hoped I could call Grandma after you went back about your business."

"I see." He opened the phone, examined it. Pressed a speed-dial button. Listened.

Crystal fought to keep any emotion from her face, to keep her fingers from tensing around the clothes.

Jack grunted. "Got Rowena's voice mail."

He pushed another button and waited. Narrowed his eyes at her. "Who is Deirdra?"

"A friend. You've met her. She runs Good Vibrations."

A third button. Then he smiled. "I'm flattered. You have Time Treasures on your speed-dial."

Crystal instinctively looked up, as if she could see through the ceiling and into the first floor. She hadn't heard the shop's phone ring. Were these old buildings constructed so sturdily that you couldn't hear through walls? Or—more distressing— had he soundproofed this room so no one would hear her pleas for help?

Quickly she masked her concern. "Of course I would. It only makes sense that when I'm out in the field looking for treasures, I'd want to reach you easily."

Another excruciating wait until he said, "Two numbers for Rowena?"

She swallowed. "Yes. The second one is her cell."

"Well, it won't do you any good. She won't be home for some time." With a chuckle, Jack slid her cell phone into the pocket of his white shirt.

Crystal shot off the chair, the chain slapping against her chest, and grabbed his arm. "Where is she? Is she here?"

"In due time, my dear. All will be revealed in due time." Shoving her gently back into the reclining chair, he spun on his heel and walked out the door. With a sinking feeling in the pit of her stomach, she heard the lock click home.

At least he hadn't discovered Soren's number.

Yet.

* * * * *

"Hell. Looks like a coal chute. No wonder they didn't alarm it."

Soren aimed the Maglite down the truncated shaft connected to the tiny basement window of Time Treasures. When they'd examined the perimeter, they discovered that only the first floor was alarmed—the showroom windows and front entrance, a pair of small side windows and the double-door delivery entrance.

The window in question was set into a jog in a corner of the rear wall. Soren theorized that in the early 1900s, when the building was new, the jog had allowed a truck to back up to the window with its coal delivery and still leave the alleyway free to other traffic.

Five-foot-wide paths of uneven brick paving separated the building from its neighbors on either side. They had parked Soren's truck so their activities would be shielded from passers-by—although at five in the morning, they hoped no one would be about.

They went to work with crowbars and whatever else Soren had stored in the tool chest in the truck bed, jimmying the ancient wood to remove the window and its connecting chute. With a sigh of relief, Soren pulled it out and set it aside.

He stuck his head through the opening, the Maglite shedding light now in every direction. "The walls look sooty, so this must be the old coal bin. It's maybe six by ten feet, with a two-section Dutch door. They're using it for a junk room. Broken furniture, old beams, two-by-fours."

"Think you can fit?" Magnus asked from behind him.

"I'll get in. Even if it strips off pieces of my skin," Soren said through gritted teeth. The opening was no more than twenty inches by twelve. If he jockeyed himself through the opening diagonally, one shoulder at a time, he thought he could just make it. "Grab my ankles. Let's get this show on the road."

When he felt Magnus' grip, Soren thrust one arm downward through the gaping hole, holding the other arm tight at his side. It took him a couple of minutes of wiggling and squirming to shove the expanse of his shoulders cater-corner past the solid stone foundation, in the process ripping holes in his sweater. Where his skin wasn't scraped bloody, he knew there would be bruises—a small price to pay for Crystal's safety.

Once he got his other arm in front of him, Soren targeted the bottom half of a two-piece Hoosier kitchen cabinet missing all its drawers and doors. He felt Magnus lift his feet into the air then lower him slowly through the opening like a diver knifing through water. Gripping the cabinet's edges with his hands, Soren placed all his weight on his arms and jiggled his left foot, the signal for Magnus to let it go. Slowly he lowered that leg until his knee touched the cabinet. Then he jiggled the other leg, and in a moment was balanced on his knees.

Soren scrambled to his feet and turned back to the window.

Magnus was already shoving the pack of tools through the opening. "And last but not least, here's the phone."

"Be sure to thank Kat again," Soren said as he took the high-tech unit. At Magnus' urgent call, Kat had unhesitatingly met them at Time Treasures to add her cell phone to his, bringing his special tools and an offer to help. Mags had shooed her back home.

Soren hooked the earpiece that would keep him in touch with his brother via hands-free phone, clipped the unit to his belt, and pushed the proper speed-dial button. Identical units, both were set to vibrate, not ring.

"How do I sound?"

"Loud and clear," said Soren in a low voice. "Let's hope I get Crystal out of here before the battery runs down." He worked his way through the discarded furniture and odds and ends of lumber to the Dutch door that still held smudges of ancient coal dust. Since there was no lock, knob or latch on this side, he unscrewed the hinges of the top half.

"Piece of cake," he said as he reached over the opened half for the latch on the bottom segment. Playing the Maglite over the room the Dutch door opened into, he murmured, "The old boiler's still here. Fat arms radiating out to the ceiling like an octopus. Geez, imagine filling that monster with coal every hour."

Wending his way around more hulking shapes of junk, he reported, "Found another door. Oh. Utilities. Modern heating unit, hot water heater, circuit box." He pulled the metal ring and opened the box, played the Maglite over the breakers. "Damn, the circuit breakers are marked only with numbers, not locations. May need to shut them all down. We'll play it by ear."

He closed the box then the door, tried another door. "Locked. This one faces the front."

Magnus chuckled in his ear. "Good think I asked Kat to bring that set of picks."

"Yeah." He rummaged in the pack and found the tools under discussion. "Got it."

"Don't forget. Oil the hinges first. Just in case."

Soren squirted them then cautiously swung the door inward. He lowered his voice to a mere whisper. "This looks like a portion of a hallway that was simply blocked off with a door, like a reverse foyer, although I can't imagine why. I see the underside of the stairway. No risers. Let's see what I can see through the treads. There's some weak light coming from the left, maybe a forty-watt bulb."

"Want me to follow you in?" Magnus' voice was a low rumble in Soren's ear.

"No. You stay there and tell me if someone's coming."

"Roger. Just let me know if you need me."

Soren peeked through the treads at various heights into the hallway. "The wall to my left has a door and the hallway goes around to the stairs. Looks like a solid wall ahead, unless there's a door that I can't see from here. I'm going to try to pick this lock."

He didn't question why Mags had a set of lock picks. As a woodworker, Mags had to have occasions when, working a piece of furniture, he came across something whose key was lost. He could only be grateful that his brother had them available and that Kat was able to find them. And that he'd gotten a crash course on how to use them.

"Got it open. I'm going in. If I hear a noise like someone's inside and I have to retreat, I'll say 'walnut' and you stand by to haul me out the window. I'm going to stop talking now, but I'll leave the line open."

"Roger."

Slowly, adrenaline rising, Soren pushed open the door to the hallway. He checked all the corners, the floor, the ceiling, looking for a security camera. Nothing. He took a half-dozen steps, noted there was no peephole then placed his ear to the door. Breathing shallowly, he listened.

Silence.

Was she in there? Was she alone? If he tried to bash the door down like a SWAT team, would Jack harm her? Use her as a human shield with a gun to her temple? Soren swore silently. He'd never been more scared in his life. What if he did the wrong thing and caused some harm to Crystal?

He slammed down on that thought. She was fine. He'd get her out of here safely. He had to. His own life depended on it.

Taking a deep breath, he tried—very quietly, very carefully—to turn the doorknob.

Locked.

Slipping a screwdriver out of the pack slung over his shoulder, he knocked the handle once, lightly, on the door. Waited with his ear to the solid wooden panel. No threatening male voice. No Crystal either.

He rapped twice. Waited.

What was that? It sounded like a clink of metal. He froze, held his breath.

Another sound, like a chain rattling.

He did another double knock with the screwdriver handle. Pressed his ear, his hand, to the door, as if trying to find a heartbeat. Please, please, let her be there, let her be safe.

Just then he heard the sound of a door opening above him. At the top of the stairs.

Soren faded back into the anteroom and closed the door quietly. He watched through the spaces as a pair of well-shod feet with heavy footfalls came into view on the stair treads, then a bulky body. Jack Healy, carrying a tray.

He wanted to jump that slimy bastard right now and beat the shit out of him, but forced himself to bide his time. He had to see where that cocksucking motherfucker kept the key. Had to be sure Crystal was indeed behind that locked door before he showed himself. He silently slipped the pack off his shoulder and let it slide to the floor.

Shifting the tray to his left hand, Healy fiddled with something around his neck then leaned forward. *The key*, thought Soren. *He wears the key around his neck.*

Soren waited until he heard the snick of the tumblers. While Healy was still stooped over, he burst out from behind the door, a screwdriver and the element of surprise his only weapons. The tray in Healy's hand clattered to the floor. Glass shattered, orange liquid spilled. Soren jumped on him like a hungry tiger, crashing both of them onto the cement.

He landed on top, knocking the breath out of the older man. But Healy was in excellent physical shape, as Soren discovered when he was flipped onto his back in a martial-arts move he didn't see coming. In seconds the kidnapper had his fat thumbs on Soren's neck, pressing into his artery. Soren swung his fisted arm to Healy's face, piercing his cheek with the screwdriver.

Healy yelped in pain and, blood spurting, loosed his hold on Soren's neck. Soren gained his feet and landed a solid kick with his steel-toed boot on the man's kidney. Still, Healy managed to grab his boot and topple Soren off-balance.

Soren crashed to the floor. Heard a gunshot.

Then everything went black.

Chapter Eighteen

ಬಂ

Holy hell, a gunshot. "Soren! Talk to me! Are you all right?"

Magnus bolted to his feet. It would take him too long to squeeze himself through that tiny window space. He ran to the delivery door in the back, slammed his six-foot-five frame shoulder first, felt the locks give and heard the alarm go off as the doors burst open. *Good.* Let the cops come. They could use the help.

Beaming the spare flashlight around the large room, he did a quick mental calculation as his savvy gaze scanned what looked like part workshop, part storeroom. On the wall to his right he saw three doors and opened the nearest one. This smaller room held junk pieces rather than salvageable works. *There!* On the far right. That had to be the door to the basement.

When he opened the door, he saw the stairway illuminated by a weak glow. He grabbed a thick slab of tabletop as though it was made of cardboard. If he was going into a gunfight, it wouldn't do his brother any good if he was shot dead before he reached the bottom. Rock maple wouldn't perform like a Kevlar vest, but he recognized that the plinth attached to the underside of the slab would help slow a bullet's velocity and reduce the damage to his gut.

Holding it as a shield on his left side, Magnus took the stairs two at a time with a Viking yell announcing a formidable and fearless adversary. The gunshot was horribly loud in the enclosed space. It crashed through the maple and pierced his left biceps. The table dipped momentarily and he fought to keep his torso protected.

"Stop! Stop or I'll shoot the man on the ground!"

Warily, Magnus peered around the edge of the tabletop. Soren lay at Jack Healy's feet, blood painting an ugly red blossom on the cement under and around his head. The gun in Healy's hand was aimed at Soren's heart.

"Get back! Go back up the stairs. Go on up or I'll shoot him!"

Magnus swallowed hard. He stared at his brother's unmoving form. Relief flooded him as he detected a slight rise and fall of his chest. *Still alive!* If he did as directed, the guy was loony enough to shoot Soren anyway. *Dear God, please tell me what to do!*

"Back up. Do it!"

Magnus' gaze moved to Soren's face. Was that a double twitch at the corner of his mouth? Was he trying to signal?

"All right. Take it easy. I'll go back. But only if you aim that gun at me instead of him."

Healy looked at Magnus as if he were the crazy one. He held Healy's stare coolly. "If you shoot Soren, you're a dead man, because you won't be able to get both of us. I'll be on you like flies on horseshit before you can pull the trigger a second time."

Time stood still. He could see Healy hesitate, waver.

The gun hand lifted. "Put down the table. I want a clear shot at your heart."

Thoughts of Kat flitted through Magnus' mind. What she'd do, how she'd react if he died. But he couldn't leave Soren defenseless, bleeding to death on the cold cement. *I love you, Kat*, he sent the thought winging its way to her. *But I have to rush this madman and try to save my brother.*

Just as he tensed to leap forward, the door to the forbidden room swung open.

"Jack, help me! I've been raped!"

Crystal appeared in the doorway wearing some kind of white nun's habit, ripped down the middle. It hung off one shoulder and bared her breast down to her waist.

"Patty!" The name tore out of Healy's gut with undisguised anguish.

In a flash Soren hooked his steel-toed boot around Healy's ankle, toppling him backwards. The gun flew out of his hand. Magnus kicked it aside and slammed the tabletop down on the kidnapper's face, hearing a satisfying crunch of bone. When he lifted it off, Healy was whimpering through a broken nose and several loose teeth, bleeding from the mouth, nose and a nasty gash on his forehead.

Good! The bastard.

"Crystal! Ohmigod, Crystal, are you all right?" Soren staggered to his feet as Crystal stood motionless about a foot inside the room, arms outstretched to him.

"Soren, you're bleeding!"

Soren engulfed her in a bear hug, repeating her name over and over. "Oh God, if anything had happened to you, I…"

Voice breaking, he cleared his throat. His hands smoothed up and down her arms, her torso, checking methodically for broken bones. "Are you okay? Who raped you? Did Healy have an accomplice? I swear, we'll get him too, and they'll never hurt you again."

He took a step back, as if just realizing she hadn't snuggled into him as tightly, as intimately, as he'd expected. "Crystal?"

It hit him then. The thick iron neck restraint, the heavy chain pulled taut behind her. The fact that Crystal hadn't moved a single step since she'd first appeared in his line of vision inside the room. "That son of a bitch!" he roared, spinning on his heel.

In two long strides he reached the bleeding kidnapper sprawled on the cement floor. He gave him a vicious kick in the ribs for good measure then grabbed him by his thick gray hair in one fist and his shirt front in the other, jerked him to his feet and slammed him against the wall.

"You bastard! You caged her like an animal!" He ripped open Healy's shirt, buttons popping unnoticed to the floor, and yanked the leather thong hanging around his neck, forcing Healy to stagger into the room after him like a dog on a leash.

He scrutinized the two keys jangling on the thong. "This damn well better open the goddamn ring you put around her neck, or you'll find yourself with my screwdriver up your sorry ass."

With trembling fingers he fitted the smaller key to the lock holding the two halves of the circlet together. The lock snicked open. Tears pricked Soren's eyes when he snapped the hinges open and saw the raw red marks on Crystal's neck.

"You cocksucking maniac!" He spun around to Healy and snapped the circlet onto the heavy man's neck. It was a tight fit and he had to push hard to get the lock to click shut. He wanted to pinch a sliver of skin inside, but it wouldn't close that way. "There, you motherfucker. See how you like it!" With a hard shove, he sent Healy windmilling backwards until he fell half on the pristine white sofa and half on the white carpet, and proceeded to bleed copiously all over both.

Healy disposed of and instantly forgotten, Soren whirled back to Crystal. Tenderly he cupped her face in his hands, kissed her eyes, nose, cheeks, ears, then bent down to drop soft butterfly kisses on the angry red marks around her neck.

He kissed his way back up her jaw, kissed each corner of her mouth, took her lips in the softest, most reverent kiss he could give her. "Did you— Did he—" Soren cleared his throat. "Do you need a…a rape kit so we can put him behind bars?"

Crystal gave him a melting smile. "No one raped me, Soren. Jack was fixated on me because I reminded him of his sister, Patty. Who *was* raped many years ago. He was trying to 'save' me from the same fate. So I figured the only way to divert his attention from you was to rip this outfit and look like I was raped."

Soren's legs almost collapsed in relief. He locked his knees and embraced her again, as gently as he could. "I'll make it up to you, I swear I will. I was such a fool to blow my stack over a piece of rock. I want—"

"Ma'am? Ma'am? Excuse me. The gentleman with the bullet hole in his arm refuses to be treated until we look at you first."

Soren wrenched his gaze from Crystal to look around. The police had Jack Healy in handcuffs and two EMTs milled around in the crowded hallway.

"Not me," Crystal said softly, looking at Soren with love in her eyes. "This man is bleeding from a head wound. I refuse treatment until you check him out."

And the two big strong Viking men could not change her mind.

Epilogue

ജ

Crystal lifted her chin, peered at her reflection in the dressing table mirror and frowned. Just one more dab should do it.

Seated at her old vanity bench, she reached a finger into the jar of stage makeup and patted the shadow of a bruise on her neck. *There. Perfect.* She wanted no remnant of last week's ordeal to mar the joy of today's special occasion.

Closing her eyes, she tried to imagine Soren in a tux, standing as best man for his brother Magnus. She couldn't wait to see him, to dance with him, hold him close to her. Between rescuing Grandma, everyone's overnight stay in the hospital for observation and treatment, talking to the police for hours on end, and helping Grandma with last-minute preparations for today, she hadn't had the opportunity to be alone with him.

Discovering that Jack Healy had erected a hunting blind in a tree that gave him a clear telescopic view into her bedroom had shaken Crystal to her core. She immediately put her Cape Cod home up for sale and moved back to Rowena's home.

Now Rowena breezed into the bedroom Crystal had used since she came to live with her grandmother so many years ago. "Ready for the festivities?" Rowena asked.

Crystal turned, looked deeply into her grandmother's eyes. "Are you sure you're okay?"

The police had found Rowena gagged and trussed up like a Thanksgiving turkey in a closet inside the office of Time Treasures, groggy but unharmed. "Child, it'll take more than an SOB of his ilk to keep me tied down for long. I'm more concerned about you."

"I'm fine. Really."

"Good. That nice detective just called me." She sat down beside her granddaughter on the vanity bench. "He pretty much confirmed what Healy told you. His sister was studying to become a nun. She was nineteen, he was eleven."

She took Crystal's smooth hand in her wrinkled one. "She came home for a visit, there was some sort of family problem involving the stepfather, but it was hushed up. Three months later, Patricia Healy died from a botched abortion. Eight years later, the stepfather died in an automobile accident. The brakes failed. Experts couldn't agree as to whether they were tampered with. Jack Healy was never a suspect in that incident."

Their gazes met. Crystal absorbed the implications in silence.

Rowena put an arm around Crystal's shoulder. "I'm sorry to just blurt this out. I should have waited until after the festivities."

"No, it's all right." Crystal tilted her head so their foreheads were touching. "I'm glad you told me. I needed to hear it. It all fits. And it will be added to the—what do they call it?— preponderance of evidence when he goes to trial."

Crystal manufactured a smile and changed the subject. "It was very generous of you to offer Kat and Magnus the use of your home this afternoon. It's a perfect setting for a storybook wedding."

The older woman shrugged. "We Platinum Society members help each other out."

"Still, I'll be happy when all the hoopla dies down."

Rowena nodded with a knowing leer. "Yes, I expect you and Soren have things to…discuss. You'll have plenty of time. As soon as the caterer is discharged, Trey and I are going to the Poconos for a long weekend. So you and Soren can *talk* to your hearts' content. There'll be no one in the house tonight except you."

Crystal's heartbeat raced. *Yes. Tonight.* Heat shot into her pussy just thinking about tonight. She wondered how many clothes they would manage to shed before—

"Excuse me, Miss Crystal, the groomsmen have arrived. My, don't you look pretty."

"Thank you, Tonya." She did a pirouette for Rowena's longtime personal assistant. She *felt* pretty in the new Caroline Herrera she'd splurged on for the occasion, a one-shoulder confection of softest, sheerest layers of peach silk with a handkerchief hemline. She'd purposely not applied lipstick, hoping to catch Soren before the bulk of the guests arrived and give him a hot, I've-missed-you kiss.

Feeling almost like a bride herself, she raced down the stairs in her stockinged feet.

And there he was.

She stopped on the bottom step and admired the broad, tuxedo-clad back, the tight buns exposed as Soren stood in a casual pose, hands in his pockets, in the foyer with Magnus. He'd removed the bandage on his skull where he'd cracked his head on the cement during his fight with Healy.

As if sensing her presence, he spun around and with two long strides stood before her. His gaze roved across her face then zeroed in on her neck. Bringing his hands to her throat, he tenderly explored her skin, running his fingertips from jaw to collarbone and around to the back of her neck. "How do you feel?"

"Pretty good, but I'll feel better if you kiss me."

Cupping the back of her head with both hands, he dipped his head and touched his lips to each corner of her mouth then placed a gentle kiss in the center. "I was so scared," he murmured. "I would have killed him if he harmed you."

She leaned into him, stopping further words with a more earthy, insistent kiss. Her mouth opened, demanding his tongue, and he obliged without hesitation. Wrapping her arms around his shoulders, she reveled in the feel, the taste of him, the unique male smell of him, soap and fresh air and deep woods overlain with a hint of citrus.

"Crystal," he groaned. "In about fifteen minutes I'm going to have to stand in front of a bunch of people. It's going to take at least that long to get rid of my boner."

Her eyes sparkled. "Just wanted you to know that I've missed you."

With that she dashed up the steps to finish dressing.

* * * * *

"He looks nervous, doesn't he?"

"He should, dear. He's the groom."

Crystal's gaze snapped to Rowena. "Not Magnus. Soren! He looks like he's going to faint."

"Probably because it's the first time in his life he's had to wear a suit."

"Grandma, hush!" Crystal hid her smile behind her program as the two women mingled with the forty or so guests in the huge foyer waiting for the bride to descend the spectacular curved staircase. At the bottom of the steps, Soren stood next to his brother the groom, knees visibly shaking.

A hush settled over the group as Kat's best friend, Lyssa, preceded the bride. On the arm of Robert Savidge, a key player along with Kat and Rowena in the Platinum Society, a glowing Kat Donaldson glided down the steps, looking ethereal and striking in a filmy ivory-colored gown that flowed from a strapless bodice to swirl around her ankles.

When Savidge handed her over to Magnus, Crystal sighed at the visible love and lust sparking between bride and groom. Then hid a smile when Magnus had to nudge Soren to offer his arm to the bridesmaid as the procession moved to the spacious living room. The guests sat in padded, blue velvet chairs in semi-circle rows around the marble fireplace decorated with orchids and calla lilies, and the minister began, "Dearly beloved, we are gathered here…"

For Crystal the ceremony passed in a blur, emotions and impressions swirling about her. As the bride and groom declared their love and commitment and made solemn promises to each other, she stole glimpses at Soren, wondering what he was thinking. When the couple exchanged rings, Soren caught her gaze, his look loaded with meaning that she interpreted as lust definitely, love maybe, and a whole lot more. She felt the prickle of joyous tears as the minister intoned, "I now pronounce you husband and wife."

Then the groom swept the bride back on his arm and gave her a swashbuckling kiss that lasted until the minister cleared his throat a third time. A cheer rose up from the witnesses, but all Crystal could think of was the moment she and Soren could share a similarly passionate kiss.

Rowena stepped forward to announce that they should all retire to the patio, where a catered dinner of beef Wellington and Chilean sea bass awaited them. Under a flawless blue sky, they found their seats via calligraphed place cards on round tables set for eight. At the head table, Crystal sat between Soren and Rolf, who considered Rowena his date for the afternoon. The irrepressible youngest Thorvald kept making suggestive comments to Crystal, earning scowls and at least one "Back off!" from Soren.

After their first dance as husband and wife, other guests joined them. To Crystal's happy surprise, Soren took her arm and led her to a corner of the portable dance floor, where he pressed her tight to the bulge growing in his trousers and shuffled his feet more or less in time to the slow beat of "The Twelfth of Never".

"How long do we have to stay?" he whispered in her ear as the music shifted to a bouncy tune. "I won't be able to walk in a minute."

"Until they cut the cake," she replied solemnly. "Don't forget, you're the best man."

A twinkle sparkled in his eyes. "And don't you forget it."

"I won't." She returned his smile, knowing the lust in her eyes matched what she saw in his.

Finally, finally, the bride and groom ran the gantlet to the waiting limo amid the flinging of rice and rose petals.

"Follow my lead," Crystal murmured into Soren's ear as they and three-dozen other well-wishers on the wraparound porch waved goodbye to the departing newlyweds.

She backed up, still waving, then slipped into the house and darted through the foyer to a closed door over whose knob hung a discreet sign which read, "No entry." Like a naughty child she opened the door, snuck inside a darkened hallway, pulled Soren behind her, and shut the world out.

"This leads to the back stairs," she whispered. "C'mon. Hurry. Before somebody gets nosy and starts exploring the house now that the main attraction's over."

Crystal raced up the steps, Soren close on her heels, and led him to her childhood bedroom. As soon as he entered, she closed and locked the door behind him, breathless and giggling. "I haven't run up those steps in years! Do you know how many there are?"

"Only one," he responded quietly, trapping her between his body and the door.

"Oh." Suddenly Crystal felt a different kind of breathlessness as he brought her hands to his mouth and kissed each of her fingers.

"Soren." His name was a sigh. He hovered over her, his mouth inches from hers.

"Kiss me, Soren. I promise, nobody will see your boner but me."

A half-smile on his face, he took a step back, placed his hands on her waist to restrain her. "What makes you think I have a boner?"

"Darn it, you'd better!" She tried to pull him closer, but he held her at arm's length. "Don't tease me. I don't just want you. I *need* you." She blinked hard, trying to hold back the sudden pinch of tears. "I need you to make me forget all the horrible memories. To make me totally yours."

Soren's smile disappeared. Killing was too easy, too quick for that bastard after what he'd done to Crystal. But he couldn't dwell on vengeance, on how he wished he had kicked the shit out of him with his steel-toed boots when the bastard was down and bleeding. He had to clear his own mind in order to help ease the trauma of Crystal's ordeal.

Restraining the urge to toss her onto the bed and fuck her blind, he lowered his head and touched his mouth to hers, a soft sweep of his lips across hers, the merest brush of his tongue into her moist, welcoming depths. He dropped angel-soft kisses on her eyelids, her cheeks, earlobes, covering every inch of her face with his mouth.

"More," she murmured, applying a surprising amount of pressure to bring her body into more intimate contact with his.

Soren easily resisted. "Do you trust me?"

"Of course."

"Good. Just stand still. How does this toga thing come undone?"

With a hitch in her voice, she said, "Side zipper. Then the shoulder just slides off."

Soren made a big production of smoothing his hands up and down her sides, brushing the edges of her breasts with his thumbs, searching for the opening. "Ah, there it is." He bent forward, his warm breath sliding across her left breast, and pulled down the zipper.

She shivered, but stayed immobile.

The peach-colored fluff slithered down her lush body. Soren felt poleaxed. "You're more beautiful every time I see you," he murmured in a hoarse voice. He skimmed his fingers along the lacy edges of her strapless bra, feeling the plump softness of her flesh, then followed the same path with his tongue. Holy hell, if she could feel his boner now, he'd probably scare her away. He ached with needing her, from his painfully tight balls all the way up to his eyeteeth, but he had to do this for her. To wash away the pain, the horror.

He knelt before her, kissing and licking his way down her ribcage, her waist. Dipped his tongue into her navel. Nibbled a path down to her bikini panties, all the while stroking his fingers along her skin, around her hips, circling behind to her butt cheeks, the backs of her thighs—she reacted particularly well to that—then down her calves to the tips of her flimsy, strappy heels.

Then he stepped back and simply admired. She was everything a man could want. And she was his. Only his. He vowed to protect her with his life. For the rest of his life.

Crystal's eyes had drifted shut during Soren's sensual assault. He had turned her into a blazing-hot, quivering mass of want. When she felt the loss of his hands, of his mouth on her skin, she blinked her eyes open. And saw him remove his tux jacket then yank off his bow tie and undo the first two studs. She licked her lips. He was gorgeous, with his burning blue eyes and mussed blond hair and square jaw, a Norse god come to life. And he was hers. Only hers.

She wanted to jump him, to feel the weight of his body pressing her into the mattress, the floor, the wall—anything, as long as it was his body. But she stayed immobile, trembling with need, her pussy weeping into her bikini panties, her breasts heavy and swollen, aching for his mouth.

And then she couldn't stand still anymore. She took three quick, wobbly steps to reach him and ripped his shirt open, scattering the studs and hearing them ping against the sunflower-papered walls. She scrabbled for the hooks holding his blue cummerbund closed and tossed that aside.

Matching her eagerness, Soren toed off his patent leather shoes, unbuttoned the pants and shucked them down his legs.

Crystal let out a little cry of delight at the sight of his tented boxer shorts. She launched herself at him. He fell backwards onto the bed—feet still trapped in the puddle of his trousers—and his arms came possessively around her.

Oh God, at last. She fell onto his bare chest and began kissing him anywhere she could reach, nipping his skin with her teeth, rubbing her cheek along the rough mat of his chest hair, grinding her pussy into his hip where she happened to land. They were half on, half off the mattress, they were half dressed and tangled, but it didn't matter. They were touching, skin to skin. He fumbled for the back clasp of her bra, and she levered up enough for him to yank the garment out from between them.

Then he pulled her up so her breast was in his mouth and he was sucking it, pulling on it, teeth clamping around her nipple and making her squirm and moan and demand more. His big hands cupped her butt cheeks and repositioned her so her pussy landed square on his cock, which felt heavenly, huge and pulsating. Vaguely she thought it wouldn't do, to have two layers of underwear between them, and he must have read her mind because he pushed her to one side and yanked down his boxers just enough to let that big, luscious cock with its purple head and thick veins spring free and point to the ceiling. She scrambled to straddle his hips, pulled the crotch of her panties to one side and, guiding him with one hand around his thick shaft, impaled herself on him in one swift movement.

Need, need, need, was all she could think. She rocked her hips, rode him greedily until they were both giving and taking, thrusting and clenching, gasping and clinging, and—condoms be damned—she wanted him to come inside her, with nothing between them, but she got there first and exploded all around him, tightening and squeezing him, milking his cock with her spasms that went on and on until she collapsed onto his chest and tried to remember how to breathe.

Then realized he was hard and motionless inside her.

Raising herself onto her elbows, she looked into his eyes, which were squeezed shut. "Soren, you didn't—"

"Christ, woman," he said around clenched teeth, "do you have any idea how hard it was for me to keep from shooting into you? I counted backward from nine hundred ninety nine."

"But I wanted…"

He kissed away the rest of her words. "I know. But *I* wanted the first one to be about you, not about me." He rolled her off him and onto her side on the mattress then stood up. "Besides, I don't like to come wearing my socks."

A laugh erupted from deep inside Crystal. Here she was, lounging like an odalisque wearing bikini panties, diamond ear studs and stilettos, while Soren stood with his back to her, the elastic of his boxers halfway down his tight butt, jiggling one foot then the other to release the trousers of his tux from its tangle around his feet. He ripped off his boxers and black socks then turned to stand magnificently nude before her, his cock rampant and glistening from her juices.

"Come here," she murmured, her gaze turning hungry as she watched his cock swell even further.

"Just try and keep me away." He knelt on the mattress, dipping it to one side, then nudged her legs apart to settle between her thighs. "I'm planning to brand every inch of you with my hands and my mouth."

Tucking his big hands under her ass cheeks, he growled, "Wrap your legs around my neck."

She did. He dipped his head and began to lap at the swollen pink folds of her pussy, setting a slow, thorough pace, tasting, teasing, skirting the hard bud that most needed his attention. When he thrust his tongue into her pussy, she moaned.

He stopped, raised his head to look down the expanse of her skin to capture her brown-eyed gaze with his intense blue one. "Did I hurt you? Should I stop?"

"No, darn you, don't you dare!"

With a chuckle, he returned his attention to her weeping slit. "You're so wet, it's dribbling down your thighs. I think you're crying because I missed a spot." And he touched his tongue to the hard nub of her clit.

Her hips jerked up off the mattress and she cried out his name. "Yes, right there, please, please," she sobbed, grabbing handfuls of his hair to press his mouth closer to the spot that drove her wild.

Then there was no more talk. Soren nibbled and sucked, rubbed her clit alternately with his tongue and thumb while stroking two fingers in and out of her pussy. Crystal slid her legs off his shoulders and jabbed her heels into the mattress, gaining leverage to buck her hips against his mouth. With an incoherent cry she climaxed again, straining against him for more, more, more, and he obliged her by sucking and licking until the unintelligible sounds of her orgasm softened into the mewling of a contented kitten and she felt herself relaxing, boneless, onto the mattress.

From some deep, faraway place of contentment, she felt herself being gently rolled to her left side. She murmured sounds of pleasure and repletion, wondering if she'd ever have the energy to repay him in kind.

Apparently he wasn't done yet. Crystal smiled dreamily. His fingers were drawing swirls across her back, her shoulders. His mouth traced every vertebra as he made his way down her spine, all the way to her tailbone and the start of her crack. Some tiny, uninvolved sliver of her mind briefly wondered how this huge Viking of a man could make himself small enough to fit on a corner her small bed as he worked his way down her body. Then she gave a mental "who cares" shrug and concentrated on the delicious feelings he was evoking in her.

She felt her right leg being positioned so her bent knee was raised halfway to her chest, exposing her slit and her anal opening to his view. His fingers traced along the crease on either side of her anus, sending shivers up and down her spine. He dipped a finger into her pussy with its residue of juices then moved the moistened finger back up to her anus, teasing it, pressing against the entrance.

Every inch, Soren had said. She'd told him of Healy's vicious assault with the loofah sponges into her every orifice, and it was obvious to her that Soren meant just that — every inch. Smiling, Crystal arched her back, tacitly giving him permission to explore. She consciously relaxed her sphincter muscle, welcoming his searching finger as he tentatively pushed inside.

"Does it hurt?"

"Only when you stop," she murmured.

Emboldened, Soren thrust harder, each time penetrating a little deeper. Crystal pressed her sweet ass into his hand, encouraging him. Soon his index finger was seated to the hilt. He slid two fingers of his other hand into her wet pussy and with both hands delved rhythmically into her tight channels.

"You need more," he growled, withdrawing his fingers. "*I* need more." He was hard as a Samurai sword and his balls ached like they were clamped in a vise.

He grabbed Crystal by the hips, raised her to her hands and knees then nudged her thighs apart and placed himself between them. With as much restraint as he could muster, he slipped his throbbing cock into her wet pussy. And groaned. It felt like he'd come home.

Bending over her torso, he reached around to cup her breasts, hanging full and loose and lush. He rolled her rock-hard nipples between his fingers and thumbs, causing her to wiggle and mewl. Her reaction was enough to start him humping. He withdrew almost all the way out of her pussy then thrust, hard, feeling her breasts jiggle in his hands.

Soren set up a steady rhythm, stroking her pussy, feeling Crystal's inner muscles clenching him. He slid one hand down to her clit and rubbed it. He brought his other hand to her sweet asshole and thrust in and out of it with the same cadence as his cock was fucking her pussy.

"Yes," she murmured. "More!"

"Greedy little thing, aren't you?"

"Yes! I want you. *All* of you!"

"You have me, sweetheart. I'll give you everything I've got."

But not in here, he thought, realizing he'd never put on a condom. He'd love to shoot deep into her, to make her pregnant with his child, but that was something they hadn't discussed—yet. Maybe tomorrow, after he'd satisfied himself and her from this overwhelming need to be with her, in her, around her.

Knowing how close he was to shooting off, he found the inner strength to pull his cock out of her weeping pussy and quickly positioned it at the entrance to her asshole.

"Yes, Soren," she begged, wiggling her ass in invitation. "Every inch!"

Soren took it both ways, as he hoped she'd meant it—every inch of her to be cleansed, and he'd give her every inch of his cock. Slowly, slowly he pushed the biggest hard-on of his life into her asshole, feeling the thick ring as the head slid inside. He knew he was slick from her cunt juices, but still he took care, pushing, stopping, pushing again, penetrating a bit at a time, taking his cues from Crystal.

Until he was as deep as he could go inside her tight passage.

It took his breath away, the trust she had in him not to hurt her. He ran his hands over the gentle flare of her hips, the incurved waist. *Mine!* Crystal was his now, in every way. It was such a heady feeling to know he was the first and, he vowed, last man to ever be where he was at this moment. He'd never given much thought to ass-fucking before, but oh, how gloriously tight she was, how hot, how sublime.

He began to move his hips slowly, rocking back and forth, his cock pulling out more with each stroke then thrusting back in more on each backstroke. Faster, harder, the pressure building, Crystal moaning and rocking beneath him, her shoulder and head now on the mattress, ass in the air, fingernails digging into his ass cheeks, Soren fucked her hard and deep until he heard her scream his name and felt her muscles start to contract and — oh Jesus, it was so different, the muscles in her asshole instead of her pussy clenching around his cock, that he felt himself spiraling out of control.

His balls pulled up painfully hard to the base of his cock. Reason deserted him. All he could do was hang on to Crystal while, with a feral roar, he spurted jet after hot jet of his cum into her welcoming body.

After an endless heaven of ejaculating, Soren sagged to his side on the mattress, pulling Crystal down with him, his slowly deflating cock still imbedded in her rear. A minute or an hour later, he wasn't sure how much time had passed, he asked her, "Are you okay?"

She moved and his limp shaft slipped out of her. Arranging herself on her back in the middle of the bed, she said, "I'm absolutely delicious. Come here."

"If I move, do I get a medal?"

Crystal laughed, reached for his arms and began tugging. Soren managed to pull the disconnected pieces of his body into enough of a coherent unit to slide himself up to her then collapsed at her side.

"Woman, you are incredible."

She flung an arm across his chest, a knee over his thighs, and snuggled close. "I think you're the one who's incredible. You did all the work."

His laugh was more like a gasp. "I wonder if anyone heard us."

"Nope. Grandma said everyone — including her — would be out of the house by eight o'clock."

"Mmph. What time is it now?"

"Five-thirty," she said primly.

Soren sat bolt upright in bed. "What? Holy shit, what will they think? Did I compromise you by making all that noise?"

The giggle told him something was fishy. He narrowed his eyes at her.

"Look out the window. It's full dark. It's around—" she looked past him at the digital clock on the far nightstand. "Ten o'clock. At night."

"You minx," he said, flopping back to the mattress and pulling her atop him. "Life will never be dull with you near me. Will you hang around and keep me on my toes?"

"Soren Thorvald, is that a proposal?"

"Um." He thought a moment. About how loving Crystal was, how much fun. How open to new ideas. How intelligent, how sexy. Definitely sexy. "You know, it doesn't matter how we met. I mean, that woo-woo crap about the crystal telling you I'm your one and only. Because you know what?"

"What?" Lying atop him, her elbows propping her up so their faces were inches apart, her eyes sparkled.

"I am. The One, I mean. For you." He pulled her closer for a kiss. "Wait a minute." He rolled her back onto the mattress, ran his fingers around her throat. "Where is that damn crystal? You're never without it."

"Tell you the truth? I don't think it has any magical powers at all." Crystal smiled up at him. "You were the magic. As soon as I saw you, I knew you were The One. I don't think I ever really needed it. But when you walked out on me because of…I think you said 'some kind of voodoo shit'…I decided that you were right. I didn't need it. Because I knew, deep down inside my heart, that we were meant to be together, and I'd do my darnedest to convince you of it."

"Okay. Convince me."

So she did.

The End

Enjoy An Excerpt From:
DANCE OF THE SEVEN VEILS

Copyright © CRIS ANSON, 2005.

All Rights Reserved, Ellora's Cave, Inc.

Kat elbowed Lyssa, inclined her head to the archway leading to the foyer. "Like him. That gladiator. I'd like to be the one to turn *him* on."

Lyssa's heart skipped a beat, then thudded back to catch up. About six feet tall, dark hair curling around his ears and nape, a narrow black mask that accented the sharp cheekbones and square jaw, the gladiator leaned negligently against the jamb, arms crossed, one leg casually crossed over the other. A gold medallion glowed against a thatch of dark chest hair overlaying well-sculpted muscles. Sandals were laced up his calves, and his thighs under the short Roman tunic looked strong enough to hold him over her in a variety of positions for hours.

She blinked. *Where had that thought come from?*

The gladiator inclined his head slightly, raised an eyebrow. In invitation?

Lyssa swallowed hard. Her heartbeat accelerated. She realized she *wanted* to go to him. But her feet felt rooted to the parquet floor. Lingering doubts about her femininity choked her.

In the background the music shifted. The frenetic opening strains of Richard Strauss' *Dance of the Seven Veils* wafted through the hidden speakers, tympani pounding, a haunting oboe solo connecting to her synapses. Her heart stuttered. It was as though fate had stepped in at this singular moment in time, sending her gaze to this particular stranger across this crowded room, the music reminding her of her costume of seven diaphanous veils tenuously held in place by a golden waist chain. In her eyes, the gladiator morphed into the lascivious, depraved Herod that the voluptuous Salome would entice into granting her deepest, darkest wish.

The gladiator moved languidly to a pile of plush cushions on the floor of a dimly lit alcove and reclined on his side, one knee upraised, leaning on an elbow. He swept his other arm out in a gesture of "The stage is yours" and waited, his mouth curled upward into a slight smile of anticipation.

You're Salome, a voice said inside Lyssa's head. *Amoral, decadent, willful. Dance for him. Seduce him.*

She thrust out her chin and posed like a dancer, the toes of one foot pointed out, one arm across her torso. She scribed a graceful arc up and over her head, then down to one hip, allowing her fingers to skim lightly up her thigh and between her breasts, as if calling his attention to the charms within the circle, ending with a graceful *salaam* gesture at face level.

Taking a deep, fortifying breath, she grabbed the edge of one veil, removed it from around her waist and dropped it to the floor at his feet. The sensuous music slowed to the *leitmotif* that was Salome's signature, infusing her blood with fire. She locked gazes with him—with Herod—and tugged another veil free. Raising it high, she allowed it to float down over her hair, then dragged it down peekaboo fashion until her eyes showed, then her nose, her lips. He transferred his intent gaze to her pouting mouth, and licked his lower lip. Lyssa felt a shock of pure lust course through her. She wanted him to kiss her. Everywhere.

The music shifted to a faster tempo, compelling her to rotate her hips, to bend and sway to the music. Her hair sifted over her face in a golden curtain. She gripped the third veil and trailed it over her breast until the sensitive peak tightened and tingled, then flung the veil aside.

Faster still, the music urged Salome to tempt King Herod to his limits, to hypnotize him, to make him *want* to grant her most perverse wish. Another veil slipped from her body, baring both her breasts. She bent toward him, teasing him, offering her hard, pink nipples to his view but just out of reach. She spun around, undulating her arms and shoulders with her back to him, then removed the veil that covered her ass cheeks. The languid Salome *leitmotif* recurred, relentlessly ratcheting up the tension. She rolled her hips in a slow front-to-back motion, imitating the sex act, as she turned slowly, slowly to face him.

The lust in Herod's eyes, the pupils so dilated they looked black, almost brought Salome to her knees. Absently she noted that his tunic tented up almost to his upraised knee. And *she* had done this to him. King though he may be, Salome knew she had spun a carnal web of obsession around him.

Frenzied now, the exotic music rushed to its climax as Salome divested herself of the penultimate veil across one restlessly moving hip, flinging it into the alcove, where it landed on Herod's muscular shoulder and slid down unnoticed. The last long obbligato sounded, the oboe trill drawing out the tension to an almost unbearable level. Salome ripped off the veil covering her golden thatch and stood before her King, triumphant, panting, exquisitely naked but for the waist chain and golden sandals, the veil in her raised fist fluttering with her harsh, hot breaths.

The music ended with a turbulent cadenza punctuated by three furious chords. Salome fell to her knees and collapsed, legs on Herod's lap, arms flung above her head, her naked skin sheened with perspiration, thighs spread apart without thought to modesty, open to her King's lustful gaze.

Panting, Salome slowly became aware of the flickering candlelight, of the muscular legs of King Herod under hers. Through lowered lashes she could see her flushed breasts rise and fall with every deep breath, the pink nipples standing erect, the areolas puckered and tight. Became aware that every nerve ending cried out for his mouth, his hands, his cock. Anywhere, everywhere, just satisfy this…this *craving*, this need for release that she'd never experienced before.

Why an electronic book?

We live in the Information Age — an exciting time in the history of human civilization, in which technology rules supreme and continues to progress in leaps and bounds every minute of every day. For a multitude of reasons, more and more avid literary fans are opting to purchase e-books instead of paper books. The question from those not yet initiated into the world of electronic reading is simply: *Why?*

1. ***Price.*** An electronic title at Ellora's Cave Publishing and Cerridwen Press runs anywhere from 40% to 75% less than the cover price of the exact same title in paperback format. Why? Basic mathematics and cost. It is less expensive to publish an e-book (no paper and printing, no warehousing and shipping) than it is to publish a paperback, so the savings are passed along to the consumer.

2. ***Space.*** Running out of room in your house for your books? That is one worry you will never have with electronic books. For a low one-time cost, you can purchase a handheld device specifically designed for e-reading. Many e-readers have large, convenient screens for viewing. Better yet, hundreds of titles can be stored within your new library — on a single microchip. There are a variety of e-readers from different manufacturers. You can also read e-books on your PC or laptop computer. (Please note that Ellora's

Cave does not endorse any specific brands. You can check our websites at www.ellorascave.com or www.cerridwenpress.com for information we make available to new consumers.)

3. *Mobility.* Because your new e-library consists of only a microchip within a small, easily transportable e-reader, your entire cache of books can be taken with you wherever you go.

4. *Personal Viewing Preferences.* Are the words you are currently reading too small? Too large? Too... ANNOYING? Paperback books cannot be modified according to personal preferences, but e-books can.

5. *Instant Gratification.* Is it the middle of the night and all the bookstores near you are closed? Are you tired of waiting days, sometimes weeks, for bookstores to ship the novels you bought? Ellora's Cave Publishing sells instantaneous downloads twenty-four hours a day, seven days a week, every day of the year. Our webstore is never closed. Our e-book delivery system is 100% automated, meaning your order is filled as soon as you pay for it.

Those are a few of the top reasons why electronic books are replacing paperbacks for many avid readers.

As always, Ellora's Cave and Cerridwen Press welcome your questions and comments. We invite you to email us at Comments@ellorascave.com or write to us directly at Ellora's Cave Publishing Inc., 1056 Home Avenue, Akron, OH 44310-3502.

THE
☥ ELLORA'S CAVE ☥
LIBRARY

Stay up to date with Ellora's Cave Titles in
Print with our Quarterly Catalog.

To recieve a catalog,
send an email with your name
and mailing address to:

CATALOG@ELLORASCAVE.COM

or send a letter or postcard
with your mailing address to:

Catalog Request
c/o Ellora's Cave Publishing, Inc.
1056 Home Avenue
Akron, Ohio 44310-3502

COMING TO A BOOKSTORE NEAR YOU!

ELLORA'S CAVE

Bestselling Authors Tour

MAKE EACH DAY MORE *EXCITING* WITH OUR

ELLORA'S
CAVEMEN
CALENDAR

WWW.ELLORASCAVE.COM

erridwen, the Celtic Goddess of wisdom, was the muse who brought inspiration to storytellers and those in the creative arts. Cerridwen Press encompasses the best and most innovative stories in all genres of today's fiction. Visit our site and discover the newest titles by talented authors who still get inspired - much like the ancient storytellers did, once upon a time.

Cerridwen Press

Monthly Newsletter

News
Author Appearances
Book Signings
New Releases
Contests
Author Profiles
Feature Articles

Available online at
www.CerridwenPress.com

Discover for yourself why readers can't get enough of the multiple award-winning publisher

Ellora's Cave.

Whether you prefer e-books or paperbacks,

be sure to visit EC on the web at
www.ellorascave.com

for an erotic reading experience that will leave you breathless.